EXQUISITE
poison

Phantom House *Press*

A N T H O L O G Y

EXQUISITE POISON

We've picked their poison,
and made it count.
Something they
can't live without.
Whether it be sweet or quietly deadly,
we've overwhelmed them with a medley.
It's more than they can bear—
Read on if you dare.

*E*xquisite Poison is a collection of poetry & short fiction in an array of genres. The "poison" can be an actual toxin of death, an addiction, a heady love story, a compulsion…read on and find them all.

~

CONTENTS

EXQUISITE POISON

A PHANTOM HOUSE PRESS ANTHOLOGY

Phantom House
Press

For creatives everywhere.

1

THE SISTERS IN THE ATTIC

BY KEIRA F. JACOBS

The ghosts in the attic are so cruel to me
They thump and they bump and they often scream.
Sisters, I'm told, three to be exact
All died the same day
100 years back.
A silly disaster
This much is true;
Rat poison fell in their afternoon stew.
Now they dwell in my attic and cause a big fuss
Over the rats that go running
Around in the dust.
The date of their death
Was September the 3rd.
Now on that day
They act simply absurd.
They rush down from the attic
And bump down the halls
And rip all the frames off my living room walls.
On the morning of the 4th
When I wake for the day

BY KEIRA F. JACOBS

I know what to expect
For the sisters can play.
They think it's so funny
And I suppose I do too,
To see brewing on my stovetop
Some rat poison stew.

2

THE COURT OF THE UNSEEN

BY A.E. KINCAID

*T*hey called her Ruen now, but that was not her name. That was *its* name.

Once, she had been Rhiannon: the beautiful, flaxen-haired heir to the throne of Tintarial. Eldest of three daughters, hers was a mountain kingdom wreathed in mists and the scent of oncoming snow. As a child, she'd shown no aptitude for dancing, politics, or languages like her other sisters; like a future queen should. But she had another remarkable gift that, in time, forgave her civic shortcomings.

Rhiannon had *power*.

Born with the Old Magic, her power knew no bounds. Depthless and devastating—with a wave of her hand, she could divert a river to drown a flock. With a single breath, she could birth a hurricane that would devastate a town. But Rhiannon did none of those things. Her magic slept within her for ten years, and during those ten years, she grew to believe herself wholly unfit as heir to the throne.

Then, when she was ten years old, her youngest sister fell ill with an arcane sickness—a blight they'd thought long-eradicated. Fearful that Rhiannon might catch it, her parents forbade her from attending her dear sibling. Healers arrived from across the kingdom, but none could help. Just when all seemed lost, Rhiannon snuck into her sister's room, stroked a damp curl away from her fevered forehead, and with nothing in her mind but thoughts of healing, she closed her eyes. Without truly knowing what she was doing, she poured her power into the girl. As she did so, the very mountain beneath her shook. All through the castle, cracks appeared in the walls and floor, mirrors shattered, and the thrones fell from their dais. Still, she flooded her sister with thoughts of respite until she felt the effort might consume her. Finally spent, she collapsed on the bed.

When she awoke hours later, her sister's fever had lifted. The blight was gone. Rhiannon's nursemaid found the pair curled up together in bed. She asked Rhiannon how she'd known to go to her sister. Rhiannon told the woman she'd had a vision. From then on the nurse-maid, whose family kept the Old Ways, whispered forgotten tales of magic to Rhiannon in the moments before sleep. For that Old Magic had healed the world and driven away the most fearsome creatures. And the woman believed Rhiannon would be called to do the same.

News of the miracle spread far and wide and people throughout Tintarial trekked up the mountain to be blessed and healed by their queen-to-be. For years, she welcomed them with eagerness, glad to have found her calling. There were so many people less fortunate—so many people in need of her, she said. She refused to turn anyone away. She'd been raised to believe that a gift of power—be that of the tongue, the mind, or even magic—should be used in service of the powerless. Even when she felt every ailment as she healed it—a side effect that weakened her for days or even weeks after—she pressed on.

Her middle sister, Freya, urged her to slow; to get proper rest. But she could not. She'd always been uncertain of her right to reign, espe-cially when Freya would have been perfect. She was accomplished beyond measure at all the activities a young woman of royal blood should be. She danced, she sang, she could speak in any tongue of the southern realms. An avid reader and master historian, she had a quick wit and persuasive tongue with which she delighted her friends and skewered her enemies. Freya should have been Tintarial's shining star. She would have been—if not for Rhiannon. And this knowledge kept Rhiannon going year after year without a thought of the physical and mental cost.

~

Near her nineteenth birthday, she had a vivid dream. In it, she stood at the foot of their mountain. She sensed rather than saw that a group of ailing people had gathered and were waiting for her—all of them too ill to make the trek to the castle. They were trapped, unseen, deep in a hole tunneled into the ground. But she could hear them cry out for her, begging her to heal them and set them free.

After that first night, the dreams became more frequent, and she began to believe that it was not a dream at all, but a vision—like the one that had helped her heal her youngest sister all those years ago. Weakened though she was from a recent rehabilitory onslaught, she did not hesitate when the dream came yet again. In the early hours of the morning, before her family rose, she dressed herself in the black traveling clothes customary for people traveling down the snow-dusted mountain, and set off.

It was midday—the sun a blinding beacon overhead—when she reached the foot of the mountain and found a fissure in the ground. Peering down into the crevice, she recognized the deep, cavernous void from her vision. It looked like a well, if that well belonged to a giant. Her scuffed boots perched at its edge, she shivered and gazed into the pit whose darkness swallowed the blazing sunlight entirely. A continuous pathway littered with debris and lined with columns and statues depicting cruel, misshapen figures wound around the perimeter. It spiraled down, smoothly sinking into the inky depths. The place thrummed so thunderously with madness and ill intent it stole her breath. She wavered for only a moment—wondering if she was a match to the terrible magic that had befallen these people she was sent to help—but nonetheless, Rhiannon steeled herself and took the first step onto the path. As she did, a torrent of wind swept in from above, hindering her forward motion. It felt like an omen—that the natural world did not wish her to go. But she was Rhiannon. Heir of Tintarial. Born with the gift to heal. *And she would not yield*—not even to the forces of nature—when there were people in need of her magic.

With each step, the darkness pressed in at her and cold sweat trailed down her spine. Fear gripped her like a hand around the neck. Her eardrums throbbed to the rhythm of her heart slamming against her ribs. It was only gradually that she realized the deep hum she'd identified at the mouth of the fissure had resolved into words. Evil words of malice and revenge. Pleas for release from the shackles of oppression. Pushing her fear aside and swallowing hard, Rhiannon continued foot by foot down the path, vowing to help these poor souls find relief.

Her knees buckled as she reached the shrouded bottom. The floor was harder underfoot than the path had been, but smooth beneath her boots. Like the cool marble of the throne room in her mountain home. She coughed as she inhaled the musty air, preparing to call out and announce herself to any who might be nearby. The sound echoed eerily in the unseen space. There was no answer, but her eyes—so starved for light she'd begun to wonder if her blindness would be permanent—caught a faint red glow just ahead. She shuffled toward it, still unsure of her footing in the dark, and called out again.

This time, there was an answer. Though it was little more than an inaudible whisper—there was definitely someone—or something— here with her.

As she drew closer, the glow resolved itself into the outline of a door carved from hawthorn wood and wrought with scrolling iron- work. She placed her hand upon it and a shiver ran up her arm as she felt the call again. Like a snake twisting through her mind, she sensed more than heard a phrase repeated over and over.

Open the gate. Open the gate. Open the gate.

There was no handle, but she closed her eyes and willed the door open. Warmth burst forth from her palms and, clearing her mind of all but thoughts of release, she funneled it into the wood. It charred, then smoldered, but would not catch. Woven within the hawthorn and iron was deep, ancient magic. She reached out with her own power and felt spells tinged with fear and loathing. With no time to wonder who in her time would have been able to create such a pattern, she pushed out further, straining the limits of her magic. The weaving stretched, pulled taut, and *snapped*. She staggered as a conflagration engulfed the door. Nothing remained but ash and molten metal.

Rhiannon collapsed in a heap on the cold, hard stone floor, utterly spent. She sat there, chin bowed and resting on her heaving chest, staring blankly at her hands in her lap. Finally, she raised her head to smile at the freed folk from beyond the door. But there was nothing there. Only darkness.

Or, that's how it appeared at first. The embers from the burned door faded to grey and all was returned to black. Even amongst such profound obscurity, she could make out seven wavering forms. Just the sight of them filled her with cold dread. She didn't know how she knew—but in that moment Rhiannon realized she'd made a grave mistake. She needed to run, to warn her family—but she was rooted to the spot. A voice rang out, reverberating off the walls and floor. It was soothing yet sharp; majestic yet maleficent.

Foolish, glorious child. Only one in a hundred years is born with the power to release us and even fewer make a suitable host. Imagine our delight when, after millennia of imprisonment, your magic broke the ground and woke us.

∽

Rhiannon thought back to when she'd healed her sister—so early in her magic. In her innocence and ignorance, the act had caused an earth shake. She remembered it well, but still did not understand.

"Host? What do you mean? Who are you?" rasped Rhiannon. Fear and exhaustion had rendered her throat raw and voice unrecognizable.

The forms were closer now, but no more distinct. They shifted before her eyes like smoke on the wind. The voice dripped with mock dismay as it continued.

Already forgotten, are we? Well, child, soon we will be as one, and you should *know me. I am called Ruen.*

Ruen paused and in that moment a story from Rhiannon's childhood unburied itself from the recesses of her mind. A bedtime tale told by her nursemaid. *Ruen.* Queen of the Everdark. Bane of the seers of old. Stripped of mortal form and banished for eternity behind the Night Gate for unspeakable crimes.

Her eyes flicked to the seven figures before her and prickle of horror traveled from the crown of her head down her spine as she whispered,

"You are...The Court of the Unseen."

Ruen's voice was pleased as she said.

Not so forgotten after all, I see. But it does not matter. We will be in the minds and on the tongues of all people soon enough. We have a plan. And it begins with you.

Suddenly the center-most form rushed toward her, quick as thought. Rhiannon tried to move, but only succeeded in sprawling on the ground. The thing that called herself Ruen swept into her eyes, her nose, her mouth and she choked on the cold burn of frost that invaded her. Writhing with tremors as her body rejected the unnatural presence, her head slammed against the hard slab of the floor, cracking her skull. But Ruen did not let go. Eyes wide with horror, Rhiannon felt the essence crawling through her veins to the tips of her fingers; tendrils spiraling up into her mind. She screamed and tore at her hair. The pain was unbearable She would be torn apart...

And then it was over.

She was aware, and not aware. Corporeal, and not. Part body, part wraith. She could change forms with a thought. But not *her* thought. As she blinked back and forth between mist and substantiality, a voice...*her* voice...let out a high, manic cackle as it flexed *her* fingers. A hellish set of images flashed before Rhiannon in quick succession. Ruen on a dark throne, an obsidian crown set atop her raven hair. Ruen overlooking a battlefield strewn with human remains;

monstrous creatures roaming between them. Ruen and her court cowering in a blinding light. Ruen, a sinister smile curving ruby lips as the door to the Night Gate burned away to ash. This was the thing she'd let out. The thing that now possessed her body.

As an unwilling passenger, she shot up out of the broken prison and into the air—six other wraith forms following swiftly behind like wicked ribbons in a gale. They soared up and around the mountain to the doors of the stone palace at its summit, the coming night pulling its indigo blanket across the sky. Ruen thrust the armored doors open as if they were nothing, plucking guards up like playthings and casting them aside. Then she strode to the throne room—the six wraiths at her back.

When she arrived, Rhiannon saw her mother, father, and sisters standing huddled together around the throne. Her youngest sister turned at the sound of footsteps and pointed eagerly over.

"Rhiannon!" cried her mother and hurried toward her. "We were so worried. Darling. . ." She paused halfway across the room, her face going pale as the snow tipped mountain. "Who are they?" she asked, pointing a trembling figure at the shades behind her daughter. Her eyes flicked back over to Rhiannon, but they couldn't seem to focus. Her brow creased in confusion at the puzzling sight before her. "You look like my daughter, but you are not. You are like her shadow." Blanching, she whispered, "What have you done with her?"

The remaining fragments of Rhiannon knew what was coming next and attempted to warn her family. She tried to force her thoughts to overtake Ruen even for an instant. To call out to her mother. But either she was too weak, or their entanglement was too permanent because Ruen sauntered forward, a cruel smile playing at the corners of her mouth. When she stood before Rhiannon's mother, her lips turned down in a mock pout.

"Oh *mother*," Ruen said in a voice like—and yet unlike—Rhiannon's own. "I'm afraid Rhiannon is gone. It's *Ruen* now."

"Ruen?" croaked Rhiannon's mother as if her throat ran dry with recognition.

Ruen tossed her hair back over her shoulder and raised up her arm as if to stroke the queen's cheek. Instead, she grabbed her by the throat. Rhiannon watched, helpless, as the ciri of life pulled away from her mother and filled up Ruen.

As if that had been a signal, the other wraiths chased Rhiannon's father and sisters across the throne room and toward the open door— Ruen opening cracks in the floor or shifting stones from the walls to halt their progress. Rhiannon's sisters stood on an island in the midst of their home and watched, horrified, as the wraiths trapped their father against the far wall. Ruen prowled over to the terrified man and drank the life from him. Then Ruen turned on the girls. With a wave, she pulled a heavy column down from the ceiling to make a bridge to their isolated place on the floor. Debris fell from the gaping hole in the roof as she stalked toward them.

Suddenly—she froze in place as someone started chanting behind her.

Bind the dark and keep it still
Let the demons do no ill
Until the day the last leaf falls
Only then escape these halls
Five hundred years the tree shall last
By this spell that I have cast.

"No!" Ruen cried as she dove off the pillar toward the spell caster behind her. It was Rhiannon's nursemaid—keeper of the Old Ways. She was holding a small silver seed in her quivering palm. Upon completing the last line of the spell, she dropped the seed into one of the cracks in the center of the hall, and the floor shook in response. Then, a stem of pale wood shot up from the fissure, branching out and flowering with silver, gold, and opalescent buds. A shaft of moonlight shone down through the hole in the ceiling, illuminating the newborn tree as it reached out—branches twisting and arcing—toward the walls and toward the sky. When its growth finally halted, it stood tall and strong, filling the center of the throne room. The scent of jasmine and wisteria hung in the air as the luminescent buds rustled in a breeze. The beauty of the tree was a stunning contrast to the death and destruction which had just been wrought in the hall.

"I'm so sorry, Rhiannon," the nursemaid whispered as tears streaked down her face.

As the last blossom bloomed, an invisible pulse shot through the room, and Ruen screamed as it knocked her off her feet.

"Now, children! Run!" cried the nursemaid, "She is trapped, not powerless," Rhiannon's sisters dashed across the stone column, stepped down to the floor, and sprinted toward the nursemaid. Ruen tried to reach out to them with her power, but she could not. Her fingers grasped the edge of Freya's skirts but Freya yanked at the fabric until she tore free. The tear-streaked horror on Freya's face as she ran from the monster in her sister's skin would have made Rhiannon collapse in despair, had she been in control of her own form.

Ruen let out a screech of frustration that reverberated in the bones.

"You are just delaying the inevitable, old crone! I have waited two thousand years—my prison is broken! This is but a trice!" she shrieked, spittle flying wildly as she tore her hair in frustration. She reached inward and tapped into not just her own, but Rhiannon's dwindling power as well. Ruen's desperation was palpable—their combined force was still not enough to break through the nursemaid's spell but she could try to limit it with a counter spell of her own. Placing a hand on the trunk of the tree she began to sing. Her was voice raw from overuse and the agony of having come so close to escape as she rasped,

Five hundred years the spell's intent
And yet when half that time is spent
This tree shall turn as black as night
And release me from my plight

Ruen went limp, but she kept her eyes trained on the tree. In the place where her hand had been, the tree darkened to ash grey, and she sneered in triumph. Hurried footsteps sounded but Rhiannon's...

Ruen's eyes were closing as she slumped back down to the floor. Her eyelids fluttered, and Rhiannon's sisters were gone. They fluttered again, and the six other wraiths gathered around, standing sentinel for their queen.

The castle was demolished. Rhiannon's mother and father were dead by her own hands. Her sisters were on the run from their home. It was all too much to bear. She pulled in the pieces of her that were left closer and closer, walling them up as she went, until there was nothing left of her at all.

Her last thoughts as she curled up within her own mind were of her foolishness. If only she'd told someone about her dream—her sister, the historian, or her nursemaid who knew so much of the Old World. She might have chosen differently. She might have understood the horror she'd walked into in the name of healing. She might have realized that she should never have come to that place, especially not in her weakened state, and that her gift was not her only value in this world. But she did not.

Ruen was thwarted, again—for now. There was no longer a reason to fight. So Rhiannon, Heir of Tintarial, born with the gift to heal, finally *did* yield. She did rest. And she was no more.

3

ONE PIROUETTE

BY J.L. VAMPA

*O*ne pirouette. One twist upon her toes against the black sandstone overhang, and it would all be over. One pirouette off the cliff.

The screams that tangle in her hair with the wind would howl no more. The blood caressing her cheek like a lover would mar her no longer. The bones of a phantom hand in hers would never again be crushed in the grip of her desperation *not* to deal the killing blow. No longer would the images behind her eyelids dig six feet under, burrowing into her skull.

Two hundred years she'd been alone. Two hundred years she'd been at the mercy of a mysterious Grimoire. One decade she was indoctrinated, and in the next she became the hands and feet of history's horrors, whilst her three Sisters dealt the glories. For two hundred damned years she'd been Sister Autumn. The witch of Autumnal Equinox.

Agatha inhaled the cool, sea salted fog, welcoming the abyss. Pushing against it was futile. It tickled her ear, whispering that she belonged there in the void. It's oil slick adulation running a gentle finger over her mouth, slipping in when her lips parted. It slithered

29

down her throat, filling Agatha with a numbness that felt like an exhumed tomb.

All the while, Mer Noir sang a siren's song, beckoning her below. *Come dance in the dark waters.* Agatha swayed on her feet coated in black sand. The call was syrupy, a sweet bane against the resounding hollow. The waves crashed against the rocks in wicked lullaby.

One beautiful note rang out over the deep, tethering her to a place of futures past, pleading. *"Stay."*

For the briefest of moments she entertained the thought. The song sounded familiar. But then memories of her indoctrination swarmed in like a hive of embittered wasps.

Everything was ripped from her at the age of eight. As she'd cried, tears dampening her soiled pinafore, an ancient woman knelt next to her on the cold, dead leaves. Dead like her parents. Cold like her soul since being wrenched from her Sisters. The woman started out kind, her gentle voice a welcomed respite and her smile as sweet as brown sugar. She led Agatha to a cabin in the woods, gave her a home with steamed milk every night and stories of magic by the fire.

When the ice began to crack along the lake outside their window, so did the crone's kind facade. By the time the snow thawed and the trees began to bud, Agatha's only relief from arduous lessons in wielding magic, and her torture for any misstep, was the Eve her captor left for a few hours. It struck Agatha as odd, at first, that these evenings occurred on each of her Sisters' days of birth. Every year until she was sixteen.

The wasps darted around in her skull, the memories they carried stinging, leaving a throbbing burn in their wake. It all began to sound like Sybil's voice.

Our burden to take, for History to make.

Fingers blistered and bleeding as Agatha bent over her doctrine writing, the switch haunting her imperfection.

The Goddess' hands of wrath and mercy, to balance History.

Gnawing hunger, to drive away the heretical thoughts because Agatha had asked *why.*

Goddess blessed above everyone. Her chosen instrument of sanctification.

Raw throat, and lashed back, for reciting a sacred text with ire because Agatha's very soul rejected it.

She was taught how to maim, kill, and gut by ten. She was taught how to wield her magic to engulf—to sanctify. She was taught to brew toxins and grow poisonous plants. She was taught how to sift out secrets and sell them like gold.

But while Sybil slumbered, Agatha drank in every word of every tome in the cottage. She taught herself how to heal. She taught herself how to wield her magic to push against the darkness. She taught herself how to brew poultices and elixirs; to grow healing plants and vegetables. She taught herself how to augur and scry.

On her sixteenth day of birth, Sister Autumn watched in horror as her caretaker died. Horror, not for the death itself, but for the crippling relief that came with it. She'd been so very naive to believe her pain was over that day. In truth, it had only just begun.

Agatha blinked at the sea, rising up on her toes, the wind biting at her cheeks. She twisted, rotating back and forth. Back and forth. Her long dress billowing out behind her like bat wings. It would be so easy to just tip forward. Like the sick she'd been Ordered by the Grimoire to inflict. People bent over, vomiting blood and bile.

It would be so easy to raise her arms, turn, and fall, like the kings she'd been Ordered to slay. One slipping in his own blood, the other landing face down on an exquisite rug.

When the latter's blood sprayed her boots, Agatha's fate was betrothed to this abyss that slipped into her veins like a poison. With the slice across his neck, the wound staring up at her like a gaping macabre grin, she'd unintentionally gone on bended knee and proposed marriage to the darkness clouding her mind; the boulder crushing her lungs; the worms feasting on her peace.

She hadn't known it then. She'd only been doing as she was Ordered, like always. But that one...that act of treachery began the slow fade of her soul being slaughtered.

The inky grief slithered up her neck, stuffing itself down her throat again. It would be so easy to succumb. Like the villages to flame, the people to poverty, the land to rot and ruin. All by her dastardly hand.

The roughness of the cliff under the ball of her foot filled Sister Autumn's mind as she shifted her back to the sea. It was the last caress of the land she'd ever feel.

The wind lashed her hair against her cheeks as she fell. The sea's song grew agonizingly loud as fog enveloped her, gently laying her down into the waves below, prepared to tuck her in snugly.

There was a clap of thunder, a bite of cold, and the abyss swallowed Agatha whole.

A voice sounded in her mind, far-off and garbled like eavesdropping with a glass against the door. Nothing else registered except the feel of her black dahlia-colored dress clinging to her, a second skin of graveclothes.

In truth, Agatha had expected either nothingness beyond death's door, or a great load of...something. Pandemonium or paradise. Anything but that same beckoning void. Vacant, yet cataclysmically painful, save for the sodden dress and the voice that began to sound like winter's hush.

"Stay with me." The words fell gently like snowflakes against Agatha's flushed skin.

It was Pandemonium, then. Mer Noir had been frigid when it took her in its arms, not hot like a lush, sunny meadow. Despite her best efforts, Agatha could not manage to open her eyes, or even wriggle so much as a toe.

"Goddess," another warbled voice broke through the snow. "What's happened?" Agatha could feel that voice as it knelt near her aching head. It was warm and refreshing, like a spring rain.

"I summoned her here to your treehouse. She arrived like this." The frosted voice sounded dreadfully forlorn, and Agatha moved to reach for it, but her dead limbs wouldn't respond. "It isn't working."

"I'll help." Ice and fire slipped beneath Agatha's skin in tandem.

A sharp gasp shot through the sticky fog. "Is she alright?" A new voice. This one sounded like the breaking of waves and carried the scent of salt and tropics.

The dewy voice addressed the newest one. "We must take her to the Burned City. To Helsvar."

"*She's not dead.*" The frigid words brought forth a chill Agatha could feel, even in the void.

"She needs to be buried, Sister."

Agatha clawed through the dirt, lungs burning from lack of breath, and eyes unseeing in the depths. The more she struggled upward, the more soil caved in on her.

Finally, her hand broke free of the dirt, cool wind licking her palm. With one final heave, Sister Autumn's other arm pushed through, and she dragged herself upward. The instant fresh air touched her face, Agatha sucked in great gulping breaths, her tongue tasting of petrichor as the soil came in with air.

Blinking away the dirt, Agatha beheld her three Sisters, all standing in crescent formation, shovels in hand, and the moon framing them in a triple-headed glow. By the looks upon their faces, she could only imagine how terrifying she appeared, rising from the ground, streaked in mud and loam, breath ragged. "Did you put me in goddess damned *grave dirt?*"

Wendolyn threw down her shovel. "It healed you, didn't it?" Sister Winter retreated back a few paces and crossed her arms.

Sorscha stormed forward, bending over until her dress hardly contained her bosom any longer. Sister Spring slapped Agatha hard across the cheek. "How *dare* you do this, Aggie?" She trembled with rage and a cold knot formed in Agatha's stomach. She'd never even considered her Sisters would be pained. Another slash against her black soul.

Seleste rushed to clasp Agatha's arm and pull her the rest of the way up from the grave. "You don't know this was intentional,

Sorscha," Sister Summer chastised, futilely brushing at the smears on Agatha's face. "Was it, Aggie?"

Sister Autumn looked at her soiled toes.

"Oh, Aggie..." Seleste's eyes filled with tears as Sorscha's burned with rage.

"You had to know it would fail." Wendolyn's finger tapped rapidly on her crossed arm. "That is not how this works. It is not how *we* work."

If Agatha thought she'd felt despair on the Isle of Ballast, living with the horrors caused by her hand, or upon the black cliffs as she welcomed death, it was nothing compared to the crushing truth of Winnie's words. There was no escape from their lot. There was no avoiding their Orders or outrunning their taskmaster—the Holy Grimoire. The Goddess Three's own Book. They were Hespa's *Sisters Solstice.*

"I think we should take her to her cottage," Sorscha suggested.

Agatha's lips parted to refuse, but it was too late. Winnie nodded, and they were standing on Agatha's front step in the next blink. She hadn't been to her new home since her lover had died. Since years before she met him, even. When she lost the prior cottage, she'd carefully crafted the current one with her magic. It was utterly perfect. A safe haven from her life. From herself. From the Grimoire. But Agatha did not deserve such peace, and had abandoned it.

"I hate this place." Winnie scowled, looking out over the autumnal grounds, nose turned up. She huffed and pushed through the front door as if it were her own.

Gathered around the table, Agatha bounced her leg, eyeing each of her Sisters. If Winnie had summoned them all, it was the Autumn Equinox already. What loomed before her crushed the air right out of Agatha's lungs. "I can't take the Grimoire." The words were hardly audible, climbing up her parched throat just as she'd clawed out of the grave. "Please, don't make me take it." She hated the pleading lilt of her tone almost as much as she hated the pity in Seleste's gaze.

Sorscha reached out and grasped her hand under the table. "We're right here with you."

For now.

Winnie nodded at Seleste, and Sister Summer let out a slow breath. She held out her hand, and a tome as old as Time itself landed in her upturned palm. Agatha's stomach soured further. Seleste gently laid the Grimoire in front of Agatha on the scarred table. "It's time, Sister Autumn."

She made no moves to open it. "I have it now, and I'm not dead. You may all go. We must be near the Witching Hour by now."

Something very near to hurt slashed across Winnie's face and she disappeared. Seleste stood and ran a tender thumb across Agatha's cheek. "I'll see you at the Winter Solstice, Sister." And she was gone.

"Not on your life," Sorscha drawled when Agatha looked at her expectantly. "I'm here with you until the last possible second. We open the Grimoire together."

A knot of emotion unfurled in Agatha's throat and she nodded, blinking tears away.

"What happened, Aggie?"

What *hadn't* happened in the last two hundred years of abomination? "Sorscha, while you three are out there making history in the most astounding of ways, influencing the rise of great kings, and uncovering riches to hand to the poor, I'm sent time and again to destroy things. *People*." She'd never admitted so much to Sorscha, or anyone, before.

Unphased, Sister Spring took her hand. "What happened last autumn?"

Agatha was not ready to speak of last Autumn. The blood. The screams. The loss. Her heart seized, longing for that cliffside once more. She shook her head, the movement almost imperceptible. But Sister Spring knew her Sister Autumn, despite their forced separation.

Sorscha grimaced. "What about the Autumn before that?"

"I sowed seeds of discord between three men."

"That doesn't sound so terrible…"

Agatha frowned. "It wasn't *difficult*, no. Lord Thomas had a daughter. Lord Bingham loved her. Lord Franc was betrothed to her, yet he was in love with Lord Bingham."

Sorscha leaned forward. "*Saucy.*"

Despite herself, Agatha smirked at her Sister's depravity. "I pitted them all against one another." She looked at her hands. "Then I was Ordered to kill the woman. She was just a girl, really."

Sorscha blanched, for good reason. "Then what happened?"

"When the blood bath ended between the three men, who all accused one another, Lord Bingham won. I believe you know him as King Louis." Sorscha's brows rose to her hairline and Agatha shrugged. "The Kingdom of Eridon had to come from somewhere, I suppose."

"That is...gruesome, but the rise of Eridon has helped so many."

"Has it, though?"

Sorscha's lips pursed. "Perhaps Hespa's Orders this Equinox will bring you something good."

She wouldn't call Sorscha an optimist, but she continually did all she could to hold Agatha up. As much as she was able, whilst forbidden from seeing her Sister outside the Solstice or Equinox.

She might not relish the chore, but Agatha could slit a throat without a wavering hand. She could brew the wickedest of poisons and administer it calmly. She could deal secrets with the efficiency of a rampant plague. But opening the Book that Ordered her to do so filled her with crippling dread.

"I have to open it eventually," Agatha said quietly, almost to herself.

Her fingers trembled as they hovered over the worn cover and Sorscha reached out to squeeze her hand, giving her a nod of encouragement.

Agatha cursed in four languages and opened the Grimoire.

4

MIRROR, MONSTER, MOTHER

BY AUTUMN KRAUSE

ow

The mirror needed tending.

Since gaining its soul one hundred and fifty years ago, it always did.

"I hear you, I hear you," Emiko Nomura said, shuffling in from the garden, hands pressed to her ears to block out the mirror's shriek. She slipped out of her boots and into house slippers.

The mirror's scream grew in an escalating soprano that went beyond any human scale. Shrill notes blistered Emiko's eardrums, filling them with a liquid fire of sound. The mirror shook, the glass shaking in its wood frame, and knocking against the tarpaper wall.

"You'll break yourself! Is that what you want?" Quickly, the old woman grabbed the bucket off her kitchen counter. It was always there, always ready to go. A bottle of neon blue window cleaner rested in it and a dishcloth—crusty from being sprayed with cleaner and then left to dry before being sprayed again—draped over the bucket's rim.

Emiko reached for the thin strip of fabric tied to the bucket's handle first. She slipped it over her eyes and tied it behind her head with practiced ease, securing it above her low, gray ponytail. Then, with one hand grasping the bucket and the other hand before her, she felt her way into the side room where the mirror hung.

"There." Her hand, its back ridged with blue veins, birdlike bones, and mottled age spots, touched the mirror. Its rage was apocalyptic. It screamed and angled itself to catch the setting sunlight and flash it into Emiko's face. She could tell what it was doing, the sphere of light reaching through the blindfold and turning the backs of her eyelids red.

Even though Emiko did it every day, her hand shook as she squirted cleanser onto the glass and raised the dishcloth to swipe it across the glossy surface. The mirror was already clean, she was certain. There was no way that a single fingerprint marred it, nor a single bit of dust resided on it.

There wasn't a cleaner mirror on all the island.

It didn't matter.

The mirror needed tending.

It always had and she served it as a faithful daughter should. After all, it had granted her wish.

Then

When Emiko was a girl, she worked on a sugarcane plantation with Mama. It was their home and had been for as long as Emiko could remember.

Mama harvested the leafy green shoots with a cutting blade and Emiko tore off the thick leaves. It was humid, as though the earth itself was in an angry frenzy, sweating and exhaling over them. Hot winds blew and hot rain showered down and hot air hung close to the ground. Everyone else wilted, but Mama glowed, the humidity creating a nimbus around her head as it frizzed her dark hair and flushed her cheeks a burning pink.

Emiko thought she looked like a beautiful angel and Mr. Hale, the owner of the plantation, did too. Often, he would have Mama over to the plantation house. But when she returned, she was dimmed, tired, old—wavering, like the heat mirages rising on the road running by the plantation. Emiko felt as though she could put her hand right through Mama and that there'd be no skin or bones to stop it.

"Don't worry, Emi-chan," Mama said, her voice as tattered as the old green, yellow, and red flag whipping about the post by the road.

"I'll find a way to stop him," Emiko vowed.

"You mustn't. Leave things as they are. Otherwise they might get worse." Then Mama whispered again, "don't worry."

But Emiko did worry. She worried and raged and hacked the leaves off the sugarcane shoots, wishing the shoot was Mr. Hale's face and that she could drive the blade into his eye and then bring it across his throat.

"He has an ungaikyō." A voice whispered in Emiko's ear one day when Mama was with Mr. Hale and Emiko was left in the field. Turning, she saw a small woman behind her. The woman was roly-poly of three sequential bumps: round head, rounded shoulders, rounded middle. "A ryōshi owed him money and gave it to him."

"That's just a fairy tale," Emiko said, violently running the rusty blade down a shoot but finding no release in the action.

"Perhaps. But the mirror is coming of age. It'll be one hundred years old today. It'll get its soul."

"But the fairy tale says that..." she trailed off.

"I know," the old woman said. "It's dangerous. Maybe too dangerous."

She turned and shuffled away. Emiko, though, was still. Then, she ran to the plantation house, heron-like legs flying over the ground.

Once she reached the house, she rested her back against the wall and sidestepped along its length toward the door. Plumeria bloomed around the house in a great white profusion of blossoms. It dripped sticky tears of dew down the walls and back gnats dotted the trails, trapped in the sweetness. Strands of Emiko's hair caught and slid through it but she hardly noticed because, as she passed beneath a window, she heard it.

Loud breathing, every other pant punctuated by grunts.

Mr. Hale.

She entered the front door, passing over the white and black checkerboard tile to the salon.

The ungaikyō hung on the wall, toothy dragons and papery cheery trees carved into its frame. If it'd gained its soul, she wouldn't dare see her reflection in it. If she did, her own self would poison her. Tip toeing forward, she bowed reverently before it. Then, turning her head away, she took it down, facing it outward.

It was heavy. The weight of it hung between her hands, slick yet hefty. Her fingers felt like fragile twigs, ready to snap. But she didn't drop it. Nothing could make her drop it. She carried into the salon. Mr. Hale and Mama faced the opposite direction, but at the sound of her footsteps, Mr. Hale twisted around, pulling his trousers up.

"Emiko?" Mama cried out, afraid. Not for herself but for Emiko. Mama's face went papery white beneath her sun-warmed cheeks, and she reached for Mr. Hale. "She'll go. Don't be angry."

"What in—" Squinting at her, Mr. Hale's face contorted in confusion. "You snooping on us, girl? What's that you have?"

He barreled toward her, a tsunami of coiled muscles and clenched fists, and all Emiko could do was hold the mirror in front of her, a shield between her and Mr. Hale. Just a foot from her, he careened to a stop. Staring into the mirror, his muscles went slack, as though the skull had evaporated from beneath his skin. His jaw fell open and his lids flared wide in horror before drooping over his eyes, as though the sight he saw in the mirror was too much to behold.

"No..." he whispered and he reached forward toward the mirror with a shaking hand. "That can't be me."

The mirror screamed. Mr. Hale clutched his chest.

The scream was a shrill discordant note that pierced the air and it rose, higher and higher, louder and louder. It shook the entire room, sound pulsating in waves. Emiko was certain her eardrums would burst. Vibrations pummeled the house, shattering windows and bursting doors off their hinges.

Emiko screamed. It was overpowered by the mirror's shrieking howl. Wood began to splinter beneath her feet. The floorboards tore apart. Cracks spiderwebbed across the ceiling and down the walls, jagged fissures that spread with each moment.

Something struck Emiko on the head, and everything went black.

Now

Taking off the blindfold, Emiko made her way to the kitchen with the mirror's cleaning supplies. She set the bucket down on the counter and looked out the window. The sun hung low in the sky. Far below the shack, the sun played with its reflection, dipping itself band by band into the rippling glass of the ocean.

Time for dinner, a bit of reading, and bed.

Knock, knock.

Emiko blinked. No one visited and she knew why. The rumors. Her fellow islanders said she was a hapa haole witch who cursed anyone who set foot on the abandoned, haunted Hale sugarcane planation. The thought made her smile. Certainly, she wasn't a witch. If only they knew that she was the one under a curse.

Knock, knock.

Making her way over to the door, she opened it a fraction. A man stood on the step. A hat was pulled down over his eyes. It was the sort that tourists wore—straw, boater style—but Emiko had never seen one in black.

Despite the setting sun, sunglasses, the lenses perfect circles, obscured the man's eyes. It was typically warm and humid, but a long black jacket enveloped him, collar turned up and leather gloves covered his hands.

"Can I help you?" Emiko asked.

"Yes, actually. My car broke down. May I come in and phone for help?"

"I don't have a phone," she responded, trying to see the man beyond his attire. "Sorry. Head east down the road. There'll be a gas station."

"Water, then. I've been walking for hours. May I come in and have a drink?"

She should tell him no and send him on his way. Something about him reminded her of a spider. His words were soft yet thin, like silky threads meant to reel her into his web.

Wafts of gardenia emanated from the man and enveloped Emiko in a thick, heavy cloud. She hadn't smelled the scent for decades, not since she tore all the gardenias on her land out by the roots and she knew how to avoid them when she walked to the store. She wasn't fully certain why she detested gardenias, though, only that she did and that it had something to do with the mirror–

"What's your name?" she demanded, shaking herself from the gardenias' spell. "Are you a tourist?"

"My name is Amdis. I am on holiday. So perhaps you can forgive my intrusion. Truly, I only wish to come in and have a sip of water before I continue on my way."

It was a lie, Emiko was certain of it. Perhaps his name was Amdis but he didn't only wish for water. There were houses nearer the road. Hers was far up; miles in. He would've had to trod across crushed sugarcane stalks, all of them entangled with weeds and grasses that'd grown unrestricted for over a century. No, this man was seeking her for a reason. But Emiko wasn't afraid of him.

She only feared the mirror.

"Come in," she said.

His lips lifted in a courteous approximation of a smile and he crossed the threshold. Once inside, he took off his boater hat and sunglasses. He set the hat on the bench she used to take off her shoes and set the sunglasses on her little side table.

Emiko got a good look at him. His skin was as white as the under-belly of a fish. The unnatural hue distracted from his otherwise attractive features and dark hair, which was cut close on the sides but rose on top in a cresting wave. He was...young. Or at least, there wasn't a single wrinkle across his forehead. But the sagacity in his eyes hooked Emiko. Such a look was earned. Over time. Lots of time.

"How did you know I was here?" then she sighed and answered her own questions. "I suppose you heard the rumors. The ones about the hapa haole withc on the abandoned sugarcane plantation?"

"Perhaps. Only I don't believe you're a witch. I believe you're only an old woman, alone, with no one in the world."

"When you put it that way, it sounds practically tragic," Emiko said dryly and it was enough to twitch Amdis's mouth into a real smile.

"I live the same way as you. Alone. Old. Only I don't look it."

"Well, believe it or not, I'm older than I appear. I do age...just slowly. Much too slowly."

"A blessing," Amdis said, a hand ruffling through his perfectly coiffed hair. The tousling somehow only made his hair more rakishly attractive.

"A curse," Emiko responded, more sharply than she intended. Her tone caught his attention and he nodded, ever so slightly. One long moment of silence passed and they stared at each other, a connective energy of understanding sparking between them. Then Amdis stepped catlike to the side.

"I must say, you almost had me," he said. "You almost made me believe that you are indeed someone like me, someone who's been touched by the left hand of the Devil. I do know there are all sorts. Men who turn to dogs at the full moon, men trapped in this realm as ghosts, men sewn together with thread and brought back to life." He circled her, the steps getting tighter and closer. "They say you are the hapa haole witch but there's no witchery here."

Amdis stopped right in front of her. With cold fingers, he lifted her chin until her gaze met his and smiled. His eyes turned black, as though the pupils were yokes that'd been pricked so they spread and filled the egg white. His incisors lengthened right before her eyes. They pushed forward from his gums, two pointed fangs.

"I am hungry. I must be fed."

. . .

Then

Emiko emerged from the darkness with a gasp. She sat up. Lights punctuated her vision in a shower of painful shooting stars. It was mercifully silent, but her ears rang, echoes reverberating through her brain in agonizing bursts.

She stared.

Mr. Hale's body was twisted on the ground. His face was a frozen masque of fear, but his eyes were glassy, sightless orbs.

Nothing had touched him. At least, nothing on the outside.

Then Emiko saw Mama.

Mama was curled on her side, her hair creating a halo around her head, just as it always did. But her body was heavy on the ground, every limb limp against it, a trickle of blood running down her forehead. Emiko knew.

She crawled to Mama and laid beside her, as close as she could. There was no breath. There was no warmth. There was no spark of light burning far inside her eyes like geode within rock.

Child.

Emiko heard the voice. It was oddly high, yet low; indeterminately human. She didn't respond. There was no reason to. All the good in her life was Mama, and Mama was gone.

Child. You are my daughter now.

At that, Emiko lifted her head. The mirror leaned against the wall, unbroken from what she could see. For a moment, she had the wild idea of throwing herself forward so she could behold herself in the mirror. If she did, she would see the monstrous girl that she was, the girl who had ignored her Mama's plea to leave things alone. If she was lucky, she would have a heart attack like Mr. Hale.

You will serve me, as a dutiful daughter does. All I ask is that you tend me. In return, I shall lengthen your days.

"I wanted to save Mama," Emiko whispered. "I deserve to die."

But you did save her. She prayed every night for two things. The first: to be saved from Mr. Hale. The second: for you to be cared for. You granted both with your faith in me. Now tend me.

"And if I don't?"

To be free of our entanglement, you must look full at your reflection and see your own poison...but if you do not, you must tend me.

So, Emiko did. If she ever went too long without tending the mirror, an invisible thread wrapped around her neck, tighter and tighter, until she stumbled to the mirror with a cloth in hand. Only then would the thread snap and she'd be left gasping. Once, she tried to cover it with a blanket over it, but the same effect occurred, until she pulled it off.

She tended the mirror as years unspooled both long and short around her. Eventually, she wondered if she'd lived before the mirror —if there had been such a soul as Mama. If there had been a childhood spent slipping through the maze of sugarcane stalks. If there had been other faces, other voices, other hands around her. It often seemed as though those memories were fever dreams stolen from someone else's life, and that she'd been born of the mirror. That it was her and it; bone and glass; daughter and mother.

Or monster and monster.

Because even as the past receded, one thing remained. A splinter in her soul. While her memories drifted into specters and then those specters drifted into ether, the splinter remained. Festered, as though time was sun and water that made it grow.

It was guilt. The knowledge that she'd killed Mama, even if she couldn't picture Mama's face or quite remember who she'd been to her. And with it came the knowledge that one day, Emiko needed to face herself in the mirror.

Not to set herself free but to remove the splinter—and pay for the extraction with her life.

Now

. . .

Emiko laughed at Admis.

"You must be fed," she said. "The mirror must be tended." Exasperated, she threw her hands into the air. "Mystical beings are so high maintenance."

Admis arched an eyebrow at her, his lips still drawn back to show his fangs. Then, he let out a sigh and the fangs retracted into his gums with a soft click.

"I'm hungry," he said grumpily.

"There are plenty of tourists to eat."

"It isn't so simple. If I devour a family of five from Montana, it's likely to draw notice."

"So that's why you came here. No one will notice I'm gone."

"That was the thought," Admis said. He considered her carefully. As he did, the black recentered in his pupils and he donned his human self once again. "You've long outlived a human's life...you are one of us. Touched by the left hand of the Devil."

"It's just a side effect of caring for an ungaikyō," Emiko said.

"What is it exactly?"

"A haunted mirror. It gained its soul and when you look into it, it shows you your own soul and every bit of evil that's in it. You see a monster." She felt as though she was reciting a fairy tale no one believed.

"And where is it?"

"In the living room."

With decisive steps, Admis strode to the room. Emiko ran after him. She stopped in the doorway. If she didn't, there'd be no way to avoid her reflection in the mirror. For a moment, she thought of running for the blindfold.

Admis walked straight to the mirror and stood in front of it. He looked like a fighter anticipating a knockout blow. But there was no fear in him. Only determination. Then his shoulders slumped and his head hung. One minute ticked by. He cleared his throat and straightened up.

"I thought I might..." he trailed off, returning to her in the hallway with heavy steps. "I thought I might see myself again. But there was no reflection. Curses honor other curses, it would seem." He shook his head. "Though I'm glad I realized you aren't merely an old woman. If I'd drank your blood—who knows what dastardly thing would happen to me. I was friends with a fellow like me once. He made the mistake of drinking a sorcerer. Let me just say, it was not good. Now, I shall leave you in peace. Unless–"

"What?" Emiko asked warily.

"Would you like me to turn you? To do so, you'd have to drink the Devil's Communion. My blood. If you did, you wouldn't have a reflection and—"

"The mirror wouldn't have any hold over me," Emiko finished. Her mind raced, pulsing hot with the possibilities. She could be free. A sip of Admis's blood would deliver her from the mirror's hold. She could stare straight into it and no image would return to her. The mirror would have to release her. It wouldn't matter that she hardly had any memories. New ones could be made and it would be as though that phantom childhood of hers had never been.

Yes. She would say yes, and drink the Devil's Communion. Loophole her way out of her curse. Never mind the splinter that had become an oozing, open wound. Never mind the woman whose face Emiko could no longer see.

The woman.

Mama.

Emiko sighed.

"No thank you, Admis."

After Admis left, Emiko took a deep breath. For the first time in a long time, she felt alive. Every nerve was awakened, every beat of her heart was poignant with being. Before he'd come to her door, she'd been inoculated by the endless march of days and years, a train on an eternal track. Admis's visit shook off the decades of lethargy, like a rag passing over dust and cobwebs.

She would do it now. If she didn't, she'd have the gaping wound but no reason behind it. Eventually, time would take away Mama's name. It'd already taken away Mama's face.

Slowly, Emiko walked to the living room. The mirror sensed her. It rarely spoke, but today it said,

Daughter?

"I am going to see you, Mother," Emiko replied. "And then I shall see myself."

Before she could think or waver, Emiko threw herself in front of the mirror.

She stared into it.

Shaking. Shrieking. Shattering. She was so certain about what would happen that she almost thought it had. Her body was braced for an onslaught of sound and movement. Then she realized all was quiet and that she was staring straight into the mirror.

A person stared back at her.

The image was young. The cheeks were flushed with heat and life, the hair circling the head, the eyes bright and keen.

Emiko said the person's name in a voice that sounded like a child.

"Mama!"

5

WHAT WE BREATHE

BY DAVID LASLEY

It's so easy to take a deep breath
Inhaling sinister fumes
We deceive ourselves

Everything is never enough, lest
We admit our wounds
Truths we'd never tell

Everyday life is a litmus test
From the watchers' views
Am I faring well?

I see the over-connected,
clamoring crowd's unrest
Yet if it approves
I'm further compelled

So I hold this ache deep in my chest
Breathing in value
From somebody else

Seeking to be a god instead
Of finding One who
Needs nobody else

The time has come: respire, rest
From this grim pursuit
Suffocating us

And to draw in better truths He's said
We, beloved, needn't prove
Any more of ourselves

6

THE ASSASSIN'S KISS

MORIAH CHAVIS

"*W*e agreed, only one more. This is the one I choose."

Ky glances between the curtains and into the ballroom before his eyes settle on me. "That was before you walked in looking like-" He waves his hand in front of me.

"What's wrong with the way I look? This is what I always wear to fish." I run my hands over the thighs of my outfit, a silky black dress that expands into a plume of fabric in various shades of red, black, and cream.

"Celene-"

"Tonight, my name is Hyacinth, according to my dance card. It will never be *Celene* again. And after tonight, you'll have no right to my new name."

Ky's eyes soften, reaching for me like he's wont to do. I imagine the gentle caress of his fingers as they slide an errant strand of hair behind my ear. But it stays firmly in the land of dreams, and his hand hovers in the air before falling to his side.

"Now, if that's all-" I step toward the curtains, and candlelight flickers across my face.

Ky's eyes harden and he grabs my wrist. "Your lips are swollen,

Ce-Hyacinth. They've never been this bad before. How much are you wearing?"

"Enough," I snap. "It won't kill me. *This* isn't the first time I've worn it, and I followed Madame Prim's regime, to the dime." I think back to the nights I stared at the ceiling as my lips burned, the endless scrubbing never completely ridding my mouth of the poisonous residue. "I'm not new to this—I know my limits."

His hold doesn't loosen, and I let myself memorize this touch, adding it to the list of other moments I'll have to forget in order to leave.

"What did you use?" he asks, voice insistent.

"It doesn't matter."

He takes a step closer. "What did you use?"

I chew the inside of my cheek. "One of her newer creations. I've tested it on a few of her marks."

"Celene," he says, and this time I don't correct him. "You shouldn't have done that. Did she test it first?"

"She didn't need to. I know what I'm doing. I've been here longer than anyone." I rip my arm from his grasp and step back.

"But—"

"Am I dead? No. Leave it alone, Ky. I've got to go."

"You're wearing black—to a wedding," he rushes to say as if that's evidence enough that there's something wrong.

Not using a new poison.

Not cutting myself off entirely from the only life I know.

He's stuck on *me* wearing black to a wedding, but it shouldn't surprise him after all these years. A knot forms in my chest.

All these years.

And after tonight, we will never see each other again.

Why, Ky? Why do we have to keep doing this? Why can't we have our last words to each other be what we said at the Sanctuary?

"I love you," he said. *"I'll always love you."*

"Mantises aren't meant for love, Ky. We're made for one job."

Murder. *The word hung silently in the air between us.*

He placed his hands on both sides of my face. "But if you weren't?"

52

"Ky—"

"But if you weren't?" He searches my face, gaze pleading.

Tears sting my nose, making it hard to breathe. "Then...it would be you, Ky. It will always be you."

His kiss had been more awakening than the dawn, but I was made for the night. The love I could have had with Ky would have lived in the day, brighter than the sun. The world we belong to hides us in the shadows.

"Black is my color," I say, pushing the memory into the locked box, the one I'll never open again. "Black hair, black eyes, black heart. The killer three, as Madame Prim says, with a dash of a red lip. Now, let me do my job. I'll send word through Mela—"

"You're too noticeable—"

"One. Last. Job!" I hiss. "Madame Prim wants me to attract the target, and this dress always works best. Call it my swan song. Let me have this."

I can't have anything else.

I can't have you.

Ky's jaw clicks. My fingers itch to run through his mess of brown curls, my palm to rest against his flushed cheek, to slide my hands under his doublet. But I can't do that, not again. If I want out, I have to get out now, and I can't drag someone with me who doesn't want to go.

Lock it in the box, Celene—No. Celene is gone.

Celene died when Fritta did.

Ky knows where he belongs, even if he doesn't fully understand what it means to belong to Madame Prim. I used to know where I fit; my path was clear. Take care of Fritta, punish those who deserve it, and wake up the next day to do it again.

After tonight, all that will remain is an empty shell and a satiated hunger for vengeance. I knew when they brought her body to the Sanctuary, this would be my last hit. Even when Madame Prim begged me to stay, promised me *this* hit would be mine—but not my last. The Mantises already look up to me, she had said, but I didn't want it. Part of me believes in what we do, but the part that buried

Fritta questioned if what we did even mattered. I can't do it anymore.

Not if I have to do it without my sister.

"I'll do this one," Ky says. "There are other ways. Mela can assist. Please, let me do this. It will be my gift to you and Fritta. She was family to all of us–"

"No," I say, my voice sharp. "I will do it. Here. Take some gold, have the servants dim some candles, pay for a spicy number, and let me do what I'm here to do. One last time, signed in blood. I'm not doing this again." The hair on my arms stands, and I fold in on myself. I lick my lips and feel a slice of pain, numbness from the poison. But it is nothing more than a weak comfort now.

"Now, stop hovering in the corner. Madame Prim will think I've lost focus."

"Are you sure you can do this?" she asked, not once but twice.

I would have said yes a third time, and a million times after that. If this is the thing that breaks me, I want my scattered ashes to stand for something.

I push through the curtains, slide my mask back down over my face, and step into the wedding. A hum of excitement dances across my skin, almost thicker than the magic flying in the air. White and gold drapery hangs from the ceiling, and I walk like a shadow in the mist. The music glides from the stringed instruments, plucking the guests from their shells and creating an ambience of celebration.

The bride and groom sit at the head table, another noble pairing, another girl trapped in a life of fine food and empty promises. According to Mela's hurried update when I walked in, they hadn't looked at each other all night. The new Lady of the House's eyes are trained on another below, seated at the two tables of guests, stretching one-hundred people on each side.

Ky wasn't wrong. My dress is...unconventional for a wedding, but it isn't the most outlandish outfit at the wedding.

I whip out my fan and cover the bottom half of my face as I study the room.

Look at me.

Each guest is aware of me, but the masks allow them to hide who they are and ignore the others in attendance as their eyes follow me through the room. Paired with the heavy-laden drinks emptying as soon as a servant sets down each chalice I'm only the woman in the mist, not the devil in disguise.

Except to the one I'm after.

Look at me.

Blue eyes catch my face, and I smile, the look barely visible through the red lace of my fan.

The groom leans over and whispers something to his new bride. His eyes never leave mine. She nods absentmindedly to him, her gaze barely leaving the person she loves seated below as her new husband's laughter fills the room. Characters like him are what make my job easy. When the guards search for the groom, no one will remember me. Everyone will remember *him*, the boy who made even the new lady of the house laugh.

They won't remember me.

They never do.

And if they did, well, I'll be gone without a trace.

I slide into the corridor, hugging the shadows. I feel Ky's absence like a physical wound, but I press on, cauterizing my bleeding heart and cleaning the blood with a promise of vengeance. He won't follow; he knows the rules. The game has begun, and we never show our hand to our rivals.

The music in the hall picks up, and the wine flows freely. I ache to rest. Between preparing last night and getting ready today, my stomach is hollow, and my back aches. My lips are swollen, but not enough for anyone to notice or consider why. Besides, once the groom figures out what I am, he'll be halfway to his death.

The truth is, I've been doing this so long I almost don't feel the effects, not after Madame Prim's stiff regime.

Poison.

Wait an hour.

Antidote.

Poison.

Wait three hours.

Antidote.

Poison.

Wait six hours.

If it doesn't almost-kill or kill you after three rounds, then you can wear it all night without any effects. Except for the swelling.

It's not uncommon to lose Mantises in the first few assignments, which is why I refused to let Fritta join. I had to do this to survive, but Fritta had me—even when it felt like I needed her more.

The groom walks out, and he almost stumbles into a servant. My chest tightens until she speaks.

"My apologies, my lord," she rushes to say.

Mela.

Thank the stars.

A part of me expects Ky to slide from the shadows, and I hold my breath as I watch their interaction.

"Nothing to worry about, miss." He clears his throat. "I, uh–"

"Third alcove," she whispers, and I almost don't hear her voice.

"Excuse me?" the groom asks.

Mela turns her face up, brown skin and dark hair falling over her shoulder. "I believe the third alcove has the answers you seek."

"Oh!" he says. "Oh, well, yes. Thank you." He clears his throat again and rushes past her. Mela's dark gray eyes catch mine in the light, the ghost of a grin hovering at the corners of her lips. She winks before disappearing.

I count the groom's steps as he makes his way toward me. My dress fans out in front of me, exposing the high slit and absence of clothing beneath. "My, oh, my…" I tsk. "Aren't you wound tight?"

"What's someone like you doing alone?" the groom asks, his charm taking over.

I smile, cheeks aching.

"I'm not alone," I say, pushing away from the wall and running my hand over his arm. "You're with me."

I lean in, catching the smell of him, like cedar and money, dull and steady.

But money can't buy everything.

This was it. The thought slips in unwanted. *This was the last thing she smelled.*

I falter, and the illusion breaks. "Miss–"

"My apologies, my lord. The wine." I wave my hand. "Maybe a room with a bit more light would do me some good. Private, of course. I would hate for the wedding guests to see me like this."

His smile returns. My lips twitch with impatience, but I cover it with another smile.

"I know just the place," he says, offering me his arm.

I take it and push down the vile words rising in me. We walk through the halls of the manor, each more endless than the last. Finally, we stop at two double doors. The groom pulls out a set of keys from his pocket and fiddles with the lock before swinging open the door and ushering me inside.

Moonlight stretches across the floor from a large, cracked window facing the cliffs. Waves crash against the beach and rocks, and the sound drowns out the thud of my heart thundering in my ears. Two towering shelves of books outline each side of the window with a lounge chair half hidden beneath a cozy blanket; the perfect place to escape.

"What do you think of this, my love?"

I smile at him, brushing my fingers over his. "This is perfect. Should I let someone know when I leave?"

The groom falters, and my smile widens. He responds in kind and he lets go of my arm, closing the door behind him with a soft click. My heartbeat picks up, and I walk toward the lounge, taking off my shawl and spreading myself on the seat.

"What a lovely view," I say, digging into my bag and reapplying my lipstick.

My lips heat up, and I let out a heavy breath after I finish adding another coat. I glance over my shoulder, fluttering my lashes.

He walks over and reaches to brush back my hair, but I stop him. His wrist isn't as frail as I would've imagined. Part of me has been picturing him as a monster, not a lord in a castle on a hill. This man, somewhere between, with soft hands but sturdy bones, would have easily tricked anyone into believing he didn't harbor evil behind his charm.

Too bad he tricked the wrong girl.

"Two rules, never touch my hair, and I will kiss you when I'm ready," I say, and he nods.

He kisses my forehead, and I have to hold back the tears as a memory washes over me.

"Can we run away, Celene?" Fritta asked, watching the snowfall from our window at the top of the Sanctuary. "Can we run away one day and never come back?"

I lean over and kiss her forehead. "One day, maybe."

He moves to my cheeks, and I have to fight the waves that threaten to crash over me. It's never been this personal for me.

"They found her body near the river," Ky said.

I stared at my sister, only fourteen years old—clothes ripped, virtue stolen, and wrists slit.

"I will kill him."

It had taken a year, but I found him.

Now, he kisses my nose. His hand slides up [60] my side before dancing over the fabric at the collar of my dress.

"You're so beautiful," he whispers.

I lean over and kiss him, imagining he's someone else and hating myself for it. Ky doesn't deserve to have his kisses wasted on this monster. The groom's breath catches in his throat, and he leans into me. His hand moves around my waist and fiddles with the strings of my stay.

All thoughts of Ky go back into their locked box as I push into the man in front of me, slipping my tongue into his mouth and holding his head in place as the kiss deepens. I want to vomit, to spit in his face and watch as remnants of poison fester on his flesh, but I don't.

I bite him—hard, tasting blood.

He jerks back.

"What the—"

I pull back, lipstick smudged, the outer edges burning my cheeks. The groom's eyes slowly open, and he peers closer.

"Don't worry about it," I say, reaching into my purse and pulling out a handkerchief. I rub my lips until they're raw and toss the rag out the window. "I've done this for years."

"Been a..." He coughs. "Whore?" He coughs again.

I arch a brow. "Oh, I'm not a prostitute, if that's what you mean."

He can't stop coughing now. His hand rubs the center of his chest, and he falls back on the lounge. I take a step closer to him, cocking my head to the side and watching him as the poison seeps into his skin; his blood.

"What..." *cough* "have...you..." *cough* "done?"

His hand tugs at the collar of his shirt. I take a step closer to him. His breathing grows labored, and a sheen of sweat breaks out on his forehead.

"Who...are...you?"

"Who I am doesn't matter. Fritta James. Do you remember her?"

"Fri-" His cough cuts him off.

I grab him by the collar and yank him toward me.

"Fritta James!" I hiss. "Do you remember her?"

"No!" he croaks. "I've...been...with..."

I slap him. "She was fourteen!" I keep my voice low, not wanting to attract attention, but I spit the words in his face. "Fourteen!"

His eyes widen in recognition, and fury builds inside me. He tries to hide it, but it's too late.

"Do you know what we do to men who hurt women?" I say, voice low, filled with venom. "This is almost a kindness. You deserved worse. But-" I study him. "But the horror will almost be enough. When your heart races—the room spinning. Knowing you are dying alone, with no one to save you. No one truly caring. Will they even notice you're missing? Are they used to you disappearing with whatever girl you've tricked next?"

His eyes are already starting to glaze over. When they find him, the pupils will be a cloudy gray, as if someone reached inside and stole the color.

"Your body will fight it, but it doesn't matter. It's in your blood now. It doesn't take much—just a kiss. A teasing tug of the lips; poison in a wound. That–that will do the trick."

His breathing goes from labored to sharp wheezes. He slumps back on the lounge, hands tugging at his collar, but his fingers aren't working anymore. His muscles are giving out. Come morning, he'll be dead in his filth.

"Did you stay with her?" I whisper as life goes out of him. "Did you watch her die? Or did you have someone else do it for you after you stole her innocence?"

His eyes meet mine, lips parting and almost forming words before his last breath falls from his mouth. I can't decide if I want to know the answer or not.

I let the tears fall as I stare at him, ignoring the smell of death now permeating the room. The waves crash outside, and I stare out the window for longer than intended. Memories of my sister float to the surface; how she dreamed of a wedding like this one day. My mind wanders to the bride, staring at the man she loves as the one she married followed me to his death.

For a moment, I imagine my sister's laugh crashing into me.

"One day, I'm going to marry, and it will be out of love," she said, watching as I donned the night's outfit. "Then you won't hate weddings anymore."

I ruffled her hair. "I will always hate weddings. But I'll make an exception for you. I might even smile."

I leave the room without a backward glance, locking the door behind me. Mela meets me outside the kitchens, taking my dress and hiding me from view as I change into a simple brown frock, tying a scarf over my hair, and watching as she tosses the dress in the outside fire.

"Where will you go?" she asks, handing me my bag–everything I've ever owned in a satchel.

I shrug. "Anywhere to escape this poison."

"You can never escape the poison," she whispers. "There's no antidote for what we've done."

I meet her gaze. "Well, I'm going to try," I say.

I'm halfway to the woods when she says, "And if I need to find you? Who do I ask for?"

Our eyes meet. "Goodbye, Mela." I step into the trees and don't look back.

7

A MIND THAT FADES

BY BRIANA URBAN

Poison is time slowly chipping away.
A mind that fades,
Slowly at first and then
Suddenly-all-at-once
"Where am I? How did I get here?
I'm scared, Jenny,
I can't remember where I was driving to."

Poison is a phone conversation on repeat,
A question asked over and over.
"How many cats do you have now?"
"Just the two, Mom."
You talk about the weather,
The zoo shows on TV,
Your kids and their jobs.
"How many cats do you have now?"
And you say, trying not to cry,
"Just the two, Mom."

"Are you safe from the hurricane?"

You reassure her, yes,
It will miss you completely.
She is happy. She was worried,
She's been following the news
And it looks like a bad storm.
The phone call ends, a short one today,
One with few questions.
But tomorrow comes and the phone rings,
And when you answer she says
"Are you safe from the hurricane?"

It's laughing when she says something ridiculous,
When it's a good day with few questions.
You talk about the vet shows
And the zoo shows,
You talk about your daughter the zookeeper,
And the one who fixes cars.
You talk about your two cats,
And your brothers and their families.
It's laughing now, while you can,
Because the other option is crying
And you're so tired of crying.

Poison is her checking the grocery list in
Every
Single
Aisle
At the store,
Because she can't remember everything on the list.
And every time she says
"I think they moved things around recently."

It's her anger at having to shop for clothes,
It's wondering if she should use the stove,
It's helping her send out birthday cards.

BY BRIANA URBAN

It's every little thing that you have to change
About how you talk to her,
Trying not to take it personally
When she gets angry and mean
Because it's not her, not really.
It's how you talk about her
To your daughters
And your brothers and your father,
How you all have to adjust
And try to understand what can't be understood.
It's your brother in denial,
"It's not that bad, she'll get better,
I want to come see her."

Poison is your daughters seeing this,
Your mother and her struggles,
And remembering their great-grandmother
Who suffered the same.
And now they wonder,
Will this be me?
Is this our fate?
Is old age the greatest poison of all,
Stripping away our minds and leaving nothing behind?

How many cats do you have now?
Are you safe from the hurricane?
I'm scared, Jenny,
I can't remember where I was driving to.

8

SNAKE SKIN AND PLEATHER

BY CHRISTIANNA MARKS

*T*he first time I saw The Huntsmen, the crowd roared so loud at the end of every song that they almost blew the roof off the venue. But I screamed for one man and one man only. As I stared up at him, all long legs and long hair, I fell in love instantly. He might not have known I existed as I clung to the rail...right below the stage, but I knew that man was my future.

But Robb wasn't mine. He belonged to the bitch next to him, her voice harmonizing with his like honey, where mine sounded like vinegar. Her belly already straining against the silk slip dress she was wearing. The ring on her left hand connecting her to Robb in a way that ninety percent of the females (and some of the males) in the audience would kill for.

That was six months ago, at the beginning of The Huntsmen's 2000 North American Tour, and I've seen every single show since that fateful day. The first day I laid eyes on Robb Barr, and every day since, I've wished his wife was dead.

Tonight's show is no different. Me, yearning for something totally improbable, but still swinging my bra in my right hand. Trying my hardest to draw Robb's attention as he strums his guitar and makes sweet music with his wife.

"Thanks for coming out tonight," Robb shouts into the crowd with his native- Californian vibe.

"It's been a pleasure, that," Georgie Barr cuts in as they begin the last song of the night.

Is it because she's from the home of the Beatles? Is that why he fell for her, because she's British? Is it because she's brash in a way that I'll never be able to emulate, no matter how many leather jackets I buy, or how dark my lipstick is, or the nose-ring glistening in my left nostril?

"As It Ends," their last song, is coming to a close, and I know what comes next. Robb will play the last chord, and then throw his guitar pick into the audience, and someone else will grab it out of the air because he never sees me.

But tonight is different. Tonight he's looking right at me, and he winks.

I stare back at him brazenly and throw my bra at his feet.

At the exact same time, he tosses his pick into the crowd, but I'm too worried about whether or not he's noticed the bra to see where it goes.

He usually only has eyes for his wife, who's starting to look like a balloon. She's due to bring their offspring into the world in a month or so. Just another thing I'll never get the chance at.

I feel pressure all around me, people trying to get next to me, pushing against me, and I'm on the rough wooden floor before I know what's happening.

"I got it! I got it!" some dumb bitch says as she plants her Doc Martin boot in the middle of my sternum to keep me down where I fell. She's got Robb's pick in her grubby hand. He tossed it directly at me, and I didn't even realize.

I throw my hands up to cover myself when another pair of boots almost lands on my face. And then I grab her ankle, trying to trip her, but she's too fast.

"Aye," a loud voice booms from above me, "if you's can't act like ladies, then git."

It's the band's manager. He's an older guy who's always close to the Barrs. His accent matches Georgie's so he must be from Liverpool

SNAKE SKIN AND PLEATHER

too, but that's where the comparison ends. "How's about a hand up?" he asks as the girls move away to fight for the pick out in the parking lot.

By the time the old guy pulls me to my feet, Robb and Georgie, with her fiery red hair, are gone. Completely gone.

I'm usually outside the venue by now, waiting to follow them to the next show in my beat-up 1977 Ford Bronco. A vehicle that's only a year older than I am. I need to get to the Bronco, and fast. I lost track of the names of the venues a couple shows back, so I'm only vaguely sure where they're headed next. I need a visual on them. Unless there's someone to ask...

"Wait, where are they playing next?" I ask the old guy.

"I've seen ya' before. You're one of them, aren't you?"

"One of who?"

"One of the birds who can't see that Robb there loves Georgie more than the air in his damn lungs."

I clench my hands at my side. He's not going to help me out and I don't have anymore time to waste on him.

"Nah, I know he's stuck on her and I can't have him," I say as I give him a knowing glare. "But it doesn't mean I'll be over him anytime soon."

I know it like the ground knows when it rains. The thought turns to music in my brain, as Robb's voice sings the line in my head, the same way he sings it on the CD.

"I'm not gonna tell ya' where they're off to. I know this comes with being famous, the crazy birds, but those two kiddos deserve a little bit of normal." He's useless. I turn on my heel and head quickly toward the side door. "However, I can't stop ya' from doing whatever it is you've been doing the whole tour," he shouts after me as I leave him behind.

My legs burn and my heart rate spikes as I run for the driver's side of the Bronco. I stalked the van when I got here and found it parked around the back of the venue. I'm hoping it's still there. I need it to be there. Or else I'll be left behind...again. Just like so many times before.

By my dad who didn't even stick around to see me turn one. By my mom when she died of an overdose in a trailer-park. By a system that claimed it wanted me, but spit me out into the world as soon as I turned legal.

I go after what I want now, and now I want him, in whatever way I can have him. Even if it's mostly just taillights and once-in-a-lifetime eye contact.

The van's pulling away from the curb right when I round the corner, and I'm glad I didn't waste any more time on the old man from Liverpool inside. I would have lost out on everything. Aside from air, this is the only thing keeping me moving.

It's a warm summer night, and the air-con stopped working last year, so the wind gets to cool me off. Which is my only option since someone stole my hard top three months ago.

I recognize a few other vehicles as we follow the van onto the freeway. I'm not the only one who's following The Huntsmen, but I'm the only one who's been following them the whole tour.

What does that say about me? That I'm devoted? The rest of the cars keep dropping off one by one as the tour goes on. Sometimes they don't even make it to the next stop. They give up before we get there.

We've only got a couple more weeks left, and then Robb and the woman who scooped him up before I could are done with music until after that baby in her belly is out.

I pop their album into my stereo, and turn it up, so that it's louder than the wind in my ears. Others might think it's too much to follow them while listening to their music, but it makes me feel like I'm the one living in the fairytale. Even though girls like me don't get the happy ending. We get whatever is left over, and an early grave... if we're lucky. The women in my family have never been lucky. We try to make our own luck, but even then, we rarely ever win. I don't see why the pattern would change with me. It's never worked that way before.

We've all been driving in a caravan for about four hours when the van pulls into a gas station. It's about time too. My bladder is about to explode, and even though I'd pee in the cup sitting next to me, I really didn't want to.

At this point, I don't care if I run into any of the band members while I'm inside the service station. I used to be more careful, but they know I'm following them. They also know I haven't tried to kill any of them yet, so I might be the freak who's following them, but I'm harmless.

It's a good thing my thoughts can't become reality, because then Georgie would have been six-feet-under months ago.

Everyone beats me inside and I have to wait for the bathroom.

Which is shit.

I stand there waiting with my legs crossed, my thighs pressed tightly together, but at least I'm not Sandra, who's behind me. She's been following along for the last couple of weeks.

"I've gotta pee," she says as she runs her hand through her chic mullet.

"Me too."

"These people have bladders of steel."

I laugh, because she's right.

The door in front of us bursts open and I'm staring directly into Georgie Barr's face.

"It's all yours," she says with a grimace. She holds her belly with one hand and the door open for me with the other. She recognizes both of us, but she doesn't say anything else. Which is fine, because I don't know what I'd say back. If she was Robb, I'd ask him to leave her and marry me.

Maybe I wouldn't, but I've never had the opportunity.

On the way back out I grab a stale donut and a gas station soda that's as big as my upper thigh. Getting jacked up on copious amounts of caffeine is the only option, because stopping to sleep isn't one.

I slip a jacket over my bare shoulders when I get back to the Bronco. It's cooled off a bit.

I don't know where the other cars went, but it's just the Bronco and Sandra's Jetta. We're the only ones who've followed through tonight, so she's my only competition . Though I've heard through the grapevine that Sandra's here because she's got a lady-boner for Georgie, not Robb. She's nice enough, but she's still an obstacle.

Even though we shared a laugh in line for the bathroom, I have this mad thought, just for a second, of swerving into her little car and watching it roll down the side of the hill we're driving on. It makes me feel warm and fizzy for a half-second, but then I wake myself up from my deluded nightmare.

I can't kill someone.

If I did, I don't think Robb would ever look at me the way I want him to. I caught a brief glimpse of that look tonight, and all I want to do is swim in it forever. I can't do that from behind jail bars. Good thing he can't see my diabolical daydreams.

Daydreams and reality are two totally different things.

I pull my hair up into a scrunchie, steering with my knees. My pleather pants grip the steering wheel just right. It gives me something less wack to focus on. Plus, I've gotten enough strands of hair in my eyes in the last five minutes to last me my whole life.

The van swerves outside of its lane. In six months, I've never seen anything but steady driving. It doesn't matter what time of night it is, the driver is always a straight shooter. It swerves again.

Something's up.

Nothing better happen to that van; it's got precious cargo in it. It's got my future and everything I love inside. I don't know what I'd do if I had to watch Robb die tonight. I think I'd die too, right on the spot. Just straight up die of a broken heart. Right in the middle of the road, next to him, blood running from all the places my tears should be.

I don't want us to end like that.

Can something end that hasn't even started yet?

Sandra catches up to me and gives me a look from the warm inside of her car. She's worried too.

The van straightens out but speeds up. A lot. It feels like we're all racing; against what, I don't know. We're going somewhere with urgency, and the van holding my lifeline is the only one who knows where.

Sandra and I tag-team, keeping the cars on the freeway behind us, because every once in a while the van doesn't stay between the lines. We've both silently agreed we're the gate-keepers for our favorite band to ever exist. We're going to keep them safe.

The guy behind me is honking his horn, but we're going to permanently cock-block him from going anywhere fast. This is a state of emergency.

The van pulls off the freeway and Sandra is right behind it.

I almost miss the exit, but I cut the asshole off that's behind me and jump over a bit of a plant where the ramp and the freeway verge away from each other. My ass slaps against the driver's seat, but the Bronco is made for it.

I'm bringing up the back, totally clueless as to where we're going. It feels like something is about to change for all of us.

I can feel it coming in the air tonight, as it whips a stray piece of hair into my eyeball. Again. I just hope and pray (to whatever God has never been there for me before) that something isn't wrong with Robb. I just need Robb to be safe. I need to live in a world where I know that he exists. One where he will continue to make music. So even if he's not mine, at least he'll be in my life forever.

I know he's supposed to be in my life, the same way I know I would die if I couldn't breathe.

The van makes it through the intersection in front of me, and then Sandra's car does, and then the light turns yellow before I even make it to the white line on the street. I have a split second to make a choice. Run a red light or be left behind and hope I don't lose them.

I run the light and dodge a car that comes barreling toward me. Their horn blaring.

Don't they have eyes? Can't they see that I don't give a flying fuck about the rules that they're so carefully following? I could crush their little car with the Bronco's tires. They'd be the ones in trouble if we collided, not me.

I'm going so fast that I almost run into Sandra's back bumper when the caravan slams on their breaks.

I'm glad I'm sober. There are too many nights I don't remember. Too many nights when I didn't think I needed to be sane enough to make it through to the next one. And then The Huntsmen happened and Robb Barr saved my life one note at a time.

Our story could be one of fantasy, but instead, this whole night seems to be turning into a nightmare. I don't know where I'm going, but I know this feeling. It's the same one that I had when I went into the system. The system that didn't give a shit about me because I was too old and wasn't cute enough, and had a thing for dismembering Barbie dolls in the bathtub.

I just wanted to cause something else pain so I didn't have to feel my own.

I've been causing pain my whole life because I don't want to get swallowed whole by the feeling of not being enough...for anyone. It's the only way I've been able to put one foot in front of the other, until now. I will protect Robb Barr with everything that's inside of me. Every harmful instinct disappears when he's in my orbit. I'm only better because of him.

The van hangs a left into the parking lot of a hospital, and it's like all of my worst fears are coming true.

He's dead. I just know that Robb is dead.

I can't have nice things. Life won't let me have a single good thing. I'm the girl who was made for heartache and bad things. A life filled with poison, and no matter how hard I try to turn the tides, they never turn in my favor. Ever.

I slam the Bronco into a spot that's a few rows away from where the van parks. Sandra parks right next to me. The nerve of her. Trying to share the role of savior when she's only going to feel like shit when she realizes Robb is dead.

Or maybe she'll be elated. She's after Georgie anyway, right?

The driver's door of the van pops open and Robb, thank God he's alive, rushes over to the passenger door. He practically carries Georgie out of her seat and I can tell the bottom half of her dress is soaked. Even from back here, even with the terrible lighting.

The baby is coming, and it's early.

Honestly. Robb might as well have died, because the knowledge that his baby is almost here brings the death of my dream. Of course, I have to be here to witness it. Everyone else will get to read about it in a couple of days. This was supposed to happen after I bowed out because the tour was over.

But no, this kid is going to be the poison that separates me from Robb.

I shouldn't be here, and yet I am, and I can't pull myself away. Not even as I watch Robb rush Georgie through the automatic doors of the hospital.

I wait thirty minutes and then it's like my body decides that I need to be inside and all of a sudden I'm heading into the waiting room. I pass Sandra's car and she's already got the seat tilted back, snoring logs. I can't hear her but it's obvious from the way she's breathing. The whole car's gonna fog up in no time.

The chairs in the waiting room are made out of scratchy fabric, and the armrests are just a bit too high to be comfortable.

This is a bad idea, but I've never been one for good ideas.

As long as no one asks me why I'm sitting in here, I should be fine.

After spending so many hours driving in the dark the hospital lights are jarring. It's almost like the stage lights from tonight happened a year ago. That's how long this night feels. One hour slowly dripping into the next. They've stopped being their own time-keepers.

"You okay?" A nurse asks as she comes over to me.

"Yeah, I'm fine. Just waiting on someone," I answer under my breath.

In venues, parking lots, gas stations, and driving down the freeway I've never felt like I was doing something dodgy. But in this waiting room, I feel like, if I opened my mouth and actually said what I was doing here, people would judge me. That they would point and laugh at me for something that a lot of people do. This place makes me feel like I'm back in one of the shelters. Being judged for existing, for just breathing the same air as everyone else.

I grip the armrest and look at the girl sitting across from me. She's trying to stop the blood that's trailing down her face from a cut on her eyebrow. It looks bad. She's gonna need stitches. Lots of stitches.

I'm in an emergency room, which makes sense, because Georgie is definitely in a state of emergency.

I'm just glad Robb is safe.

Even if my dreams are dead, he isn't. Even if everything I've ever hoped for dies in this shitty emergency room in the middle of God-knows-where.

The rest of the world doesn't matter when your whole world revolves around Robb Barr. And it does. My whole world is singularly devoted to one man. One man I'll never have. If he knew I was out here waiting for him, would it change anything?

Like an answer to my silent prayer, Robb is suddenly in the lobby. He looks exhausted. He looks like he's barely held together with string. Like if you cut one end, he'd unravel into a mess on the floor.

"Hey," he says as he sits in the empty seat next to me. "It's nice to see a familiar face."

My heart stutters. I don't know if this is a gift, or if it's the worst form of torture.

"Hey," I respond as I reach for the scrunchie in my hair. I don't know what my hair looks like as it falls around my shoulders, but at least I don't look like I'm twelve.

"You were at the show tonight, right?" He rubs his eyes like it'll clear everything away. They're such beautiful eyes.

And I'm sitting here wondering when he's going to bring up the fact that it's weird that I'm here. I'm the thing that's out of place. I'm the thing that shouldn't be taking up any of his time. But he looks like he's happy to find me here. Or if not happy, at least glad.

"Yeah, I might have thrown my bra at you." I mean a for it to sound flirty, but it comes out sounding wrong.

Still, he laughs. It sounds strangled under the weight of everything that's going on, but he's laughing outright. "I remember," he snorts.

It's cute. I shouldn't be thinking it's cute, but I can't stop myself.

"You're forgiven, even Georgie thought it was funny." Reality comes crashing back in. He looks worried, and even though she's not physically in the room, she hovering over this moment. The only moment I've had with Robb.

I hate her all over again.

How can I hate something so completely that Robb loves? If he loves it, shouldn't I? Isn't that what love is?

"How is she?" I grind the words out of my mouth.

"She's fine. The baby's coming early."

"I figured."

"A month and a half early. I don't know why we thought we could tour and finish up with a month to spare. We were supposed to have the kid back in Liverpool. Georgie wanted to be near her family. Instead, we're here." He says it like it's the most normal thing in the world, touring until you jump on a plane and fly halfway across the world to have your baby.

"It's all gonna be okay." I reach for his hand, but drop mine right before it gets to him. He watches the trajectory and lets out a breath when I deflect. Does it make him happy that I didn't touch him?

"You're right. Everything is going to be fine. We're all going to be fine," he says as he rakes a hand nervously through his hair. Pulling it back from his eyes.

His damn eyes. They're too distracting up close.

"So where are you headed now that the tour's over prematurely?"

His question feels stilted, jagged against our conversation so far.

"I don't know. I guess I'll have to figure it out, won't I?"

It feels like I've been hit with a ton of bricks. I'm never going to see Robb again, but at least I have this moment. It's more than I ever thought I was going to get. I wish I could push him up against a wall of the nearest empty corridor and kiss him until he forgets about everything but me. Until I'm the only thing his world revolves around. I want to make him feel what he makes me feel, but this is not that kind of moment. Not when Georgie's having his baby in the same building.

Not when I'm just some random girl who he's never going to talk to again.

"Why wouldn't you go home?"

"Home is wherever...I am," I blurt, sounding like some country song playing in a honky-tonk. I almost said, "you are," which wouldn't have been any better.

"A lone wolf, huh?" h e asks.

"If I'm being honest, I'm more of a snake." The words slip out like I'm shedding my skin. I don't want to lie to Robb. He might be the first person I've never wanted to lie to.

He's some fictional part of my life that I'll always get to keep for myself. Tucked away for a rainy day, because God knows there's been more rainy days than sunny ones in my life. He's a secret I get to keep for myself and no one else.

"Okay." He raises his eyebrow like he's intrigued. I gave him an answer he wasn't expecting, and he doesn't know what to do with it.

That's something I am good at—surprising people. Even when they don't want to be surprised.

"I like to go where things are warm. Places where there seems to be some form of light to drag me towards it."

"Sounds more like a moth to me," he replies. "A moth to a flame," he adds when I just stare at him.

Here I was, going for worst case scenario and he finds a slightly better one, because moths have wings. He'll never know how well it fits.

How can someone who will never be yours get you so completely?

"Robb, Robb Barr," a nurse says as she opens one of the two swinging doors into the waiting room.

Robb stands, holds his hand out to me, and I shake it. Cherishing the moment that our skin touches.

I need to imprint the feeling in my brain. Flesh against flesh. Warm skin against warm skin. My elevated heart rate beating against his palm.

"Thanks for the distraction. It was nice talking. Have a good life," he says.

He's not being a jerk. He's not being an asshole. He's being sincere.

"You too. Congratulations," I respond, almost choking on the last word.

"Thanks," he says as he looks back over his shoulder at me.

This is it; the last time I'm going to see Robb Barr, until The Huntsmen go on tour again. I know it in my bones, so I look good and hard. I stare at his ass as he walks away, and I don't feel bad about it. When the door swings closed as he follows the nurse, I stare just as hard at the spot where he used to be.

We breathed the same air for a second. Even if it wasn't as sexy as my fantasies, it still happened. We still shared the same space and acknowledged each other's existence.

The bleeding blonde girl across from me leans forward. "Was that THE Robb Barr? Like from The Huntsmen?"

"Yeah."

"He's gorgeous. I should have said something. Why didn't I say anything?"

She must be all of 17. She doesn't stand a chance. Well, neither do I and I'm 22, but at least my age isn't the thing holding me back.

"Why's he here?" She leans forward.

I could tell her. And maybe, if she was from a tabloid and I'd get money out of this shitty night I would, but she's just some random who smashed her face on the right night.

"What happened to your face?" I ask.

"Ran into the corner of my mom's upper kitchen cabinet," she says as she puts the blood-soaked kitchen towel back on her eyebrow.

"And where's your mom?"

"She's at work. I drove myself here." She says it like she's all proud of herself, but I think her mom should have been home to take care of her. Everyone should be taken care of.

"Did you tell them you're here?"

She looks at me bashfully. She's just a kid, but that doesn't stop me from thinking that she's dumb as a brick.

"Hey, can't you see this girl is bleeding everywhere?" I say it loudly, directing it at the lady behind the front desk.

Everyone turns to look at me. Like they have from the moment I walked in here. Hanging with rock stars and yelling at nurses. What else is new?

"Oh," the lady says as she looks up from the computer she's been working on. "Oh, let me get you the paperwork."

The receptionist stands and walks over to us with a clipboard.

"Thank you. I'm Cadence," the girl says as she takes the clipboard.

"Cathy," I say. I haven't told anyone my name in so long that it feels like foreign word on my tongue.

Her pen scratches quickly across the forms, and then she's whisked out of the room, and it's almost like she was never there to begin with. I'm alone again, with no one but strangers.

Leaving this overly- hygienic room makes me feel like I'm abandoning Robb, but if I don't leave soon, I'm just going to be setting myself up. I'm just going to feel like a fool when he comes back out here, hours from now, and I'm asleep in this ridiculous chair with drool all over my face.

We already said goodbye. There's nothing else that needs to happen here.

I'll sleep some of this exhaustion away in the Bronco, and then I'll pick a direction and drive into the unknown when the sun comes up.

It's still not very cold when I step back into the night. The darkness and the stars envelop me like a blanket and I guess that's a good thing since I don't have one of my own. Mine blew out on the freeway multiple cities back.

I lean the driver's seat all the way back, throw another sweater over my shoulders and pass the hell out before my eyes have even closed.

Sunlight wakes me up, and I realize the sweater I covered my head with has slipped onto the floor. The sun is piercing my eyelids, forcing me into conciseness.

And a sob cuts through the pain in my eyes. It's loud and it carries across the blacktop. Sandra's still dead asleep in her car, so it's not her.

"How the fuck am I supposed to live?"

I'd know that voice anywhere. It's the voice that sings me to sleep. It's the voice that took the time to talk to me last night. Robb Barr sounds like he's dying. Robb Barr sounds like he has nothing left to live for. There's a little bit of hope bubbling up in my chest. I can be what he lives for.

I slip out of the Bronco.

And make my way over to the sobbing rockstar on the curb.

"The baby?" I have to ask about the baby first.

He shakes his head. "The baby's fine. More than fine. She's alive," he says, his voice breaking as he looks up at me with tear-stained cheeks.

I sit down next to him.

He puts his head onto my shoulder and lets out another earth-shattering sob as his arms go around me. It feels like I'm the only thing keeping him in place. I'm the only thing making sure he doesn't float off into space.

"It's okay," I say into his hair. "It's all going to be okay."

"She's gone. She's gone and I have to raise our baby by myself. Once Billie Jean's out of that glass coffin of a NICU, I'll have to take her home alone," he sobs into my neck.

Georgie is dead.

I think the words, but I'm having a hard time making myself believe that the man of my dreams has just lost the only thing standing in our way. Or that I'm the one here to pick up the pieces of his life.

"It'll be okay," I say again.

I can't help the smile that spreads across my face.

This is the beginning of my fairytale.

9

BABYLONIA

BY JORDAN NISHKIAN

He handed me an apple once
and after I watched him
devour its parts—its hide, flesh, core,
its cyanide seeds that call him for
more—the sanguine fruit began to drum.

Bleeding from spasming chambers,
the arterial stem contracts.
My fingers reach, linger, pray for beyond
ivory-enameled gates. He smiles,
cardial tissue stuck bare

in his gums. "My Delilah," warm vermillion
sprays. "My love." I wipe his grizzled chin
with stygian locks—the same that washed
his feet, that trickled up open thighs.
No giving him up, I'd rather split him in two.

BABYLONIA

Hands grip at sable hair;
tugging at twisted roots, they want
to pulverize his samsonic frame,
break him, make him search
for a strength self-made.

1 0

AN EASY MARK

BY AMANDA HAVILL ADGATE

*H*e said he loved me.

The cell door clanks, and I can hear them, the chattering birds, wailing and jabbering in their cages. It's become background noise, the constant stagnation of life on hold, paying for their sins with time and sanity. I don't get to leave my cell—it's so close to my trial date— so they are faceless voices, echoing across the smooth cinder block walls, a sort of rhythm to the madness. Clanging cups in the morning, the metal-on-metal rattling my teeth, then it's yowls and murmured words, thick like syrup dripping down the walls until lunch. Then come the prayers, whispered or screamed, the tears or the outbursts, like a car bomb, shrapnel and cruel words or fists flying. That's when the guards are busiest, hurrying back and forth down the slim corridor lining the cages, and I listen to the noises that will soon be a memory. I can feel the smile curling my lips, stretched over my face like a circus clown's, red and crude. I am pleased no one can see me.

Forty-seven days I've been here, thinking about those three little words, listening to the clamor, feeling the bars rubbing my skin raw, chafing my soul. Waiting. I decided forty-eight days ago that I was done waiting.

That's where it started, the beginning of the end of the world. Three little words.

I met Kit outside my building. Snow drifted in lazy clouds through the air as my boots rested against wet concrete, the world weighted with the promise of endless winter. My apartment was a matchbox with peeling paint, haunted by the ghosts of past tenants. Better their ghosts than my own. *Home* was a word I never understood. Childhood hadn't been easy for me—a mother with abandonment issues and a father with a penchant for booze and tomfoolery. By the time I turned seventeen I was out of there, scraping enough money together to catch the bus to the first big city on the schedule. The past has a way of creeping up on me, claws sinking into the soft flesh at the base of my skull, and for whatever reason, that day I hadn't been able to shake off the shadows. They lurked at the edges of my mind, whispering between the steady beating of my heart. I only ever wanted one thing, one thing to change my days from survival to *life* and I longed for it with every nerve ending, every cell in my body hungering for that future.

Kit leaned against the wall of the drugstore on the corner, leather jacket rubbing against the worn brick, smoke twisting in a lazy spiral from between his fingers. The sight of him chased away the shade in an instant, a behemoth smashing through the memories, like getting high off of helium. I floated, weightless, anchored by his ink-black eyes. Infinite possibilities—the freedom of the future—laid out before me like starbursts in the vastness of space. *This is destiny, Sunshine. Ordained. Fated.*

I just...knew.

He was the one I'd been searching for.

Our relationship began as a whirlwind of fisted sheets and wild nights, biting kisses that morphed into feelings whispered against slick skin faster than the winter thaw. If I close my eyes now, I can still smell his aftershave mingled with clove cigarettes, taste his salty skin against my tongue. Those months were a glorious time of shifting perspectives and coiling thoughts. My head couldn't keep up with the possibilities of a life with Kit in it.

It was magic, destiny—it was completion at the next level. Kit was addicted, I could see it in his eye, the need fulfilled, but only for a moment. It was a look I had known my whole life, as familiar as the back of my hand, as the tiny constellation of freckles aligned on my wrist. The details didn't matter: we were world-worn lovers, finally finding purpose and intention in the beating heart of another.

"Never leave me." His words brought tears to my eyes.

Yes. I'll never leave. This is forever.

I was overcome, splicing my soul to grow roots into his. A new creation of heated words and longing looks and grand plans.

The idea—a tiny seed that had grown over the years spanning between that bus ride and Kit's first kisses, a weed reaching for the sun, resilient and ruthless.

"Life's hard, Sunshine, you know all about that. We need to fix it for us, don't you see? Money is the root of all evil. We are cutting it out at the root, helping ourselves for a change. No one has ever looked out for you, but *I* look out for you, baby."

He stroked my cheek with a rough finger, and my mind cast back to those years, slashed red and black—my ghosts, the memories that haunted—that I breathed into his ear the night before, feeling the heady pulse of his heart beneath his ribcage. Words describing my mother and her weak spine, depicting my father and his strong back-hand. It was freedom, revealing my past, sharing the pain that poisoned me, coating my insides in rot. Our souls melded together, melting to become a new creation, one with willing hands and a sharp tongue.

"Yes." The word hissed from between my teeth—his favorite word.

With him, all things were possible. He accepted me as I was. He made my wildest fantasies a reality.

"Hey." The guard rattles the bars, forcing my gaze to his face. "Fifteen minutes."

I dip my head, blonde hair falling to hide from his inspection, his greedy eyes tracing my form. Revulsion claws at my throat, but I remain still. He may stare, but I've already disarmed him. He's too dim-witted to see the signs. I wait until his footsteps retreat before lifting my eyes to the small window, light filtering through to touch the white cinder blocks.

Kit's plan was simple—he spent evenings in the dim light mapping his marks, a red pen clenched between his glinting teeth as he researched bank locations, penciled in estimated response times, and scoured the internet for locations nearby that would conceal us effectively. His obsession was a delight, bonding us together in a way that transcended any other romantic entanglement I had ever experienced. We were made for each other, it was clear in those days. His fever infected me, racing through my veins and setting the world on fire. It didn't matter that his grip became rough. I wore the bruises that bloomed across my skin like badges of honor, proof of my devotion to the man that turned his dark eyes on me and altered my world. It didn't matter then, that I looked into the mirror and saw my mother staring back at me. He loved me. This was what I wanted.

"I love you." He whispered the words after a particularly rough night, raking his fingers through his hair, pleading with me to understand—and I did. Of course I did. I couldn't give up on him then, not when we were *so close*.

Days passed slowly, the television blaring about rising temperatures and spring break plans. "Sunshine, this is it." Eyes wild, he turned to me, his jagged nails scraping against my skin.

I imagined sparks spilling from those scratches, blood dripping to the floor. A thrill raced through me.

"We're going to do this, and then the world will be ours." He squeezed harder. "I'm all you have, and we are in this together."

I nodded. *Yes, I am with you.*

Four banks turned into seven, and with each additional stop added to his crudely drawn map, my stomach swooped lower. The sheets lay tangled at the end of the bed, neon lights casting bold colors across the pale fabric, untouched by his skin.

And then it was time. Swept up in the allure of breaking rules and persuasive kisses, we packed the car, Kit's rusty old Honda, and worked our way across the state.

The first bank was easy—a small target, the guard's face dumbfounded when he saw the gun in Kit's hands. No one tried to be a hero. The money smelled like ink and endless possibilities as the teller loaded it into the bag, and Kit kissed me, all teeth and tongue and intense longing that I thought I would die, right there in front of so many terrified eyes. We made it out of town before the police even knew we were there.

We were invincible, and I was floating, edging ever closer to the sun. *So close.*

From there, the robberies blended together—the whites of the witnesses' eyes, the distant blaring of police sirens that never caught up to us. He would kiss me at every hit, as the tellers stuffed bags with cash, violence swirling in the air like the smoke from a campfire. It was heady, *romantic.* The bruises started marring more of my skin, but it didn't matter. Five banks down, and the bills were crammed into three suitcases, lining the trunk of the Honda. Kit whooped in the motel room when his face popped up on the television screen.

"We did it, Sunshine. Fame *and* fortune. They'll never forget us now!"

The smile strained my lips, powered by sleepless nights and manic thoughts, of secret hopes curled into soft flesh that bruised easily. I couldn't tear my gaze from the map, smudge marks from his hand marring the page—so much like the darkened blots defacing my body.

"Hazards of being a lefty," he joked, but I saw the insecurity creeping into his eyes, muscles tensing up, as if waiting for my ridicule, to give him a reason to show the proof of Kit's love, a language I know so well.

As if I would find him lacking. *Never.* He was the answer to so many prayers that I uttered, alone at night hiding under the covers, hands clenched until my knuckles were white while the shadows lurked, waiting for blood. My childhood was soaked in the scent of alcohol and arnica, my mother's floral perfume.

"Two left." The words tumbled from my mouth as he watched the news, a sharp excitement turning his face into a stranger's, stark and shadowed. His inky eyes turn to me, gleaming, a predator's stare.

"You still up for this?" He slid closer, pulling me flush against him. The buckle of his belt caught on my hip, and I bit back a yelp.

"Of course. This next one, it's the biggest on your list." I willed my body to stay still. I wouldn't mess this up. *It was all I ever wanted.* "We could be set."

His cold nose nuzzled my neck, the scent of cloves and aftershave sticking to the back of my throat like a film. His fingers tightened at my back, kneading my spine—a threat and a promise twining around my bones.

"And we *will* be set, after these last two banks. Then we can travel to Mexico, live on the beach and sip Pina coladas until we are old and gray." He dropped a kiss on my cheek, lingering. His teeth scraped against my earlobe and I shivered.

"I can't wait to see what you look like with gray hair." My fingers slip into his dark curls, and he groans. The rest of the night is spent tangled in scratchy sheets, his words saying what he couldn't show me. The dawn arrived quickly, my eyes tracking the progress of the sun through dusty motel curtains.

~

The inmate in the cell next to me starts yelling, slamming beefy hands against the metal bars. My thoughts flutter, papers caught in a sharp breeze, while the guards work to calm her down, threatening and cajoling, before the cacophony begins to fade. It's always like this when my mind curls in on itself, as if that can keep me from shattering into pieces. I can focus again, on the story I won't ever be able to tell another soul—the secrets I clutch close to my heart, a treasured pearl, my most precious possession.

The last job started off without a hitch. The bank was almost empty of customers, and the tellers cooperated quickly, filling the bag with little difficulty. The guard was occupied with Kit, his voice muffled underneath his ski mask, growling threats and gesturing wildly. My heart was racing in my chest when I met the bank manager's eyes, and suddenly my moment had come. Emotion surged over me like a tidal wave, raw and overpowering. I was ten again, watching his fist connect with my mother's jaw, feeling his nails dig into the soft skin of my arm. His hair had grayed, but the rheumy eyes of my father were the same as I remembered. Those fists had left bruises on my skin that matched the scar tissue on my heart, and as I raised the gun, staring down the barrel into those eyes, stretched wide at the sight of a predator, at *me,* a thrill of pure delight slid up my back to rest against my left ear. *Finally.*

A hand closed over mine the next moment, and I couldn't drag my eyes away from the man who ruined my life—"father" wasn't the right word for what he was to me. *Monster* fit better.

Kit's whispered words clogged against my eardrums, not making sense. His fingers tightened over mine. When I slid my gaze to meet his eyes—pitch black as the nights I would shiver on my bed while my mother's screams echoed through my skull—I relaxed my stance, enough that witnesses would see me surrendering, putting the gun down. My father heaved a sigh of relief, and Kit's eyes swung over to him just as I tightened my fingers one last time around that trigger.

The anger that surged through me at that noise, the idea that he was *free,* that he would be walking away from this, ignited a fire as cold as ice inside my chest, cracking through the room like an avalanche.

Time passed in fragments after that—I was floating again, the air tasting of cotton candy and the grit of stardust. The memory of those hours are pieces, the edges jagged and sharp to recall. The bank manager's name tag, the gold around the edge gleaming in the fluorescent bank lights. Kit's hands, the fingers trembling on the steering wheel. His mouth was moving but I couldn't hear a word over the wild laughter bursting from my chest. I rubbed a hand over my face, only feeling the blood when it stuck to my cheek, viscous. What once was life clinging to life. It coated my fingers, the red under my nails so vibrant it didn't look real. Chipping like paint, flakes falling onto my blue jeans like a red snow storm.

"Shit, Sunshine. *Shit."* Kit's eyes roll in his skull, like a frightened animal. He turned the corner sharply, throwing me into my door. The laughter spilled from my lips, and I couldn't stop it even if I tried. The sirens wailed behind us, growing fainter as Kit drove into a corn field, the stalks barely reaching the top of the car.

"Is he dead?" The words rolled around my mouth like hard candy, sweet and jagged. I could feel Kit's eyes on me.

"Why did you do it? Why did you shoot that guy?" He shook his head, those black curls dancing in the sticky air, and I trailed one crimson finger down his cheek, relishing his shiver, the mess I left behind. That was the moment he *saw me,* the entirety of me, down to the depths of my soul, and his discovery had him reeling.

"Why did I kill my father?" I chuckled and leaned back into the seat before my mind wandered again. "Did I, though?"

The flashes get worse from there, my memory scattered like ash in the breeze, and I have to close my eyes to concentrate, to recall the last delicious bits. Savoring the ending of the greatest story of my life. The sounds around me—the inmates, the guards, echoes of the isolation and insanity—batter my eardrums like a ship at sea, but reliving those moments feels natural. My hands tighten around the metal of the bed frame, an involuntary reflex at the thought of the cornfield, those final moments. It had been thrilling, like racing the sun or cliff diving in the dark.

I remember words tripped out from behind Kit's white teeth like dominoes. "They're almost here, Sunshine. You gotta distract them, let me hide the cash. Do you hear me?" The creak of the car door, and the steady *thump* of police-issue boots approaching filled my senses. I could feel my heart beating fiercely against my ribcage. Knew that *this was the last loophole to close.* It was so perfect, the way he framed his suggestion—his *order*—to me that I was nodding my head before the words had a chance to sink in. *Of course, of course I will do this for you.*

This one last thing.

The officers were there in a blink of an eye—maybe I was distracted, my mind whirling with vicious exhilaration at crossing off the number one item on my to-do list. Their badges gleamed in the fragmented sunshine, the rustling of the cornstalks like a windstorm.

Kit did the rest.

A fascinated horror filled me at the sight of him, shoving past me to escape into the waving green stalks. I crashed to the ground, scraping my knees as dirt embedded itself in the red decorating my hands. My view from the trampled corn stalks littering the earth was unimpeded—I watched his body shuddering to the ground, the bag slipping from his grasping fingers as the bullets hit his back. The world was a distant roar, like standing before the ocean, and I couldn't tear my eyes from him, reality seeping slowly back in, color leaching back into a black and white television program. Questions were asked in stern voices, one after the other until my skull was pounding with them, a maelstrom of gruff men barking for answers that I was sure they didn't want to hear. It's all about the narrative, isn't it? Belief in *your own beliefs.*

So I lied. I told them what they wanted to hear.

Monsters are hidden behind shy words and coy smiles, a mask of innocence that fits the narrative of strong men in power. Monsters are *made,* created from cruelty and despair. Crafted from the scattered bits of a world that broke them into jagged pieces—and monsters just decided they wouldn't take it anymore.

It was easy, conforming to the story crafted behind closed interrogation room doors, coffee cups and sympathetic hand pats. They took one look at Kit, his tattoos and the way he dressed, and had everything figured out already. *Poor thing. An easy mark. What kind of a man targets such a sweet girl? It must've been so horrifying for her.*

I heard them, the judgments coming before the investigation, low voices putting me in pegs before I spoke a word. With one glance it was plain to see my designated role—like slipping back into an old suit, mildew festering in the pockets, but no one ever looks that closely.

The judge, rigid and unmoving as a mountain, cracked as I sat at the defense table so demurely, his ideal posture for a woman. But I was a snake, buried in the brush—at first glance there's nothing there, but the poison sits just under the scales, waiting for the right moment to strike. I keep the venom close to my chest, confident it isn't necessary. I am nothing if not prudent.

His words are stern, a father lecturing his daughter, and I play my role. Meek and helpless, the quintessential qualities in a woman. Easier to manipulate, delicate bones against soft skin.

"Yes, Your Honor." Fragile, like gossamer threads.

My father's eyes flash in front of my mind again, the recognition right before I pulled the trigger. I promised myself I would destroy my pain, and I did. It was easy, conning Kit into doing exactly what he was tempted to do—killing two bastards with one stone, I mean. Greed and love of money was his downfall, and simply I led him to the edge, taking care of a little unfinished business on the way. My father won't get another chance to break me again. The therapist at the hospital was right—processing my trauma has been very helpful. I feel free, for the first time in my life. His heavy hand, the one that bruised me and broke me before I knew who I was, won't touch me again.

I've had a lot of time to think about this, ponder the purpose of my life and choices as I sat in a jail cell, doubling down on my role as the poor, helpless female, gaslighted into participating in robbery, progressing to murder. They believe what they want, and I'm happy to let them. I live to serve the patriarchy, of course. But *we* hold the real power—it was as effortless as talking Adam into eating the fruit, twisting him around a finger to listen to the serpent's hissed promises. Woman was made to charm a man into doing what he should not. Gentle fingers, casual words, and the plan unfolded before Kit's eyes, dazzling him with his own brilliance, the light blinding him to the truth. I am the puppet master, pulling all the strings. Revenge has been served boiling hot, and my plans don't include prison time, so I continue my role with a fearful glance, curling in on myself. *Help me, I need saving.* The heroes come, swarming like flies on a corpse.

A spike of glee fills my chest, and I mime wiping away a tear. The judge eats it up, his eyebrows pulled low with barely-concealed concern. *My hero.*

The sun is warm on my skin as I leave the courthouse, free from the shackles of the law, from the film of men's eyes. It's my right, taking power from under their distracted noses—too busy looking for the next challenger. Reveling in the applause of their great feat, they miss the mouse scurrying away with their very souls. *Who is the real victor?*

If Kit could see me now. It is a shame—those inky eyes inspired me, and now they stare without seeing inside a wooden box in a pauper's field. I made sure of that.

Men are fools—they are the easy mark.

11

THE SWEET KISS OF DEATH

BY ANNE J. HILL

Death kissed her lips and
wouldn't let her go.
He caressed and entrapped her
in an intoxicating love affair.

He wrapped his icy fingers
around her waist and planned
to hold her within his embrace
until the end of all time.

He wiped her tears and
whispered sweet nothings in her ear,
until her guard was down
and her fight was gone.

The sweet kiss of Death
was poison on her lips.
A cruel master that dealt harshly
with his victim in the night.

But a whisper flowed through her,
a memory of a peace she used to know.
Her soul fought against his weightless void,
a spark within setting ablaze.

And then he robbed her of body
but not of soul.
For Death holds power over
her flesh alone.

12

THE WELL

BY K.C. SMITH

*D*eep in the thick snow-dusted pines, where the sun's warm rays never shine, and the cold winds of winter do not blow. Where the mockingbird's mimic does not reach, and the low hum of summer can not be heard. Where shadows move on their own accord and a simple whisper echoes through the trees like a shout through a cavern's maze, there is a well.

In appearance, the well sits like any other. A circle of stacked weathered stones with mud hardened into crumbling dirt between the cracks and pale green moss snaking its way along the sides. But its story is one that has echoed throughout time. No one knows who built it or how the well came to be.

It has simply always been, existing through time as if it had come before all else. The world built up around it until it was left forgotten in the deep gloom of the forest.

That is, until a young boy lost his way and ventured too close, unable to avoid being trapped in its web. The well, hungry and desperate, sensed the presence of life. It drew the boy closer, singing him a song of longing and wonder like a siren reeling in its prey.

And so, our story begins paving the way of history with little more than a coin and a stone.

Torsen was a fine lad, a boy of great strength and sharp wit who enjoyed exploring. He wished to learn and further his mind; to create and invent. His greatest joy was discovering new plants and animals, and how the elements could be used in different ways, creating something else entirely. It was his curious mind and wandering spirit that had Torsen exploring so far from his home, from any place he had ever gone before.

The world was big and full of marvels. It was Torsen's greatest wish to see all of what the world had to offer. To travel from coast to coast and over the sea to other lands. And so it was on this day that Torsen's keen curiosity finally pushed him beyond his usual distance.

He walked across the sprawling green hills surrounding his home to the towering white-capped mountains that no one in his village had ever visited before, following the line of monstrous rocks and stumbling upon a forest of giants.

As he progressed through the dense wood, he listened to the sounds of nature: the rustle of leaves beneath his feet, the creak of branches above him, the low whistle of the wind as it moved around tree and rock. These sounds were what Torsen adored above all else, more than the singing women of his village and even more than the wooden pipes that were blown through to create soft melodies. No, it was the sounds of the things that had existed long before he and his village, the original song of the earth.

So it came as no surprise that when these sounds could no longer be heard Torsen took notice, searching through brush and pine for a reason why a hush had fallen over the wood. A bleakness seemed to bleed into this place, as if the forest there was dying, crumbling before Torsen's eyes.

Torsen cocked his head of golden blonde hair to the side in fascination, trekking onward through the strange place, undeterred by the sullen scene around him. With each step, the ground seemed to soften as if it was slowly rotting the further he ventured within. He looked to his feet to find tendrils of inky black earth spreading out like a web of venom seeping into the land.

The further he walked, the colder the wood grew, causing his breath to fog in the air before him. Still, he kept his pace, growing even more curious yet faintly uneasy about what was at its center.

When he began to shake with cold, wrapping his arms around himself in an attempt to stay warm, thoughts began to flit through his mind of turning back. But it was then, as those very thoughts passed across him, that his vision caught on something.

Through the dying trees, intense green was laid out like an animal pelt upon the ground, and sitting in its middle was a circular stack of gray stone—a well.

As Torsen drew closer to it, the air grew warmer, chasing away the frost that had clung to him. The colors of the forest faded from browns, blacks, and grays to a world so vivid he squinted his eyes against its brightness. A singular point of life within a dying forest. The abnormality reeled him in like a fish caught on a line until he stood upon the lush green grass before the well.

Torsen peered into the circle of stone covered in soft, delicate moss. A low hum began to vibrate around him. It rang in his ears and was oddly soothing. He extended a hand out, letting it hover above the black, eerily still water, lowering his hand slowly and stopping just before he touched its dark plane.

It was then, just before he was about to touch it that a wayward thought broke the trance he had been in. As if someone—or something—had delicately placed it just in the forefront of his mind. He became acutely aware of the weight that hung within the coin pouch slung around his waist. This was a sacred place, and an offering should be made. He should throw a coin into the well and ask for this place to bless him. This circle of creation was something different, a place of reverence.

A single bronze coin glinted in the sunlight between his fingers. Torsen held it above the water and released it, sending out a wish for the unique protection of this place to follow him for all his days.

Torsen watched as the coin simply vanished beneath the well's surface without a splash or ripple of water. The coin lost to the darkness. He gazed at it, curious, when something began to show within the water. A slight whiteness grew bright and solid as a stone began to rise from beneath the water line until it sat upon the immovable surface no larger than the very coin he had just thrown in.

Torsen reached out, his palm tingling as he held it above the stone, hesitating to pick it up. Suddenly, he rocked forward, feeling a shove from an unseen force. His hand plunged into the pitch black waters around the stone. Torsen's eyes widened as he pulled the stone from the surface, letting it rest within the palm of his mysteriously dry hand. He hadn't a moment to consider why his hand was not dripping with the dark waters of the well, for the stone began to push into his skin.

A cry of pain escaped Torsen's lips as he attempted to pry the stone from his palm, but it only dove further into his hand, tearing through skin and cracking bone. Torsen fell to his knees, crying out in terrorized torture as he clawed at the stone, trying to pry it from where it burrowed into his flesh.

When the searing agony finally ceased, he looked down at his throbbing hand, expecting to find mangled flesh, but what he saw had him pushing up to his feet, bewildered. There was no blood, not even a small gash in his hand. His skin was perfectly intact, but left in place of the stone, marring his skin, was a black spot the same size as the stone. Torsen flipped his hand, inspecting the unharmed smooth skin. The stone was gone.

As Torsen looked back at the well, it had changed. No longer were the waters dark and foreboding. It was clear, looking as any other well. The ground and surrounding forest had also transformed, looking as any other forest would. Gone was the vivid liveliness of this place, and the strange black tendrils that had wandered from it.

Torsen shook his head looking once more at his palm. The black spot remained, permanently inked upon his skin. A breeze wrapped around him, sending his hair standing with goose flesh. He turned, no longer aware of where he was or how he had gotten to this place.

He had never been this far within the forest before, and each branch, each tree began to close in on him as if they were reaching down to tear him apart.

Suddenly, those very trees that had loomed over him like angry beasts, creaked, their branches arching, until they were all pointed in a single direction. Torsen's fear had begun to coarse through him long ago and he took the opportunity, sprinting through the path that the forest had cleared for him, hoping it led him back home.

But when Torsen made it through the rows of trees, breaking free from the edge of the forest, he was not home. He breathed in large heavy breaths, chest heaving, lungs burning from the excursion and terror of fleeing from that strange place.

Torsen had come upon a small village he did not recognize. Straw-roofed huts were scattered about, with few people ambling between them. He recognized no one and instinctually felt that he was an exceptionally long way from home. Outside of the nearest hut sat a woman tending a large pot of stew over a fire. A wayward thought flitted through his mind as he observed the pot swaying slightly as it hung over the fire. At first just a small thought, although not one he had ever experienced before. It was an unkind musing, something entirely foreign to Torsen.

In his village there was only goodness. He had only ever felt goodness all of his days, but this felt wrong. None from his home had ever treated another unkindly, it was an unfamiliar concept and

Torsen did not know where it came from.

As Torsen took a step toward the woman tending her meal, an urge so powerful and all-consuming gripped him, taking over his senses until all he could think of was the horrific thought that had wormed its way into his mind. His hand itched to knock over the boiling pot of stew that dangled above the burning embers.

He attempted to shake the peculiar thought away like an unwanted insect that had been hovering by his ear. He needed to know where he was and if these people might help him to get back to his own village.

Taking another step toward the woman, his body went rigid, only his leg moved, kicking out at the smoldering pot and knocking it off its pendulum above the flames, its contents spilling across the dirt.

The woman squealed, jumping back as the scolding contents splashed, burning her flesh.

Torsen only watched as the stew slowly seeped into the earth. It was as if that singular cruel act opened the doors of malicious intent and flooded through him. A slow, malevolent smile spread across his lips and he grabbed a flaming log from the fire, noticing how he did not feel its heat. He threw the log onto the roof of the nearest hut, watching in thrilled interest as the fire quickly engulfed the entire hut, spreading onto the next one.

"Why are you doing this?" the woman cried, watching as her home and all her belongings were incinerated.

"Because I wanted to," he said simply.

He looked down once again to the black spot in the center of his hand, only to find there were black branches sprouting from it, spreading through his hand and up his arm like lacework. Horns suddenly sprang free of his forehead, blood trickling down his face from their protrusion.

Power, unlike anything he had felt before, coursed through his veins. Torsen clenched his hands into fists, feeling the utter rapture of the unexpected force.

The woman stared at him in horror. "What are you?" Her voice shook with fear.

Torsen looked back to her, cocking his head to the side like a vulture inspecting its next kill. He thought about her question. He was no longer Torsen, that name felt distant. No, he was something much different now.

He was hate. He was famine. He was despair and destruction. He was a poison so foul and wicked, who only wished to spend the rest of his days infecting the world.

He was decimation.

He graced the woman with a baleful smile before saying, "I am the devil."

13

THIS MORTAL COIL

BY TEAGAN OLIVIA STURMER

*H*e comes to me in the dead of a midwinter's night, all dark hair and eyes so green they might be made of poison. I can feel his fingers brush my cheek as he whispers sweet-nothings into my ear, words breaking across my skin like a million feather-light kisses. But when I wake up, blinking in the cold moon-light that streams in from the window at my feet, he's gone, vanished into nothing. And my heart cracks along its own fissures, finding myself still alone. Still waiting.

This is how it's been every day since he left. His mother's death was too much for him, it weighed too heavily, and when he left me standing on the veranda, the summer wind ruffling the dark curls that spilt along his brow, it broke me. Shattered me like some reflecting mirror.

"I'll return," he'd whispered against my neck, his breath so hot it boiled my blood. "I'll return when the snows come."

And with that, he was gone, taking all the jagged shards of me with him.

I stand at my window, wrapped in a shawl, watching as the snow drifts lazily down from the midnight sky to land against rock and tree and briar, and a smile hints on the corners of my lips.

"When the snows come," I whisper to the bubbled glass. "When the snows come."

The next morning, my presence in the house is forgotten by the few still breathing here. Why should I be remembered when my blood is not the same blood that built this house? I am of hardly any more importance than the rosy-cheeked girl who lights the fires every morning. The house—its lofty, dark-stained beams and wood-paneled walls—bustles with anticipation for the arrival and I am thrust aside. I hear the large oaken doors creak open, the sound of heels clicking against tile, and drag my fingers along the wood bannister, breath hitching in my chest, curling up through my throat like vapor.

I see Lucien first, my heart nearly bursting out of its confines of ribs. My older brother takes the carpeted stairs two at a time, travelling coat billowing out behind him like a great, grey ocean. He sweeps me into his arms, crushing me against him and all I can do is laugh, like I did when we were little and carefree and just wisps of things.

"Ophelia!"

His voice is deeper than I remember it and when he pulls back, I can see fine lines cut into the corners of his ocean-blue eyes.

"You got old," I say, a smirk teasing my tongue.

He laughs, big and barrel-chested. "And you haven't changed a bit."

I want to tell him how wrong he is, how much the big empty house has changed me, how often I have found myself wandering its many dust-covered passages alone and weary and so heavy I might crack under my own weight. I've lived here for years, but never have I been so alone without my brother.

But then I hear a different voice, *his* voice, echoing down in the foyer below us, ringing low and true, like some ancient bell. My gaze cascades down over the bannister, but all I can see are the checker-board floors—polished to a pristine shine.

Lucien smiles knowingly, reaching for my hand. But I pull it away. I can't see *him*. Not now, not in front of everyone. Instead, I turn to my brother, acting as though the man who is my undoing is not standing just below me.

"How was America?" I ask, a stupid, dull question.

Lucien runs a hand through his honey-colored thatch of hair and opens his mouth, but it isn't him who gives me an answer.

"Dry. In more ways than one."

The breath catches in my throat, scraping the edges raw, and I look down, finding *his* eyes already trained on me. My skin flushes at the sight of him—all dark curls and poison-green eyes—and all I want in this moment is to get lost in him. Get lost in the way his breath emits from full lips, the way his black hair—longer on top—falls over his deep-set eyes. I want to sink my skin against his until I no longer know where my body ends and his begins.

But he is not alone, flanked on two sides like he always is. His aged father—the Lord Sutton—is all broken lines and grey skin and weak spine dressed in a suit that has not fit his frame in nearly a year. And his stepmother, like a crow perched on his shoulder, her talons digging sharp and iron-strong. I want to say *his* name, to let it brush against my tongue and teeth and lips and remember how it tastes. Like I've bitten into an apple so red it could be made of blood. But I can feel her eyes on me, his stepmother, Cyrilla, who saw fruit ripe for the plucking in a grieving widower and swooped in like he was carrion. She has never liked me, not even when her sister and brother-in-law took me and Lucien in after our own father died amongst his books and papers. She was not sad when her sister died— I don't remember a single tear spent over the corpse which now lies in the family mausoleum.

I smile demurely over the railing at the young man standing on the tile. "Hello, Mr. Sutton."

The sting of my formality washes over his face before he sets it back to stone. Red lips tighten around his teeth and he inclines his head.

"Ms. Gray."

The desire to throw myself over the bannister just to touch him, just to feel his teeth tease my skin and taste his mouth against mine, shimmers above my surface, my whole being vibrating with the desperate, naked need for it. And I can see he feels it, too. The way his fingers curl and uncurl at his sides, skin pulling white across his knuckles. But before I can go to him, before I can throw myself down the stairs to land in his arms, his father is pulling him away, and Cyrilla is giving me her familiar crow-eyed stare.

Once they're gone, I find a coat and walk with Lucien out to the gardens. The snow crunches beneath my shoes, the air crisp and cool and filled with so many secrets. I loop my arm through my brother's and lay my head against his shoulder.

"How is Heath? Really?" I ask, knowing that if anyone knows that boy I love with the dark curls more than I do, it's my brother.

Lucien sighs, looks back to make sure we are far enough away from the house, and then breaks away, gaze snagging on the bitter barren landscape beyond.

"He's, uh"—he pulls the cap off his head, wringing the thick wool between his hands— "he's not well, Ophelia. It started on the boat just after we left, always brooding, always rambling about his mother's death. He's..." A shadow passes over Lucien's face. "He's convinced she didn't die of natural causes."

My chest tightens, sharp and stunted. Lady Amelia Sutton had always been kind to me and Lucien. I had adored her and when she'd fallen ill, I'd been the one who had taken care of her. *I* had switched out her bedding when she'd soaked it through during the night, *I* had wiped up the scarlet blood when she'd had one of her coughing fits, and *I* had held Heath's hand when his mother had slipped off into whatever awaits us when eyelashes tease skin for the last time.

I feel the cracks around my heart widen as I turn my eyes back to my brother.

"Cyrilla?" The name slips off my tongue before I can stop it, and for a moment I feel ashamed to even think that the new Lady Sutton would kill her own sister. But I have felt the suffocating, black-feather wings of that woman firsthand, know the greed that swims behind her eyes like some death elixir.

The shadow on Lucien's face grows darker. "Heath thinks so, yes.

He's...he's changed, Ophelia." He reaches a hand out to brush my shoulder. "I don't want you to get hurt."

Dread sinks claws into the soft flesh of my stomach, squeezing at the viscera until I feel like I might drown in my own blood. It makes sense—*yes, yes,* of course it makes sense. Everyone in the parish knows the story that has haunted the gilded corridors of Yorrick Hall for twenty-three years. Before the three of us were born, when the current Lord was just a rotten boy with no title and the dark curls now worn by his son, Gerard Sutton crushed the heart of one sister and won the hand of the other. Now, *Lord* Sutton, sitting on his tarnished throne built on the backs of dried-up silver mines, is a broken, weary man. And when his wife died, his spine cracked, and Cyrilla sunk her teeth into weak and willing flesh.

I blink as snowflakes kiss my eyelashes, melting on my cheeks to run down my skin like tears. It is not the shock of Heath's accusation that spills across my soul like poison, it's the fear. The fear that soon, this belief of his will turn into an obsession, a madness with no method to it.

I reach for Lucien's arm. "You must be there for him," I say.

Lucien smiles uneasily and pats my gloved hand. "Yes, of course. I would die for that man, always a brother to me. But you, you will be there, too."

I try to smile as we make our way back to the house, snow falling in great swaths now. I cannot be there for Heath, not in the way Lucien can. Cyrilla has made sure of that. Not in words, but in unspoken threats. She has high hopes for her stepson to marry wealthy and pull Yorrick Hall back to its days of glory, back to the sun. And I am nothing. Just the daughter of some clerk who the late Lady Sutton took pity on and welcomed into her home.

It was like winter-weary earth welcoming sunlight; the way love grew between Heath and I. Slow and soft at first, just glances across the room, gentle brushes of skin when he'd ask to see the book I was reading. But the summer before his mother died it had turned into something more. Something that dripped lush and heady and hungry. Something as intoxicating as the blood red wine Lord Sutton kept in cases in the cellars. The same wine Heath and Lucien had smuggled into America just months ago, the only way to pay for the failing silver mines.

It all was kept secret, our love affair. Heath knew the desires of his stepmother, but he only wanted me. Wanted my skin against his skin.

I shiver with the memory and Lucien smiles down at me, thinking it's just the cold. Once we get inside, we shake the snow from our boots and furs, and I make some excuse about books waiting for me in the library. His lips part knowingly, and he dismisses himself.

I smile as his back vanishes beyond the curl of a corridor and whisper a silent thank you for his discretion. The last few months have been torture without my brother. And without Heath.

The thought of Heath sends tingles along the stretches of my body, a deep ache carving itself in the lower reaches of my stomach. I turn toward the stairs, trying not to race to the deep oaken doors, praying I do not run into Cyrilla and her bloody hands.

The library greets me with warmth and dark wood and the smell of old, yellowing books. This has always been my favourite room in the house, the room that has felt most like the heart of Yorrick Hall. Everything else is a shell, a golden sheath to cover the rot beneath the walls.

I can smell his cigarette smoke before I see him, the scent of tobacco warm and inviting. I run a hand through my blonde waves, then down my dress. I fill my lungs up with steadying breaths and round the corner.

From a distance, he hasn't changed these last six months. His hair is cut short on the sides, curls spilling long over dark, brooding brows. The cuffs of his shirt are rolled back, silver cuff links forgotten on the table by his elbow. There's no book in his hands, no paper, he's just sitting there, lazily, the cigarette burning to a pillar of ash between his fingers. A smile breaks out along his lips, rakish and so devilishly handsome I fight the urge to throw myself on top of him and sink my teeth into it.

"Hello, Heath," I say, finally finding some breath in the space between us, even though it feels dangerously thin.

His grin widens and he stands, knocking the cigarette into a silver ashtray. His hands are on me before any words can pass between us, fingers hot and searching. The air rushes out from between my lungs to curl around my lips in a sigh so delicious it tastes like forbidden fruit. Suddenly, all thoughts of Cyrilla and smuggled wine are erased from my mind, replaced by *need*. I want to feel Heath's heart beat against mine, want to tangle my fingers in his curls, and whisper his name over and over again until the only shape my lips know to make is the sound of it.

His lips brush my collarbone, the curve of my throat, the line of my jaw. I sigh against him and his hand travels around to grab the small of my back.

"Shit, I've missed you," he breathes, hot against my skin.

A laugh lilts on my tongue and I hold him close, somehow only needing him closer.

"I missed you, too."

His lips find mine and then we are falling into the chair, all tangled limbs and searching hands and hot, steaming breath. I've missed this, this undying desire just to hold each other, just to know and be known. With Heath, the loneliness melts away until it is vapor on wind. His fingers peel back my collar, scooping the fabric off my shoulder and planting hot, heady kisses on the skin. I shiver against him, only wanting to burst, to shatter into a hundred, thousand shards of diamond dust. He pulls me against him, and I can feel his heart beating beneath his ribs. He moans into me, and then his teeth are biting—sharp and dangerous and delicious.

We have always danced this line, between gentle brushes and devilish devouring of one another. And sometimes it scares me, this intoxicating inhalation of one another's souls, but then I remember that soon enough, we'll die, and when my time comes, all I want to remember is the fire that dances on my skin when Heath holds me tight and consumes me like a fever.

When we're done—when the stain-glass windows have turned to steam and we're both slick with sweat—we fall apart on the floor, and he lights another cigarette, staring up at the ceiling. Silence sits between us, cooling the heat that wavers through the room. I lay one hand over my belly and take his in my other. His hands are calloused, probably from hauling the crates of contraband wine.

"How was America?" I ask.

Heath blows a long stream of smoke out from between his lips, watching as it catches in the yellow sunlight spilling through the windows.

"I hated every bloody second of it," he says.

I turn my face to watch him, see the way his eyes study the ceiling above us, and I can tell he's already a thousand miles away, his mind caught up in things I should know nothing about.

I squeeze his hand. "Lucien told me. About Cyrilla."

Suddenly, he's sitting up, hand pulled away like he's been bitten. His eyes are wild and it scares me. I sit up, heart racing.

"I'm sorry—"

"What did he tell you?"

His voice has changed. No longer does it hold the sounds he moaned against my throat, now it's something harsh, accusatory. I fumble with the buttons on my bodice.

"He…he told me you think she killed your mother. And I—"

He scrambles to his feet, cursing under his breath as he stubs the cigarette out and runs shaking hands through his hair.

"I don't think these things, Ophelia," he says, voice low and vicious. He turns around on me, eyes dark, the shadows on his face darker, like some mask. "I know them. I fucking know them."

My chest tightens, but I fight against it, trying to draw breath to my lungs. I take a step forward, stretching out a comforting hand.

"Will you help me see it, then? I want to know what you know, Heath. I want to help if I can."

He seems to soften at this, letting me brush his face with my fingers. His arm wraps around my waist, pulls me closer, nuzzles his face in my neck.

"I'm sorry," he whispers.

I kiss his curls, feeling tears grow hot in my eyes. "I want you to feel like you can share things with me." I take his face in my hands and lift it to match my own. "I love you, Heath Sutton."

A sigh curls from his lips, soft and sorrowful. "Damn it, I love you, too." He smiles. "I want to tell you, I really do, but I'm afraid you'll react just like your brother did." He breaks away, running fingers down his chiseled face. "You'll think I'm crazy."

I want to laugh, to tell him I already think he's crazy, and I love him for it, but I don't, I just draw him back to me, holding him steady as his body shakes.

"I don't think you're crazy."

Another sigh, heavier this time, filled with things unsaid. Weights that no one should carry alone.

"I saw her, Ophelia, on the boat the first night we left. Luc and I, we'd loaded the wine into the hull and no one had been the wiser. We'd shared a beer and then called it a night. And just before I feel asleep, damn it, just before I could have gotten a fucking good night's worth of sleep, she just showed up at the foot of my bed."

A shiver traces fingers up my spine, to settle like ice in my throat. "Who?" I ask, already knowing the answer.

His eyes grow haunted, whites wide and bloodshot. "My mum. It was my mum. Half-dead. Gods, it was awful. Skin—" he shakes—"skin like, like old fabric, all cracked and dry and shrunken. But it was her eyes, Ophelia, so blue, so fucking blue—" His voice chokes with sobs, and I can see the truth of it all, there in his face.

"I believe you," I say, and he sags gently against me.

He takes a rattling breath, mouth thick with saliva. "She told me what happened, the truth of the whole bloody thing. She told me how Cyrilla had been poisoning her for months, and she didn't realize it until it was too late. Until she was so sick, she'd forgotten how to speak."

His words bring back images of his mother, so weak and pale you would have thought she had been made of snow. Too weak to even open her lips to drink water, let alone expose her killer.

"I'm so sorry," I breathe, knowing my words are nothing against the pain he must be feeling.

He shakes his head. "It is no secret that Cyrilla has always wanted this house, this"— he brushes the silver cufflinks off the table to where they clink on the floor—"this goddamn money. She planted the seeds long ago, seducing that spineless idiot I call father. Everything she wanted was within her grasp, she just needed to get rid of my mother. So she did, poisoned her until she couldn't even speak and then played the part of a grieving sister, all the while digging her nails into my father's soul until he bent to her will."

I shouldn't be surprised, none of this should come as a shock. Cyrilla has always been a snake, but the truth of it sears across my skin like poisoned fire. And I feel so helpless, standing there beside Heath and not having a damn good thing to say. Nothing that will take the pain away, nothing that will bring comfort. So, I reach out to cup his jaw again, to wipe away the cold tear that trails down his cheek.

"What are you going to do?"

For a moment, there is silence, and it echoes around in my ears. And then he pulls away, so sharply I fall forward against him. He leaves me there, alone, and goes to the window. His eyes have darkened again, clouded against the light that shines through the colored glass, and my hands shake at my sides like downed birds.

"I'm going to do what my mother told me to do, Ophelia," he says. And then he turns his eyes to me, hard and sharp and so full of hate my blood runs cold. He reaches for my hand. "I'm going to fucking kill her."

That night, before dinner, I stand in my room and trace the bruises on my wrist from where Heath held me. They molt purple and blue, like a sunset in January, and my throat chokes with tears. The Heath I fell in love with, the Heath who snuck me bouquets of lavender and wrote me letters to slip under doors when Cyrilla wasn't looking, would never do this. Sometimes his kisses could get rough, but only because he wanted to consume me, only because he wanted to hold me so close and somehow closer. But he's never hurt me before, and it scares me. It makes my marrow run cold. I reach for a pair of white satin gloves, slipping the soft fabric over my hands and up to elbows, thankful for the concealment. I take another look at my reflection, hands running the length of my blue evening gown.

I will never be what Cyrilla wants for her stepson. I could be the prettiest thing north of London, but without a penny to my name, I am no use. Cyrilla only wants something she can sink her teeth into, something rich and dripping with so much gold, she can make a bed from it. And I am not that. Unlike Lucien, there is no place for me in the new family business of smuggling wine. I know that as soon as Cyrilla finds a suitable match for Heath, I will be thrown out to make my own way in a world that bruises women.

I suck air between my pink lips and ground myself to the decaying walls of the house. That time has not come yet, and all I need to think about right now is getting through another dinner with Lady Cyrilla Fucking Sutton.

Lucien is waiting for me on the other side of the door, all pressed coattails and perfectly combed hair. He smiles, white teeth shining in the candlelight, and I should hate him. Should hate how perfect he is, how he is everything in the eyes of the Suttons I am not. Useful, smart, angry and violent when they need him to be.

Male.

But I don't hate him, I love him so much it guts me.

"You look beautiful," he says, and I whisper a silent thank you that he can't see the bruises forming on my wrists.

We follow the corridors of Yorrick Hall until it spits us out before the grand, wooden doors of the dining room. I can hear voices on the other side and my skin prickles. The doors open and my stomach drops to the soles of my feet.

Lord Sutton sits on the far end of the table, his face thin and dark, preoccupied with the lace edging of the napkin in his lap. Cyrilla sits opposite him, wearing a dress so red and pink it might be made from the spilled viscera of some poor creature. She smiles up at me with beady, dark eyes, lipstick bleeding out into the wrinkles around her thin and ugly mouth. Heath ignores my gaze, and when I turn my eyes to my seat, I see why.

A woman sits in my usual spot. I have seen her before, at parties, always laughing, always the center of attention. Her body drips in emerald, hair as black as midnight oil.

Rose Guilder, the sole heiress of the great Guilder Empire, their gold pouring in from far-off tea fields and cargo ships. She glances up at me, eyes glinting in the candlelight. Suddenly, I want to run away, I want to run and run until the cold has turned my feet blue and I'm dragging night air into my lungs like ink. Lucien must feel the panic rising in my chest, because he tightens his arm around mine and glares at Heath.

"Oh, my darlings," Cyrilla trills out, her voice like a magpie. "Come sit, come and meet our new friend."

She says the word *friend* like it's some rich secret and I have the sudden urge to sink my nails deep into her throat until I can feel her veins pulsing beneath my fingers, blood spilling hot against my skin.

Lucien helps me to the empty seat beside Lord Sutton and then goes to sit next to Heath, eyes like stones. Rose turns to me and smiles.

"You must be Lord Sutton's ward, Ophelia, yes?"

Her voice is smooth and rich and for a moment all I want to do is listen to it as it pours from between her ruby lips, but then I picture some death elixir being mixed into Lady Amelia's wine, and my face sours.

"Yes, Lord Sutton's ward." I meet Heath's eyes burning through the candle flame. "Amongst other things."

Lucien chokes on his wine. Through the glow of the fire, Heath's jaw spackles red, his fingers curling white-knuckled around the edge of his silk napkin.

I watch Cyrilla's jaw punch out against her skin and then she lifts the little bell on the table, gives it a sharp ring, and dinner is served. I catch Heath's eyes once more as Rose tries desperately to corral him into conversation. My knife slips into my meat, tender and soft as it bleeds against the white china of my plate.

Revenge, they say, is best served cold.

But I like mine hot, so hot it burns like desire, like acid on skin.

Like poison.

The ceiling above my bed swims red. I can still feel the candlelight burning against my eyes, watching Heath as he tries to hold steady conversation with a girl he cares nothing about.

Fucking Rose Guilder.

With her emerald earrings and gold dripping from her fingertips. Gold Cyrilla craves. It is an obsession for her, a sickness. A rot that sinks into her bones and carves out space between her organs, ravaging her spirit, her humanity. I claw at my pillow, wanting to draw blood, but I don't even rip the fabric.

I want to hurt someone; I want to open my throat to the sky and scream until my very soul spills from my tongue. And gods, I just want *him*.

The moon slips white beams of light into the window at my feet, and I sit up, looking out at the stretch of dark lawn below. A figure slips across the snow, making its way to the mausoleum hidden amongst trees and frozen river.

Heath.

Heart racing, I slip my feet into a pair of boots and grab my coat from where it hangs against my door, slinking out into the silence of Yorrick Hall.

Outside, the chill bites through the wool and claws against my skin. I shiver, plowing forward against a wind that threatens to leave me breathless, gasping for air in the moonlight.

I find him, tucked against the riverbank, a dead and dried sprig of rosemary in his hands. We'd planted the herb together, the summer before, at the foot of the mausoleum. McConnell's Blue, his mother's favourite.

It's a frostbitten thing now, all wild tangles and naked spikes. He hears my footsteps crunching in the snow, but doesn't turn around, just straightens.

"I'm supposed to marry her, you know."

The words are like ice to my heart, even though I knew they were coming, even though I've *always* known the truth of them. I sit down beside him, reaching to turn his face toward mine. There are tears in his eyes, frozen on his cheeks. I wipe them away, wanting only to press my lips against them until they melt. But I don't.

"She seems awful," I say, trying to bring light to the heaviness pressing in from all around us.

A smile cracks his lips and then vanishes. "I'm not sure if I can hear about the five varieties of black tea for the rest of my life. But"—he holds the branch of dead rosemary up against the moonlight—"it will be perfect, perfect for the family, perfect for making the business official."

And that's when I know his words aren't his own, that he's just repeating a script, an actor on life's vast stage. We all play our parts so well, in the end. And who would suspect alcohol and opium and other contraband when the crates are topped with tea?

I pull the dead sprig from his hands, tucking it into my coat pocket. "Rosemary for remembrance," I whisper against his ear. "Tonight, for remembrance's sake, just be with me."

My name whispers out from between his lips, tinged with tears, and then he's pressing me against the ground and I don't care how wet and cold the snow at my back is, I only want to feel him, *know* him. His gentle brushes turn to fevered desire as the ground around us melts and the stars above shine silver-white light down on us. He's like a drug, like a crystal glass of straight gin. He fills my veins with fire until I feel like I just might explode, and when I finally do—when I am undone there in the starlight and snow—I roll his name around on my tongue like wine before it spills from my lips.

He drops to the snow beside me, chest heaving. "Goddamnit, Ophelia. How am I supposed to be with anyone else?"

He rolls to his side and sweeps a thatch of hair from my face. And then I'm scrambling up on my knees, ice biting into the skin, and grabbing his hand.

"Run away with me," I say, unable to stop the words. "We could go anywhere. Rome, Madrid, Boston. I don't care, Heath, as long as I'm with you."

A cloud moves in front of the brightly shining moon, but it's the look on his face that makes everything go dark. He gets to his feet, brushing my hand away, like it's wrong.

"You can't be serious, Ophelia. Are you—" He runs a hand through his hair, kicking violently at the snow, making me flinch. "I told you about my mother, I told you what Cyrilla did. And what? You expect me to just leave? To pretend like none of it fucking happened?"

I feel tears pour red hot into the space behind my eyes, making them ache and burn. I stare at the snow, dead white in front of me, like some burial shroud.

"I—"

"*You!* You only think about yourself, don't you?"

He bends down, face inches from me, eyes wild and bloodshot, and I can see it, the sickness. The same sickness that swims in the eyes of Cyrilla, that lust, only his isn't for gold or riches or power. It's for revenge. And I'm terrified it will kill him.

"Heath, please—" My throat is thick with saliva. Thick with emotion.

He throws himself back, hands cutting through the winter wind. "Damnit, Ophelia, don't you see? I can't be with you, I never could be. I'm a curse." He holds his shaking palms out in front of him. "I'm a fucking curse. This whole family is."

He turns to go and I scramble to my feet, reaching out after him, fingers brushing his coat.

"Wait, Heath. Heath!"

He turns back around, face haunted by the ghosts of his past, present, and future.

"Heath." The name is heavy on my tongue—sweet communion wine. "I love you."

For a moment, his eyes soften, his shoulders slacken, and in the end, that's what breaks me. The softness and goodness of him being turned to stone. The man I know and love so well turning into a mere bitter imitation, drunk on revenge.

"I know," he says. "I know."

He turns away, footsteps crunching on snow through trees, leaving me all alone in a pool of moonlight. For a moment, I am frozen, a girl made up from marble bones. And then, the marble cracks, the façade I've worn for so many years crumbles to dust, and a laugh breaks from my lips, cuts across my skin, streaks up toward the sky.

Everything I've been holding onto, everything I've held myself together with, shatters like thin ice.

It's Lucien that finally finds me the next morning. He guides me back to the house, helping me into bed and ordering a bath drawn. I am a ragged mess of a thing. Stained and soaked nightdress, ice and snow matted in my hair. I don't remember how long I was out there, but it was long enough so that the world shimmers at the edges now, blurring reality from imagination.

I envision Lady Amelia at my bedside like Heath described her, skeletal, skin as thin as paper. She lifts a cup to my mouth and I drink, wincing at the bitter taste.

"It's good for you," she soothes. "You'll feel better once you've drunk it."

And even though I know it's the same poison Cyrilla gave her, I do as I'm told. Because I am just as broken and bone-weary as the rest of them.

Sometime later in the day, after I've refused bath and bed alike, I slip from my room, sneaking through the corridors until I reach Heath's door. I can hear shouting. *Lucien.* He's angry, hungry for an explanation of why his sister lies frozen and half-mad in her bed. I giggle stupidly into my hand.

And then I hear the word. *Duel.* And my giggle sharpens at the edges, turns to iron spikes. The door is thrown open, and I see Heath, eyes red and rimmed with tears. He looks ragged, half-alive. *Cursed.*

His gaze snags on me and his face twists. Sorrow, rage, guilt, all covered in revenge. Bloody revenge. All he wants. I want to scream at him, but my fingers brush something in my pocket and when I pull it out and hold it up to him, a laugh cracks against my teeth.

"Rosemary for remembrance," I say and crush the sprig in my palm.

~

The lawn is cleared of snow late in the afternoon. Duels have been illegal for nearly a hundred years, but that doesn't stop the blood pumping hot in my brother's veins. I want to tell him it's stupid, foolish, what's the goddamn point? But all I can do is laugh. Laugh at the futility of it all, the mortality.

And just like Heath, a bloodlust has washed over Lucien, an all-consuming desire for vengeance. Gone is the love-like-brothers between them, my brother has turned into the rabid animal Cyrilla has always seen him as—the muscle, the protection turned to the uncontrollable rage of a mad dog.

But aren't we all a bit mad? Here in this poisoned house. Even Lord Sutton and Cyrilla can't stop it, can only add their own kind of madness to it all. Their own lust. And so Cyrilla decides to turn the whole thing into a show. The lawn is cleared, the table is laden with wine and fruit, and the players are set.

Lucien's sword glints silver in the sunlight. I don't know if it's the warm light or the melting snow or the look of death in Heath's eye as he looks between his stepmother primping on the sideline like some bird of paradise and the man he once called friend, but I step forward, reaching for my brother's arm. Clearing my mind of all the fog and mist, I let a single word slip between my lips before I'm giggling madly again.

"Don't."

But I'm too late. It is all too late.

Too late for Heath to carry out his promise to his mother's dead corpse.

Too late for Cyrilla to sheath herself in gold and marry her stepson off to Rose Guilder.

Too late for Lord Sutton to save his son, to save his own damn soul.

And too late for me to live a life with the man I love.

Swords are drawn, a whistle is blown, and then they clash. Like two mad wolves, snarling and swiping and cutting through the thawing air. I claw at the trunk of a tree, watching, only broken laughter spilling from my tongue.

Sword against sword, body against body, and with each crack and clash, I feel myself break more inside. From the corner of my roving eyes, I watch Cyrilla take a flask from the pocket of her dress, dropping two drops of some ruby liquid into Lord Sutton's glass while he watches his son fight for his life.

Of course, this has always been her plan. Kill the wife, marry the husband, and then kill them all. Until everything is hers. Without thinking, I run across the field and take the cup, holding it high.

But I am too late. Always. Again. Too fucking late. Lucien's blade finds its mark, sinking deep into Heath's side. A cry breaks from my lips as blood runs red against snow. Heath heaves a shuttering sigh, crashing to the ground, and I do the only thing I can think of. I take the cup before Cyrilla can fight me, and I ram it between her lips. She coughs and gags, ripping at my fingers, but I don't pull back, I only push harder. She chokes, splutters, coughing ruby onto my nightdress. But already it's done its work, already the poison is leaching into her system. She screams my name, slaps me in the chest, and I fall to my knees. My eyes lock with Heath and I can see the tears, the film of death slowly pulling over them. Lucien stands over him, sword poised to make the final blow, so caught up in his own bloodlust, he's missed the carnage behind him.

"No!" I cry, lurching forward, crawling across the snow to Heath, but he's already slipping away, already losing his grip on this barren earth.

I look at the cup shaking in my hand and then up at Lucien. But now it's his turn, to be too late, and before he can stop me, I'm pressing the silver rim between my lips, taking the wine into my heart, my lungs, my cursed soul.

The poison is bitter and all-consuming and I relish in it, feel its heat like Heath against my body. The cup slips from my fingers, rolling in the snow as the corners of my eyes go dark. Lucien is at my side, crying, screaming, turning pale, but I hardly see him. I feel Heath on the earth beside me, and then his hand drops into mine, flesh cool against flesh like river stone. And maybe this is how we'll lay forever, until we have been worn smooth by the ages, taking root as the rest turns to silence.

14

A TASTE OF ACONITE

BY ALEXANDRIA BRAZLE

"Cheers." I turned away from the violet haired barista, clutching my flat white between my hands, letting the warmth seep through my slate fingerless gloves. I sighed. Coffee is the life blood of a secondary school teacher. I adored my job, but teaching sniveling kids the value of mitochondria and osmosis when all they wanted to do was snog, was really starting to grate on my nerves.

As I walked out of the shop into the slowly warming spring air, I turned to my reflection in the shop window. I fluffed my curls up a bit, running a finger over my lipstick to make sure it wasn't smeared from drinking my coffee. *I hope Grant's at home, and I don't miss him,* I thought. He'd been working from our home office all day and I managed to escape parent teacher conferences early in hopes to surprise him.

I smiled in anticipation for this evening. We decided to order in Chinese food tonight to celebrate the start of Easter Week and for some uninterrupted time off together. I'd been dreaming about this date all week. Midterms are always busy, and I have a hard time being able to keep my head above water. It was difficult to not bring work home the last two weeks. Grading essays, arguing with parents about missing work, and tallying up grades for report card scores is enough to send anyone over the edge. Nonetheless, doing it while managing a bunch of antsy, hormonal kids. But it's over. I'm done.

I stepped up my pace, excited to get home, and put on the new lingerie I ordered just for this evening. A cute forest green number. With lace three quarters of the way down the arms and a deep v plunging neckline. I always felt my best when I wore green; my mom always said it complimented my skin tone.

I pulled my phone out of my cardigan pocket and sent a quick text to Grant. *Can't wait to show you what I got for us tonight.* I added a kissy face emoji for good measure to make sure he got the point.

Skirting around a covered bus stop, a drop of rain hit the top of my head and I shivered. I didn't remember rain in the forecast, and I forgot to pack my umbrella. Rookie mistake of moving from New York to London number one: Never forget an umbrella. I'd been in the UK for a little over two years now, but I was still clearly learning and adjusting.

I rounded the sidewalk corner and shifted my purse back up on my shoulder, wrapping my knit cardigan around my middle a smidge tighter. I weaved around a pigeon pecking at the ground and I rammed into someone in the process. "Sorry," I mumbled. Walking was dangerous business. London was a cool city, but the likelihood of me tripping over my own shoes or, you know, even the air, was too high for me to chance gawking at the scenery. But this time, since I knew I was close to my apartment, I kept my eyes up. And I wasn't sure if it was a good decision or not.

There was Grant, standing outside of a black cab, forearms resting on the open window, smiling at someone with a seductive look that I thought was only reserved for me. The breeze made her blonde hair fly out of the window in long wisps as she leaned her head forward to meet Grant's awaiting lips, kissing her for longer than he had kissed me in weeks. My coffee cup slipped from my paralyzed hands and splattered onto the concrete, soaking my canvas shoes. A shot of irritation zipped through me; another poor decision to add to the day. Even from where I stood, feeling like the wind got knocked out of my lungs and dumbfounded on the sidewalk, I could sense the longing of them having to part, the anticipation of another secret meeting to come. Jealousy, as green as the depths of Grant's eyes, swallowed me whole.

"No," I whispered. *It can't be. He chose me. He chose ME...* I looked down at the vintage ring on my finger, eyes returning to the back of the head of *the woman,* envy wrapping me into its embrace, coloring everything dark.

My fiancé stepped back, hands hanging onto the cab window until the last possible second, watching the woman drive away as she turned around and blew a kiss to him.

He walked back up the steps of our flat, running his hands through his very misshapen hair, a ghost of a smile still lingering as he closed the screen door behind him. I couldn't move. Not one muscle. Like someone had frozen me to the spot to watch their whole interaction like some sadistic prank. Thralls of people weaved around me, huffing and side-eyeing me on their way home from the long week. Could no one else see the pieces of my heart shattered on the sidewalk, seeping into the cracks in front of me? My tears blended into the little rivers of rain beginning to pour from my hair. A horrid cry sounded out from behind me, and I whirled around looking for the source, only to find a few people looking at me with fear in their eyes. Making a wide berth to stay away. Then I realized that the awful sound came out of my own body. Wretched and terrible, the cry of someone getting their heart ripped out while they stood there unable to stop it. Grabbing at my throat, rubbed raw with the sandpaper of grief, my nails pierced into my skin, desperate to make this pain stop. "Please, make it stop!" I screamed.

Another drop of rain splashed onto my nose, this time followed by a few bigger droplets, before the heavens above me pulled back the curtain and let the rain come down in torrents. It was as if Mother Nature wanted me to feel the full effects of what I just saw, letting the cold bleed into my soul as my heart turned from shattered and fragile, to hardened. Icy. My shivering wasn't only from the frigid rain drenching me to my very core, but from the adrenaline and rage suddenly building in me that I didn't know I was capable of conjuring.

Grant will rue the moment he ever asked me to be his wife. Those traitorous lips will burn.

~

I was curled up on the couch in my favorite black leggings and long tunic sweater, nursing my second cup of coffee of the morning. When Grant slipped into the bathroom for his morning shower, I snuck some Irish cream into it. *I'm going to need all the calm I can muster up today.*

The red rage still simmered underneath the surface of my skin. My constant companion while I weighed out my next steps. I had hoped to utilize the time we had left in our short engagement before our early summer wedding to rekindle some of the fire we had when we first got engaged. We were excited then, blissful even. But life got busy, my semester became insane. My first appointment for altering my wedding dress was in a few weeks. I'd have to go on Pinterest soon and look up ideas on trashing the dress after a breakup.

"Hey," Grant called out to me from his shower. "Would you mind grabbing me a fresh towel from the dryer?"

Plastering on an impatient smile, I replied, "Sure babe, let me grab it for you."

I slammed my coffee down on a coaster, bitter liquid sloshing over the sides, and I took my time walking down the hall to the dryer in our flat. I flung the door open, leaving a small dent in the drywall. Sweet and ridiculous satisfaction gave me a small burst of control and power. It would be key that I keep up the facade of ignorance while still finding ways to slowly wreck his life. Right now, every kiss, touch, and smile were kindling for the fire burning within.

He will burn, I thought, wringing the towel in my clenched hands.

I sauntered back down the hallway and opened the cracked bathroom door all the way, laying the now cold towel on the counter, and pulled the curtain aside to sneak a quick kiss from him.

"Thanks." He smiled at me.

I grinned back but it felt more like a grimace, with eyes too wide for it to be true.

Thankfully, he didn't notice. "Hey, I've got the afternoon off tomorrow with the app's coding being in review and everything, and since you're on break, do you want to visit one of the botanical gardens? I know you've been itching to check out the Chelsea Psychic Garden for a little while."

Impressed that he remembered that, I genuinely smiled at him this time. I leaned against the doorframe. *This will be fun,* the rage giggled. "That sounds great, Grant. Let's make it a date. I think there's a cafe there we can go to for late afternoon tea if that's good for your schedule? Take the morning slow?"

He thought for a moment while his hands rinsed the shampoo suds out of his hair. "I have a meeting with some of the app development guys at the pub at seven later that night. That'll give us plenty of time to head back home on the Tube after we're done so I can change." He shook the water out of his hair as he turned off the faucet, droplets landing on my black shirt. His emerald eyes met mine. "I've really missed you, Meg."

My heart did a somersault, momentarily forgetting my plot. I really did love him. It made my heart ache. Flashes of skin touching skin under a cabana in Puerto Rico. Grant shaking my dad's hand after our engagement. Slow dancing to jazz music in our living room. My eyes got misty as my head tilted and I gazed back into his eyes.

"I've missed you too. I really have. Everything has just been so insane with midterms and your app taking off..." *Maybe we can figure this out. If he would just tell me, we could work through it... If he would admit it was a mistake.* I threaded my fingers through his. "This break will be good for us."

He lowered his eyes, for just a moment, and I saw unease flash across his face, gone just as quick as it came. My heart closed off again.

I can't forget. No matter how much I love him, I must not forget what I saw.

I reached across his torso and grabbed the body wash sitting on the corner of the tub. I popped it open and sniffed. "Is this a new smell? Did you use up the one I got you already?" His eyes flicked from the hand holding the brand new bottle back to my furrowed brow and accusing eyes. He chuckled just a hint higher than normal. "I don't know babe, I just use whatever is in here, I don't keep track of what you get me all the time."

He took the bottle and placed it back on the tub. His eyes returned to mine as he reached across my chest, letting his forearm graze as he grabbed the towel I brought for him. I stiffened, instantly nauseous. The red taste of fury filled my mouth, sour and hostile. I smirked at him, and he smiled like he got away with something. I pinched his arm a little too hard.

"Don't take too long getting ready, we've got a train to catch."

Grant stepped onto the platform and held my hand, helping me not to fall as I followed him off the train. His hand felt like home and familiar, but tainted. Like a home that had been ransacked by robbers and all that was left behind was broken glass and a mess to clean up.

He sighed a contented smile. "We could not have asked for better weather for our date today." He squeezed my hand, looking down at me with his green eyes. I tried to smile back at him, but couldn't hold his gaze for very long before glancing away, letting go of his hand in the process. He didn't smell like himself. He must've changed what he smelled like for *her*.

I dug in my purse for my chapstick and wallet to pay for our entrance fees. Smearing the rose-tinted Burt's Bees across my lips, Grant reached into his back pocket feeling his phone vibrate. He chuckled at the message and texted back before turning the phone on silent and sliding it back into his pocket. A glimmer of amusement remained on his mouth as we approached the ticket booth.

"A friend from work?" I asked, a pang of sorrow tearing through me.

He shrugged. "Yeah, group text. Someone sent a funny meme."

I nodded. *Good response.* "I'm really glad we made time for this today, Grant. It'll be good." I clenched my jaw, teeth grinding in the effort to bide my time. *Be patient,* the rage cooed, its tendrils tracing down my neck.

A flicker of light reflected in my peripheral vision once I found my wallet. A sliver of blonde was woven into the forearm of Grant's jacket. My eyes squinted, shoulders stiffening, like Atlas struggling to carry the weight of the globe on his shoulders. I plucked the hair off his arm. He glanced down at me, holding up his forearm for inspection. "What was that? A fuzz?"

"Nope. Just blonde hair. Must've gotten on you from the train." I shrugged, feigning disinterest. My insides burned.

He made a short laugh, darting his eyes around before gripping my hand in his. I squeezed once, letting my nails dig in just a little bit.

I paid for our tickets, and we made our way through the glass entrance. I'd love to get an annual pass here. I have always thrived in the glasshouse, in the smell of fertilized soil. My Midwest childhood knocked at the door of my memories every time I got to adventure into the heavenly world of flowers and plants. My father always said that farming and botany ran in our family, and that it was probably where my affinity and fascination with plants originated. I was the president of my 4-H club in high school, a group focused on agriculture, learning how to partner with the land, and coax her to reap a fruitful harvest. Being the group expert in foraging, I helped other students identify which plants were poisonous and which were safe to eat. I was hoping that while exploring these gardens today, my past would help inform my present.

When we opened the double doors, my ulterior motives quieted. My faked excitement about our date became real the second the smell of freshly watered soil hit my nose. *Oh, did I need this. If anything, I just needed to clear my head and forget for a minute.*

Pothos covered the walls with draping vines while potted decorative purple kale line the entrance and exits. I'd been wanting to visit this particular botanical garden because of its history. In the past, they would train apothecaries how to use medicinal plants for herbal remedies. My feet moved on their own accord looking for the path to the medicinal gardens. Above me, a glass dome let the natural light in, allowing onlookers to see the blue sky or listen to the pure sound of tinkling rain.

I pushed open the door to the greenhouse and my eyes took in every plant and its scientific Latin name. *Matricaria recutita. Echinacea purpurea. Aconitum. Also known as lycoctonum.*

I tilted my head at the last name listed on the plaque. I'd heard of 'wolfsbane' before, usually strewn throughout ornamental gardens in the ritzier areas of London, specifically near Buckingham Palace. I'd even heard of it being used against werewolves in fairy tales and in fantasy novels. But I'd never heard of it being classified as 'medicinal.'

I took a step closer to the informational plaque, noticing the warning of side effects if it were consumed or touched. Confused, I kept reading.

Used in traditional Chinese medicine, aconite was used to treat fevers and chills, used topically to treat muscle aches, and to help manage panic and anxiety.

I skimmed ahead a little bit, looking for more history about the warning signs. My pulse quickened and my excitement grew instantly when I spotted the word *poison.*

Aconite, also known as wolfsbane, was commonly used as a poison. Hunters would lace arrow points with the flower's juice to kill large wolves or leopards. If ingested by humans accidentally, it can cause gastrointestinal issues, tingling or burning of the mouth, and asphyxiation.

My breath caught in my throat as the idea lit up like a match in my mind. This. This was perfect. A modern day poison of aconite.

I would stop his heart for the way he shattered and broke mine.

I started giggling uncontrollably, and I knew I sounded ridiculous, but I couldn't stop. A mother put her arm around her young daughter and led her out of the glasshouse and it only made me laugh harder.

I took a picture of the plaque and made a show of snapping a few more of the other plants to make sure that Grant thought I wanted to research when I got home later. We meandered through the gardens for another hour before we decided to stop for our afternoon cuppa inside the main entrance's cafe. We giggled over fond memories, ate a few mini BLT sandwiches, but all the while, I was running through my mind the scenarios of how to poison my fiancé without getting caught.

Sending a bouquet of flowers? No, that wouldn't work, we rarely had fresh cut flowers in the house because of his pollen allergies. Somehow, he needed to ingest it. That was the surest way to kill him. I looked at my fine china tea cup and saucer, watching the tea and small bubbles spin around when the idea hit. Wine. I could add it to an already opened bottle of wine that I knew he would drink. Two birds with one stone if they drank it together. I smiled as I took another sammie off the platter, looking up at my darling fiancé through my lashes. He grinned back at me, leaning in for a quick kiss.

"I love you, my Meg," he whispered against my lips before they kissed mine.

My stomach ached with longing. Longing for the three most important words you could say to someone to be true. Longing to run my hands through his hair, to wrap them around his neck and throttle him.

I leaned away slowly, working to keep my bile down. I took one more sip of my black tea before saying out of the corner of my mouth, "We should probably pay and head back to the platform before we miss our boarding time. I have to go to the store for a few things we're out of at home too."

He had a meeting to catch soon after all, and I highly doubted that it was work related. And I had a plan to conjure up.

The bell rang loudly against the glass door of the garden supply shop as I stepped out of the warm, breezy afternoon. I smoothed my mousy curls back into place and ran through my plan, checking boxes off on my pocket notepad for each ingredient needed. I was still ever thankful for Easter Break and that I didn't have to spend my time teaching teenagers. Revenge took up a lot of brain capacity and mental space. It didn't leave much real estate for anything else.

"Hello dear," I heard from behind a large, ornate floral display sitting on the front counter. An elderly woman with once vibrant blonde hair poked her wrinkled face out from behind the piece and smiled at me. "Are you here for an order pick up?"

I returned the smile, thankful for a like-minded woman who loved plants as much as I did. "I'm looking for a specific flower that I've heard can be a bit... difficult to handle. I was hoping that I could place an order here with you?"

"Well we can certainly try," replied the sweet woman, clearly thinking I was talking about some plant that was hard to keep alive. "What exactly are you looking for?"

I smiled, a pristine picture of innocence. "Aconite? They're also called monkshood or wolfsbane?"

The woman's face transformed from loving grandma to shock and horror, wide eyed and taken aback. "I haven't gotten an order for those in quite some time. Do you make home remedies? The last person I had come in asking for those was a bit of a naturalist and made his own medicines."

I considered my answer before speaking. She just handed me the perfect alibi. "I'm wanting to pick it up as a hobby." I waved my hand around in enthusiasm. "I've heard wonderful things about the plant and that it adds beauty to a garden." I'd done my research, of course. But I needed to continue this oblivious front.

Her eyes were thoughtful, still a little concerned about the species I was wanting, but not wanting to lose a customer either. "It can be dangerous to work with. Touching it with bare hands can cause extreme pain and swelling while ingesting it could be fatal." My eyebrows raised. She nodded. "While I was studying botany in my younger years, my professor told me a story of someone who consumed over 40 mL of an aconite tincture, and within hours they had suffocated and died, the poor thing. I really don't know how these flowers are legal still, but when used correctly, it really can do wonders for a person. And it looks gorgeous in a cut flower or bee keeping garden."

I let some of my fear that constantly swirled underneath show through my eyes, hoping I appeared solemn and afraid. "I've heard of that happening. How horrid."

She grabbed a pad of paper and a pen from under the counter. "Well love, you seem like you know your stuff, is there anything else I can order for you besides that? And how many bushels would you like?"

I ordered a small bouquet of aconite. It wouldn't take much to make a potent tincture. I asked for a species of daisy and some seeds for chamomile as well.

"Truly, thank you for your help. I'm excited for this little experiment of mine" I told the kind shop owner. She looked so incredibly pleased to have made an order, albeit still concerned, and both reactions made my day a little brighter.

As I walked home, I ran through how to make this work without putting any suspicion on my shoulders. I'd have to plan a way out of here and I couldn't go back to New York, too expensive. I stopped by the same coffee shop that I went to the day I saw Grant make his death sentence. I ordered a vanilla latte and grabbed one of the last seats at the bar facing the street.

Drawing out my laptop, I researched some of the outlying villages around London. I'd always dreamed of us owning a cottage so I could grow our own vegetables and herbs. I double-clicked on a village and did a quick Google search. Cotswold. The pictures were absolutely stunning and my breath caught in my throat with excitement this time, not heartbreak. Looking down at my watch, gauging how much time I had left before I needed to be home to make dinner, I quickly worked at making the perfect cover and escape plan.

~

Later that night, after we finished dinner in the living room, Grant got dressed for the evening and I dressed down in my favorite hole-filled sweats and old NYU hoodie. He didn't wear his normal casual slim-fit jeans and pull over jumper. Tonight, he decided to wear his black skinny jeans, the ones that I always complimented how good it made his ass look, and his sports coat over a basic white t-shirt. It was always one of my favorite outfits he wore when we would go out.

"Enjoy your cozy night in, love," Grant murmured into the top of my head as he hugged me.

He gave me a quick kiss goodnight, waving as he closed the front door. I sighed, tucking my fleece blanket up under my armpits and began working on the blanket I was crocheting. But the rage didn't want me to sit still, urging and coaxing my doubt to act. It didn't like how I so easily trusted Grant. His tech company did host meetups at that pub on occasion, but I couldn't get the image of that blonde hair on his jacket out of my head. I had a hunch, though I didn't want to be right. But I had to be sure.

I sprang up from the love seat, throwing my crocheting work off my lap, and made a quick change into my black zip up hoodie and black fleece leggings, ensuring that I could blend into the shadows easily if needed. I checked myself in the mirror, my dark curls sticking out all over the place. I worked to smooth them down, their unruliness that I normally enjoyed, now causing me to growl and yank at my hair, ripping out tiny sections in wrathful indignation. Small ringlets scattered the sink, shock and regret boiling over. I shrieked at my reflection, hitting the mirror with the palm of my hand. *He told me he liked my unruly hair. And then he chooses some platinum* Barbie?! I punched at the mirror until a satisfying crack reverberated in my ears, little crimson lesions dotting my knuckles. I smiled, the fracture splintering my reflection.

I chose to tie my hair up, realizing how much time I'd wasted fussing over myself. Once I stepped out into the chilly open air of the evening, I pulled my hood up, shadows from the streetlights obscuring my eyes. The pub was three blocks away, so I took off at a sprint to make up for lost time. Breathing heavily, I remained close to the darkened buildings, slowing once I finally saw Grant strolling and laughing on the phone with someone, only a block away from the pub. I stayed behind him by about 100 meters just to be safe, but close enough to keep his silhouette in my line of vision. He stopped at a crosswalk on the corner, laughing as he held his arms open to someone across the intersection.

A giggling blonde woman ran into his awaiting embrace. She pressed a hard kiss to his lips and looped her arm through his, continuing down the street to the pub. I heard the high-pitched ring of her voice echo to where I stood, wrapping around my heart, and squeezing it. I could sense that there were other people walking down the sidewalk tonight, even the occasional couple lip locking and sighing against the brick buildings. But all I could see was Grant's head resting on top of the woman's, right arm wrapping around her shoulders to pull her in closer to his body. A whoosh of air expelled from my lungs, leaving me breathless and empty.

Did he think of me when his cheek pressed into her hair sprayed locks? I backed up against a building, one hand covering my mouth, one hand over my chest. It ached. *Did she fit perfectly into his body as I did? Better? Did she smell like him the next morning and wanted to keep his smell enveloped around herself like a favorite blanket for as long as possible like I did?* My breathing wasn't slowing down. My back slid down the wall, ass hitting the ground, hard.

I felt a little less crazy, a little less pathetic sitting there hyperventilating, having caught him in the act of lying to my face. This plan needed to happen. Soon. My heart couldn't take any more of this torture. It was time for his.

Five months ago

I breathed in the smell of his neck, letting his scruff scratch my forehead. *I could get used to this.* We were walking with arms wrapped around each other, not sure whose limb was whose and we didn't care who stared. We were in pure bliss. I squeezed his hand, lifting my head from his shoulder and pecked him on the cheek. He smiled, kissing my forehead. He wrapped his right arm around my shoulders and rested his head on top of mine, pulling me closer into his side for warmth.

"You really do look ravishing tonight," he murmured into my hair. I snuck my arm inside his coat around his lower back and squeezed. This was our last visit to New York to see my parents before we moved in together in his flat in London.

"You don't look so bad yourself," I winked at him.

The park sidewalk was lit with multicolored Christmas lights twinkling and waving in the soft breeze. I desperately wanted to show him the first lighting of the huge tree at Rockefeller Center. It's touristy, but it is iconic, and it *was* Christmas time.

We slowed our pace as we saw the crowd waiting and swaying to stay warm. Winter in NYC was no joke. Its wind was biting and made my nose icy, but I didn't care. Grant was mine and he made my world more modern and adventurous. I never wanted to forget this moment and how we felt.

Grant shifted to stand behind me with his hands on my waist and chin resting on my head as we waited for the lights. Classic Christmas music of Nat King Cole sounded in the background as I linked my hands with his across my stomach. A buzzing sound whistled through the air, and then fireworks of green and red burst across the starless sky, every branch on the massive tree glowing. A collective gasp and clapping resounded across the park as Christmas had finally begun for so many families.

I turned to face Grant. "Isn't it incredi—" I gasped.

"Meg Buchannon." He was no longer standing behind me, but kneeling on one knee with a handmade box splayed open, a beautiful Art Deco ring reflecting the dancing lights of the tree. "You have always believed in me and brought out the best in me. You're fiercely loyal, kind, beautiful, and such a treasure to know and love. I'm excited for the best times of our lives to be lived and experienced together and I promise to cherish you all the days of my life. Will you marry me?" His hand was shaking with nerves and I could hear muffled gasps and glee-filled whispers from those watching around us.

One gloved hand covered my mouth, and one hand went to my heart as I nodded my head. "Yes. Over and over, I will always tell you yes."

He stood up, took off my glove ever so gently, and slid the vintage ring over my left ring finger, and kissed it.

He whispered so low so that only I could hear it, "I am yours alone. For the rest of eternity."

~

Present Day

A few days after making my order, I got a sweet voicemail in the early evening from the woman at the garden supply store letting me know that my shipment had arrived. Walking a few streets over to the shop, I felt more peace than I had in a long time, seeping further in me with each stride. I opened the door to the sound of the friendly bell tinkling above me, smiling at my new friend. Or accomplice. Either worked fine. Thankfully, the woman had just begun pulling out the bag of purple aconite with meticulously gloved and cautious hands. She glanced up as I walked into the store, smiling at my stupefied look.

"With these purple beauties, you need to always handle them with gloves. If at any point a part of it touches your skin, or if you forget to wash your hands and you ingested it, it wouldn't be a pretty evening for you." She tsked her tongue a couple of times while wrapping up the lethal bouquet and smiled with adoration at the daisies, placing them all in a lovely canvas bag. Gingerly slipping the bag over my tweed coated forearm, I resounded my thanks to her again, truly grateful for her part in everything, of course, she was none the wiser.

By the time I got home, Grant was sliding on his gray robe getting ready for bed early, too tired to notice the bag I was carrying. He kissed me on the forehead as I walked into the kitchen, laying the tote on the kitchen island.

"Goodnight my love," he murmured, stroking my arm with the back of his hand before blearily walking towards our bedroom.

I bore my eyes into his back like two sharpened daggers, wishing all of this would be solved and my revenge was as easy as a deathly stare. But, good things were never easy and I had a long night ahead of me. I opened the cabinets looking for my mortar and pestle. It was time to get to work.

I tip-toed to the basement with my bags and supplies. Gloves on and donning on a mask for extra precautions while I pulverized the precious flower, I worked on grinding up the full flower: roots, stem, leaves, and petals, making sure to do one stem at a time. After each flower was finished, I poured the thick liquid contents into a measuring cup, repeating the process well into the early hours of the morning until I had 50 mL of aconite tincture.

By this point, I poured myself a small glass of merlot that I found hanging under one of the cabinets in our tiny wine storage, emptying the bottle just enough so that I could pour the lethal contents in without overflowing the bottle and still making it look like someone had half a glass. I took great care in ensuring that my supplies were cleared away like nothing had ever happened, the gloves were safely in the trash, and my hands were thoroughly washed. I crept back upstairs and I sat down on the couch as the edges of the sky slowly turned pink and orange, a truly lovely way to end my escapade. My bag of purple aconite flowers empty, the wine chilling in the fridge for the following Thursday evening, I literally patted myself on the back for my brilliance.

My head snapped up as I realized that once the plan was executed, I'd actually have to quit my job, move away, get a new name... I didn't know if I could handle all of that weight and responsibility. I started hyperventilating a little. Standing up from my seat in the living room, I walked over to the kitchen sink and leaned my forearms against the counter. I made a bowl with my hands under the cold water, splashing my face and pinching my cheeks hard.

"Get a grip, Meg!" I whispered to myself, slapping each cheek. *I have to finish this. I have to. No second guessing or backing out now.*

It wasn't even the poisoning or the getting caught that I was worried about. It was the extra details that I hadn't accounted for that must be figured out in the next two days. I wasn't much of a planner and all I had in mind so far was a village I could escape to. But if I was motivated enough like I was now, I could get shit done.

At least I planned on a girls' night with one of my best friends. That would get me out of the house and give me an excuse for that night. That's how I knew Grant would probably invite the girl over anyway, since I would be out late.

I'd bring an overnight bag and tell him not to wait up. I'd tell him I may stay the night at her house if I drink too much. And then I would make my escape. Start over with the life that I deserved.

I collapsed at the kitchen table, both exhausted from the roller-coaster of emotions and newly inspired about this new life I was dreaming up for myself. I could do this. I *deserved* this.

A few weeks later, I turned on the light in the backroom, rolling my black gloves up to my elbows, and hooking the mask loops around the back of my ears. I grabbed my box cutter as I carried the cardboard box labeled "this way up" to my worktable. Sliding the razor down the shiny tape, I popped open the box and pulled out a bag of long purple stems, laying them down on the table near the other stems I had already cut down to size for the bouquet I was compiling. I worked to arrange this particular bouquet with care, making sure none of the purple petals or leaves touched my skin. Bright hooded purple flowers surrounded the delicate daisies and the whole arrangement was edged with baby blue forget-me-nots.

Satisfied with my work, I wrapped the vase and all the flowers into a clear plastic bag, tying it securely with a small piece of jute rope. Taking off my gloves, I carefully grabbed the vase with one hand and unlocked the metal door with the other. Leaning my whole body weight against the heavy door, it groaned open. I squinted at the fluorescent lighting of the larger storage room, making sure none of my employees were loitering around as I shoved the bookcase closed, hiding the door behind my bookkeeping records.

I weaved my way through the storage area, stepping around five-gallon buckets filled with water and different flowers ready to be put into wedding bouquets or get well soon gifts. Pausing at the TV in the corner, BBC News just released more information about a case that still had no real leads.

"For those of you just hearing about this most fascinating case, a man and a woman were found dead in a downtown London flat a few weeks ago, both appearing to have died from asphyxiation. Authorities are struggling to find the source of the deaths, and cannot at this time release any information about the results of the autopsies. Police do say that they are looking for a secondary school biology teacher by the name of Meg Buchannon, who was allegedly engaged to the man and hasn't been seen since before the death of her fiancé."

I continued walking. I was greeted at the front desk by a woman still wearing her cat eye sunglasses inside and a faux fur coat, even though the air was starting to turn humid and scorching. I placed the arrangement in front of her, typing the price into the tablet.

The sound of the TV followed me into the front display room. "If anyone has any information about the whereabouts of Ms. Buchannon, they are instructed to call the authorities immediately. A photo of her can be found here on the screen."

Oblivious to her surroundings the woman exclaimed, "Oh my! My sister-in-law will just keel over when she sees these! Just intoxicating. Simply to die for." She looked up at me, winked, and handed over her credit card while still gawking at the florals.

"That'll be £122," I replied, eyes still focused on the newscast.

"That's fine honey, just fine."

Swiping her card, I grinned at the irony of the situation, picking up my midafternoon cuppa and stirring around the sugar grounds that had settled to the bottom. The picture they chose was of my school ID photo, now extremely outdated compared to my current appearance.

"Have a great day, miss." I smirked as I handed over her receipt.

I reached into the bag that I stored under the counter for my chap-stick and found my journal. Looking around to ensure that no customers were in the store, I opened the book to the middle of the page, pushing my bleach blonde hair behind my ear, running my fingers down the paper until I found what I was looking for.

"A Taste of Aconite," I wrote, right above where I scratched down the details of my next steps and decisions that I made the night of the poisoning. I wanted to ensure that I could continue my life in London, even if it was in a village outside the city. I needed to stay here, to use my knowledge of botany and biology to continue what I started. I added a check mark next to the last item on the list: "start my own flower shop."

I hummed a chuckle, shaking my head, and tucked the purse back under the counter when I heard the jingle of the shop door opening. A young woman approached the counter, nervous and skittish.

"I heard by word of mouth that you're the one to come to for, um, beautiful purple intoxicating florals?" She wrung the bag she held in her hands and looked at me, eyes filled with both tears and hope, the beginnings of a bruise blooming under her eye. I nodded at her understandingly, the familiar rage tickling at the back of my mind, and grabbed a pad of paper while walking around the counter to guide her to the back room.

"You've come to the right place, hon. We'll take care of him."

15

WOLF GIRL

BY ANNA ELZINGA

little wolf girl,
what wine dark poison
thrums through the thick of your blood?
what is it coursing within you
that you fiercely try to water down?

starving one,
what rotting fruit do you settle for,
staining the ghost pale of your mouth
like blood mottled bruises?

gloom-ridden girl,
what causes your back to stoop
curved in on yourself
as though to protect the little life you have left
flickering in your chest
wavering like a match flame in the sharp
mountain wind?

knife-edged one,
all cracked lips and split knuckles,
tar veined and weary,
what is it that gnaws you from the inside?
is it that full moon harbinger, grim mouthed and cold

ever licking at your bleeding heels?
she haunts you in all your wide-eyed midnights—
she sets your poison coursing,
making the monster inside you
howl and rattle
against the flimsy prison
of your rib cage.

little wolf girl, doomed to devour
or be devoured
again and again
cyclical dread
old, repetitive dismay.

little wolf girl,
you can cure
this curse
that corrodes
your bones—

the age-old antidote lies within you.

16

DARKENED SOULS

BY MICHELLE LYNN VILLA

*S*tupid! *Stupid!* How could you let this happen? And why, *why* did I agree to have it here at my place?

Before the knock sounds on the door, I already know who it is. It's the reporter. How could I have been so careless? I clench my fist at my sides so that I don't take a swing at the wall. What is done is done. It's time to face my reality and attempt to handle this with the utmost care. The knock comes again and I open the door to find the annoyingly handsome man standing on the other side of it.

"Hello, I'm Andrew. Thank you for having me over," he says, walking in before I even invite him. He whistles. "You have an amazing flat."

"You didn't give me much of a choice, did you?" I say, closing my door.

"Oh, come on, don't be like that. It wasn't like you were trying to hide what you were doing, now were you?"

"Well, maybe you should've mind—" I stop myself before I do or say anything I would later regret. "You know what? Let's just get this over with, ok? I have better things to do with my time, and with people who actually value it."

I don't mean for my irritation to show so vividly, but there is something about this man that just brings it out of me, and my current dilemma doesn't help. I watch as he goes and makes himself comfortable in my small living area. Seeing him sit there while he takes in my décor bothers me even more. Not that my place is a mess, but, because of who I am, there are certain things that are private. For that exact reason, I never invite anyone over. With a sigh of defeat, I make my way over and sit across from where him cross my arms and legs and just wait while he pulls out a voice recorder and a small notebook and pen from his messenger bag.

"A voice recorder," I say sarcastically, "how very vintage."

"Yeah, well, digital devices can be hacked. Okay, let's start with your name," he says pressing the record button, notebook and pen in hand waiting to take notes.

"Chloe Craft," I say.

"Is that your real name?" he asks, looking right through me.

"Sure," I say, shrugging.

He pauses the voice recorder. "Come on, you said you would give me an honest interview."

The look of irritation on his face makes me laugh. It's been a long time since I've seen that look. I lean forward, challenging him. "I said I would give you an interview. I never said how much of it would actually be true."

Thinking that he'll just go along with it, I sit back, smiling, waiting for him to just give up. He doesn't. He brings his bag back onto his lap and searches for something inside. While he does this, I take the time to look at his features. He is very good looking, but it's the way that he scrunches up his face in concentration that makes him attractive to me. You could tell by looking at him that he is intelligent. It was in the eyes. Which also tells me that he will probably see through my lies. I will have to strategize my answers.

I hear him clear his throat and that brings me back to my senses. I look at him and he nods over to what he holds in his hand. I glare at him. It was the video camera he had recorded me on. I take back everything I just thought about him. Devious creature!

"I guess I should just take this video of you and show it to the proper authorities and see what they have to say about what you're doing."

Anger builds up inside me at being blackmailed, I take a deep breath and force myself to calm down.

"And here I thought you were intelligent," I say looking him dead in the eye. "Not many would dare to blackmail someone like me and get away with it."

"And what exactly are you?" he counters.

"I'll let you try and figure that out. I could be someone who turns you into a toad. Delete that video and be done with all of this," I threaten.

"And what makes you think this is my only copy?" he grins devilishly and speaks again before I can say anything. "And before you even think of doing anything to me, I made sure to let several people know exactly where I was going with explicit instructions to take the video to the authorities if I didn't come back tonight."

Very smart man. I scrutinize him, trying to call his bluff, but see that there was none. I decide to give in and just answer his questions. He sees my resolve, and pushes record on his voice recorder again.

"Alright, let's start from the beginning, shall we? What is your real name?"

"Celestina Aimes," I answer.

"Interesting."

"How so?" I ask, knowing exactly why he finds it interesting. "Did you expect something more witchy?"

"Well, yes, I mean no," he sputters trying to find his grounding. "Your last name, it sounds familiar. It's an old name here in Arcadia."

"I'm aware."

"Are you part of that family?" he asks, putting his pen to paper, waiting for my response.

"Yes," I answer truthfully.

I wait for his reaction, but instead he starts writing notes in his notebook. I wish I could see what he's writing, but I make no attempt to ask or show any curiosity. I know if I show just how nervous this has made me, I will lose all control and tell him everything that I have been hiding and keeping secret. I can't allow that to happen. Too much is at stake and I can't let anyone else get involved. Deep down I did feel the strong urge to share everything I know, if only to stop this feeling of loneliness I have felt for so long.

"You told me that you know the mystery behind the people who disappear and come back very sick. Said they're being poisoned and only you know how to cure them. How?" he asks getting right to the point.

I wasn't ready to reveal the *how's* and *why's*, so I try to think of a way to prolong this subject.

"I'm sorry for being rude; may I offer you some tea?"

"Sure… What kind of tea?" he asks suspiciously.

"Morning Brew. I was preparing some before you showed up." Seeing his apprehension, I add, "I promise it's only tea. Nothing you need to worry about."

"I'll just have some water, thank you," he says going back to whatever notes he was writing down.

"Of course," I say getting up from where I sit and head to the kitchen. Grabbing a glass, I pour him a cup of water.

"Can I ask you something?" I ask going over to my forgotten tea cup and pour tea into the tea cup.

"You're going to interview me now?" he answers with his own question.

"Just curious about something."

That catches him off guard as he looks up from his notes.

"You're curious about me?"

"Yes, so can I ask you ask question?" I try very hard to hide the irritability in my voice. I inhale a long breath and hold it for as long as I can, and when I release it I try to bring back some composure.

"Go on then," he says going back to whatever he was writing in his notebook.

"Why do you need to know who I am? What's in it for you?"

He doesn't answer right away, he looks like he's contemplating whether to tell me the truth, and for a moment I feel he might not answer me.

"Nothing really. I'm the type of person who notices when good things are being done. Which is why I document them; so that others can see the amazing things that go unnoticed. People have been disappearing for weeks, and no one has been able to say why, or what made them so sick when they return. Then I find you, and you are just healing them. I couldn't explain how you did it, and I had to know. I was going to ask you, but you just kind of disappeared."

"So, you started asking around about me?"

"Something like that," he says.

Adding sugar to my tea, I hear footsteps; when I look back towards the living room, I notice that he is not in his seat. I look around frantically and find him looking at the herbs I have hanging by the window. He inspects each bunch of herbs carefully; feeling the texture and taking in their scent. It wasn't a craft that was done as much in homes anymore since you could easily go out and purchase any herbs you wanted at the local markets. I made them myself because they helped me do something when I felt anxious. It had been a long time since I met someone as curious as Andrew. Before he could investigate any more of my things, as I notice him making his way towards the opposite wall, I bring him over his cup of water, which he carefully inspects. I take my cup of tea and go back and sit in the same spot hoping he will join me.

"So, the people who you heal, how do you know what's wrong with them?" he asks again, not straying from the question I was trying to avoid.

"That is a long story," I say simply.

"Well, a long story is exactly what I am here for." He settles back into the seat across from me, patiently waiting for me to begin.

I think he sees my hesitancy as I sit there and struggle with my indecision of not telling him what he wants to know. Another part of me wants to tell him everything. I have never really told anyone everything about what happened all those years ago. Always feared how they would treat me differently if they knew what I had gone through or maybe take advantage of the things the discovered I could do. I sit in silence for a few more minutes mentally battling with myself on what to do. I sigh in defeat for a second time.

"To answer your question, I have to start at the beginning, so make yourself comfortable, and please, pay attention and try not to interrupt or it'll just take longer," I say, looking over at him, expecting him to say something, but he just nods.

"So, you have been to Arcadian Park, yes?" I ask and he nods not interrupting. "You see, centuries before it was Arcadian Park, it was just a large plot of wildland and forests," I pause making sure he isn't about to ask me any questions. "It was a time when magic, and sorcerers weren't as rare. In the middle of all of this there was this cottage that no one really knew about and there was a good reason for it. A sorcerer once lived in those dwellings and, like any dark being, was plotting the demise of the kingdoms. The reason most don't know about this cottage is because of the many spells that were placed on it centuries ago to keep him from being able to harm anyone."

"How did you know about this cottage and the sorcerer?" Andrew asks, jumping straight to the point, I find this odd because most people would have looked at me like I was crazy at the mere mention of sorcery and magic. That's also because most believe that magic and sorcerers have long been gone from the world.

"I was his apprentice for a time," I say awkwardly. "I might have also... maybe... been in love with him." I try to hide the blush that rises up my cheeks. I hear him snort from the other side of the sitting area. "Okay, go ahead and judge me, I was sixteen and I really didn't know any better. And in my defense, I didn't know what his plans were. He wasn't what people thought sorcerers were supposed to be. He wasn't old, or rude or abusive like I had been told all my life. He took me off the streets when my family threw me out for not wanting to marry a man who was three times my age. They could have forced me to, but they thought that if they threw me out and I saw how the world really was I would come running back and beg them to take me back. That I would agree to marry the man they had chosen for me. Well, they were wrong."

I pick up my cup and drink some tea, trying very hard not to reel in and control my emotions. It had been a long time since I thought of Gabriel. I mourned him for a long time, but he made his choice, and I was done making excuses.

"They were right about one thing: life wasn't easy on the streets and people weren't always keen on hiring a woman. But I made my way without having to resort to what most expected me to do. I had too much pride to do that, if you know what I mean," I say, hoping I wouldn't have to clarify exactly what I was referring to.

"When I met the sorcerer, he found me out in the fields collecting herbs. He offered me a room, and food, and said he would pay me. All I had to do was collect the things he asked for and keep his cottage clean and organized, and prepare the meals. I agreed. When he took me back to the cottage, he gave me a tour of the whole place, which was a lot bigger on the inside than it looked on the outside. I guess I should have been suspicious when he asked that I not go into his workroom, no matter what I heard or saw. See and hear things, I did."

I sit for a moment and remember back to those first days. There was always a flash of light, or small explosions coming from that room. Once, I could have sworn I heard a thunderstorm coming from behind the door. Not wanting to end up back in the streets, I kept my distance. Even so, my curiosity increased every day.

"He never treated me terribly, and he kept his promise. I was scared of him at first because I was a girl living with a stranger. A stranger who was not only a man but a young one at that. If it ever got out, my reputation would be ruined, not that I really cared about that. We didn't spend much time together in the beginning, except for at mealtimes. I thought the meals would be spent in silence, but he always started a conversation; first asking about my day, then asking me about my past, and about things that I enjoyed. I asked him questions now and again, interested in what things he liked. I had never before received that kind of attention from anyone. No one had ever tried to get to know who I was. Over time, I got to know him and he got to know me."

"And you fell in love with him."

I nod my head, not looking in his direction so that he would not see the tears gathering in my eyes. It had been a long time since I opened up about these things with anyone, and Andrew was making it very easy to do so, by just listening.

"After some time, he revealed to me who he was. That he was a sorcerer. It was like he wanted me to be afraid and run from him, but I wasn't. It was already too late. I was in love with him, and I couldn't tell my heart to run. I think when he saw that I wasn't going to run, he decided to offer me a position as his apprentice. He said he would teach me how to make potions and how to master magic."

"Don't you need to be born with magic, to learn spells?" he asks.

I shake my head, waiting for the real question I'm certain he wants to ask; the one I wanted to avoid. To the few I had told some of these events to, their biggest question or interest was for me to teach them magic, but with Andrew that question never came.

"Not necessarily, people don't need to be born with magic to learn it. I could teach you if I really wanted to. And don't get me wrong, there are people who are born with it, but it is very rare nowadays." I pause so that he can have time to register what I'm saying.

"I read every book he had in his library collection. These books looked centuries old so I assumed that they had been passed down to him from his family. They weren't, but I thought nothing of it. For a year I learned. I was enthralled with everything he taught me, and I learned all the magic I could. I learned about healing magic, and magic that could help gardens grow.

"Like anything else in the world, there was dark magic. Magic that could poison a person's heart and turn him to darkness. Like everything there was a balance and I learned that there were some magic I didn't want to learn. He warned me against this magic and that I should never attempt to use it, I could educate myself concerning it, and maybe how to counter it, but I should never use it."

I pause before going into what came next, knowing the pain it was about to bring back.

"It never occurred to me to ask more about his past and where he came from. I never thought about asking why he lived there. I wanted to ask him what experiments he conducted during the late hours of the night, but I didn't. I wanted to ask him what his goal was with all his experiments, but my promise kept me from asking." I scoff. "Until the day I woke up to the sound of screams; voices and explosions. I was used to the explosions, but the screams and voices I had never heard before. There were some that sounded like people were being tortured, others like they were laughing and enjoying their anguish. My curiosity finally got the best of me and I made my way to the one room I had promised to never enter. I opened up the door and peeked in. He was there inside a magic circle, chanting a spell while chaos encircled him. My mind could not comprehend what was going on at first, then I saw men and woman from the village, no older than me, tied to tables in what looked like a dark shadow trying to enter the bodies." I pause again, trying very hard to keep my anxiety levels from over taking me. There was a slight tremble in my body and I fight harder to keep my emotions under control, but I have a feeling that might not last long.

"What was he doing to them?" Andrew asks when I don't continue, sitting closer to the edge of his seat. If he noticed my trembling he pretends very well not to notice.

"He was poisoning their souls."

"Poisoning their souls?"

"Yes. You see, you can convince a malicious man to do your bidding if there is something in it for them, but a pure soul will not be convinced so easily. The sorcerer has to poison their souls and to do that, they need to be willing to sacrifice a piece of themselves. So, you can understand my shock when I saw what I saw. At first, I didn't know if it was the darkness that he was trying to put into their souls, but then I felt it, and it felt like fear, anger, and hate. Pure evil. I thought he was the purest being I had ever laid eyes on. But on the contrary, he was darkness itself."

"What was the purpose of turning people to darkness?"

I looked over at Andrew. He was no longer taking notes, but watching and listening to every word I said.

"Do you remember learning in school about the Dark Ages?" I ask him trailing off subject for a second to a separate event in history, trying to bring him to the answer himself.

"Vaguely. It wasn't a subject that was often taught because of how long ago it was. Schools prefer to teach about current events."

"*He* was the reason the Dark Ages happened." I sit silently and wait for his reaction. The one I knew was either going to make him think I was crazier than he probably already thought I was, or he would believe every word I was about to tell him. I watched him as realization hit him and he looked over at me, shock and confusion playing over his features.

"How is that possible?" he asked, confusion finally winning over the two emotions. "That would make him over..."

"Over three thousand years old, yes," I complete his thought. "He was the reason our world almost fell into darkness. He poisoned so many and made an army, just so he could live in the chaos he thrives on. Kingdoms warred trying to destroy each other. Friends became enemies and were determined to best one another. But then Adina came and stopped him. The purest and brightest soul was sent to aid in the fight against the darkness. Legend says she had vanquished him, but I don't think she had the power to do that. I believe she could only imprison him in the cottage. Light can never vanquish darkness; there must always be a balance. One cannot win over the other, or at least that is what we hope."

Andrew gets up and starts pacing my flat, running his fingers through his hair, absorbing everything I had told him so far. Then he stops and looks around at my belongings, the herbs, the books on my shelf, and the amulets that I had collected over time. What eventually catches his eye are my photos and all his attention goes to them. He walks closer to the photos and stares at them intently. Looking at the many faces that were on the frames on my gallery wall. It was my favorite part of my flat. There you can see the evolution of how paintings became photos. A true testament of my time.

"Are these all of your family?" He asks looking at a very old painting of me and my parents from before all of these things happened to me.

"Some of them," I reply.

"Wait. Are these pictures of you?"

"Of course," I patiently wait for him to connect the dots.

"Exactly how old are you? And how is that possible?" He turns really looking at me for the first time since he walked into my flat.

"That's not exactly a question you ask a lady now, is it?" I was hoping he would not push, but by the look on his face I know I might as well reveal my age. "If you must know, I am five hundred and seventeen years old."

Taking in my response, his eyebrows shoot up and his jaw slightly drops in shock. He blinks his eyes and closes his mouth as if coming back to reality and just stares at me. I had never revealed to anyone my age. I knew what would happen if I did. I would have been accused of sorcery, which wasn't entirely wrong, but even I wouldn't want to be burned at the stake. Or people acting like the selfish beings most of them were would demand that I share my secret with them. Poor mortals. Their greatest fear has always their own mortality.

"How is that possible? You look like you're barely seventeen years old. No one can live that long. Did you find the fountain of youth or something?

"Of course not. The fountain of youth is just a ridiculous myth," I say jokingly, trying to smile, knowing that it is not exactly sincere. "What happened to me is the result of what happened next." I invite him with the nod of my head to take his seat again, and he does.

"I couldn't stay with him, not after realizing what he was doing. I knew I had to leave. His idea of a future was both disgusting and terrifying to me. But, before I left, I went to the library and packed as many of the books as I could, so that I could educate myself on how I could defeat him before it was too late. Then, I ran before he knew I had seen everything.

When I stepped outside of the cottage, I saw the most nightmarish sight before me, and it made me sick. Seeing the truth of what he planned, the illusion of the beautiful cottage was gone. The land surrounding the cottage lost its magical appearance. What was once a paradise was now grotesque and diseased. There were no longer the herb and flower beds that I had worked so hard to grow but dead plants that were the color of death— if death was a color."

"Where did you go?" Andrew asks.

"To the one place I said I would never return to. I went home. I knocked on the door and when my parents opened to see who was on the other side, they were relieved to see that it was me; that I was alive. I disappeared for a whole year, and my parents— who gladly kicked me out to teach me a lesson, rushed out and took me in their arms.

They explained to me that they thought I was amongst the people who disappeared. They had been looking for me for several months, and had almost lost hope. When we came inside, they let me go to my room, which was kept the same way I left it. It was, honestly, the breath of fresh air that I needed. When everyone went to bed that night, I stayed up and started going through every book I had taken from the cottage and tried to figure out how to stop the spell he had been casting. I did the same thing for many nights. It, still to this day, amazes me that I was able to leave with so many of the books, but it wasn't enough. When I didn't find what I needed, I started asking around town about any information I could get my hands on."

"How long before he realized that you were no longer there?" Andrew asks.

"I honestly don't know. He never came for me. He wasn't able to come into town, so I never saw him once he finally did notice. One day, I felt something in the air. Something dark. Just when I thought there was nothing I could do, a kid followed me into the Grand Library and said that they had the information I was looking for."

"Seems a little too easy that someone just happened to have the answers you were looking for," Andrew says, looking skeptical.

"I thought the same. I knew he might have had his spies out there; since I was convinced the spell he performed that night was not the first time. But I didn't feel any darkness coming from him, so I gave him the benefit of the doubt. We set a time to meet later that night, and he said that his teacher wanted to meet with me since I was the first to ever come back. I wanted to ask more questions, but he said not to speak a word of it until I met with his teacher." I look over to see if Andrew is still listening. The look of concentration on his face confirming he is.

"That evening, when I went to leave, my family tried to stop me. My mother was terrified of losing me again, and no matter how hard I tried to explain to them that I would be fine, they didn't believe me. I hated myself for just walking out on them without an explanation, but I couldn't tell them about any of it. I didn't want them to be a part of what I was trying to do.

When I got to the designated location I was greeted by the same kid and he took me to some sort of backroom where he introduced me to a very tall, elegant, official-looking lady by the name of Amara. She told me she was from the Kingdom of Cresnia and that she'd heard of the rumors of one that had come back from the cottage and had to come and speak with me." I pause to take another sip of my tea, only to realize I had none left, so I set the cup aside.

"I asked her how she knew of this place when I was made to believe that there was no one who knew of it. She then explained to me that she was but one of the Guardians; and that they were the ones that had to make sure that the sorcerer could not escape. They were selected by Adina herself, before her disappearance, to make sure that he did not repeat what he had done in the Dark Ages. Over the years, they felt that the spells that kept him there were growing weaker, and they were trying to figure out how he had been able to get the victims to him. I told them how I got there and everything I learned over my year there. They couldn't believe how far from the cottage he had been able to travel when he found me in the fields. I found myself telling them everything and I couldn't stop myself. Not being able to tell anyone since my return, especially my family, was really hard. But since they trusted me enough to let me know their involvement, I, again, gave them the same benefit of the doubt. I didn't see any other choice since I had a feeling it wouldn't be long before the sorcerer would escape his entrapment and wreak havoc on the kingdoms, and those who kept him trapped.

"In the days to come, we researched everything we could about the darkness and who he was and how he came to be. What we found was that neither he nor Adina were what we thought. They are literal conduits for good and evil—light and darkness. They are the balance of everything in this world. When the great battle during the Dark Ages happened, Adina used all her strength and power to make his prison and then just disappeared. There were speculations that she had died, but there are those who believe that she used so much of her power that she had to rest and regain her strength."

"But that was three thousand years ago," Andrew says, interrupting me again, and I don't mind too much; knowing that telling him not to was too much of a request.

"It was, and it was twenty-five hundred years before my involvement, but we didn't find any evidence that she was around. So, we readied ourselves for a fight against him."

"You keep calling him 'him', does he not have a name?"

"When I was with him, he said his name was Gabriel, but I never found him by that name in any of the text I ever read."

"Did a fight ever come?" he asks.

Realizing I was coming to the end of my story, I readied myself for the incredible pain that I was about to relive. I had tried so hard for so many years to not think about this moment, but there were times when my mind would just go back. The moment when my heart broke and I made a decision for the greater good.

"It did. I spent a month learning new spells, hoping that each would be stronger than the last. We prepared, knowing that we could die in the process. Amara sent messages to the other Guardians and one by one they showed up. One by one they marveled over me, trying to explain how I did not fall into darkness when so many did. Even I couldn't explain it at the time. While I was there, I never sensed the darkness. Not once. But now that I was out of the cottage and its magic, darkness was all I sensed there.

"Then the day came, a lot sooner than we hoped. We thought we were prepared, but we couldn't prepare for everything. Attacks on the village were started by other people. Just random attacks, we thought, but then I recognized some of the people who were attacking. I had grown up with most of them. But they weren't the same people—you could see the darkness coming out of them like a dark mist that surrounded their bodies, moved to their command like tendrils reaching out turning everything they touched to evil. That is when we knew it was time to do what we planned. But everything went wrong," I say, a chill going up my back as I remember the events.

"We each went to the place we were told to be in to perform the spell, but before we muttered a word, a cloud of darkness engulfed us. He was so much stronger than we anticipated. We should have known. He had been waiting over two thousand years to exact his revenge on the world. One by one, every Guardian fell to the darkness, fell to his command and became his puppets. Except for me. The cloud that surrounded everyone else was repelled by my mere presence."

I tried to inhale, but found it hard through the sobs that came then. I did not realize I had started crying, but here I was, crying out tears I thought I had long since shed in front of a stranger. One who was blackmailing me, no less. But when I looked at him, no longer was there smugness on his features, I saw sorrow, sympathy and something else I couldn't quite describe.

"Celestina, who are you exactly?" he asks me, very seriously this time.

I looked at him and gone is the reporter. There is only this guy, who I just met, looking at me like he wants to protect me from whatever evil would come my way. I don't know when it happened, but his attitude towards me changed. Either that, or with my emotions all over the place, I was seeing what I wanted to.

"I didn't know at the time—I never could have guessed—especially not when I was surrounded by so much darkness and chaos was rampant through my town. But when I thought about all the people I wanted to protect I searched down deep and found that there was a power there that I could not explain. A light came to mind, and then it illuminated my body from within. Right before though, he appeared before me, begging me to stop. There was so much pain on his face that I almost believed he was sincere and it made my heart ache as I ignored his pleading. He begged me to save him and said that when I did, we would be able to be together. That he loved me. I wanted to believe him, but something inside me told me he was lying. I finally saw the evil deep within him. That's when I lit up like a beacon in the darkness, and when I let the light loose, it unleashed from my body like an actual living thing, driving out the darkness and pushing the darkness back to the cottage. Pushing *him* back to where he could hopefully not escape.

"When everything settled, I looked around and saw that everyone had gone back to their true selves, but I couldn't find any of the Guardians. I came to the conclusion that when I pushed him and the darkness back, he took them with him. I tried for days to bring them back, but they were tied to the darkness. Tied to him. I had no choice but to leave them."

"Who are you?" he asked again, waiting patiently for my reply.

"I am Celestina Aimes," I say slowly, "but my powers are from Adina herself."

"How is that possible? You said she disappeared after imprisoning him during the Dark Ages."

"She did, and honestly, I have no idea how it was possible. I have spent the last five hundred years looking for answers. Searching for ways to permanently stop him from hurting anyone else."

"How are you still alive?" he asks, and I search for the words to explain it to him.

"When I cast the spell that returned him to the cottage, I tied my soul to that spell. It gave me temporary immortality. That is the price I had to pay to make it work. If something happens to me, the spell will be broken and he will be set free."

"I guess that makes sense, but why are people starting to disappear now? And how do they manage to come back when no one else could in your time?"

"As he grows stronger with time, I grow weaker. Unlike him, I was born a human, he *is* an immortal. He also has the Guardians in the cottage giving him more power to bring down the spells that I put up to stop his escape. I am out here fighting alone." I try to think of a different way to explain it but it's the best that I have. It's the only explanation I can come up with.

"How come I've never heard of this incident?" he asks pulling out a handkerchief from his pocket reaching over offering it to me.

"It was an isolated incident." I accept and wipe the tears from my face. "All I did was stall what could have turned into his next reign of terror. I spoke with the kingdom heads of what happened and we took the proper precautions to make sure no one ever went near the cottage. Which is why the south part of the park is closed off to all. But like I said, his power is growing stronger by the day. It will only be a matter of time."

"Is there a way to help you become stronger?"

"There have been rumors of artifacts that were scattered around the kingdoms. I read that it helped Adina to magnify her powers, but when she disappeared, the Guardians were afraid they would be used for darkness, so they scattered them and left clues on how to find them. I have searched for clues and I've found riddles, but I have never been good at deciphering riddles." I look away in embarrassment, shaking my head and wiping the rest of the tears from my face. "That is the story as to how I knew how to help all those people. What you saw was me using magic to help them come back from the darkness. So, now you have your story, and if you don't mind, I have things to do, people to help."

"Wait, you said there were riddles, I'm good at riddles. Maybe I could help,"

"That's very kind of you, but I can't get anyone involved. I don't think you understand the dangers that come with what I do. Plus, there are other reasons that I don't let others get involved," Getting up from where I sat; dismissing anymore questions or arguments I know he was about to throw my way.

"Give me one reason why I can't get involved," he challenges me, like I knew he would.

"I am over five hundred years old," I say looking straight at him, ensuring that he got the message. "I eventually got tired of outliving those people who were connected to me."

He must have sensed the sadness in my voice because he packed away his things and started walking towards the door. Still standing at the door as he passes through the threshold, only to turn around on my doorstep, determination in his eyes.

"No, I don't accept that reasoning. Let me help."

"What's in it for you?"

"Helping someone save the world! I like this world and from what you described, I would like to keep it that way."

Such a simple reasoning.

"You have your story, isn't that enough? It could take years to find the answers I seek. Past your lifetime. I can't let you waste your life on something that could take that long. *Go*. Live your life. Fall in love and have a family. Live to the fullest, so that you don't regret not living."

"Last I checked, it was my life, so I make the decisions and I am going to help you," he says turning around and walking down the steps onto the sidewalk. "You need my help, and I am going to give it, no matter what you say."

"I should have turned you into a frog," I say to him.

"But you didn't," he smiles. "I'll see you later."

He waves and walks away. I watch as he walks down the busy sidewalk. Unable to control my smile at his enthusiasm, I make my way toward the door.

That's when I hear something, "You have become weak as the years have gone by my dear." I freeze at the sound of his voice whispering in the wind.

17

THE MIDNIGHT MASQUERADE

BY KAYLEE RENO

The evening is young and yet the darkness pools around me like midnight. The moon hangs full in the sky and its alabaster shadow falls across my path, illuminating it brightly—a stark comparison to the faded blue shadows of dusk. The silent night is peaceful in an unexpected way and the *shushing* of my gown against my legs is the only sound in my ears as I ascend the steps to the grand ballroom. Around me, others follow suit, one step at a time, silent all, save for the brush of fabric against flesh and the dull clack of heels on stone.

Silent as the grave, I think darkly.

Their faces are sober beneath their masks, their mouths set in grim little lines. As if they are loath to be here. As if the ball were a funeral and the guest of honor the dead.

I shudder, despite the warm summer air. They are wise to think this.

As I approach the tall, narrow double doors, I adjust my own mask, a flicker of anxiety sparking in my belly. The ball is a masquerade—a yearly sort of grim tradition with a fearsome and tenacious host—and I'm grateful for the illusion of something to hide behind. A cloaked figure allows the person in front of me to enter and

I watch as the guest pauses, draws in a breath, squares their shoulders, and plasters a ghostly smile across their face. They enter and the doors close slowly behind them, the sound hollow, echoing, final. I lick my lips, my heartbeat quickening. I am next, I know, but it is several agonizing moments before I can gather the courage. A wave of nausea threatens to be my undoing, but I clench my jaw, determined. The moment passes and I approach.

Though I cannot see the face beyond the shadow of the hooded figure, I keep my eyes down, my gaze averted. I know not to look too closely. I know that doing so would result in naught but nightmares for many nights to come.

If I am even fortunate enough to survive this night. If I am fortunate enough to leave this ball at all come morning. I must keep my wits about me. The figure stands between me and what lies beyond like a hallowed guard. An unsettling and macabre warning. The doors before me swing forward on silent hinges, an oddity of itself, I think, and a blackness so thick it seems to ripple, yawns on before me. I halt suddenly, unsure. Fearful. But when I steal a look behind me, the nameless, faceless figure is looking at me, looking *through* me, and I startle violently. I have hardly a moment to steel myself before I stumble forward into the blackness, tipping into the ballroom like a vase might tip over the edge of an unsteady table.

Where a moment before there was silence, now music and laughter, joy and weeping assault my ears as I cross the threshold, and I distantly wonder if it is because there is some enchantment placed over the room. The thought is vague though, as I am accosted with a thick, pungent mist that dulls my sense of time and awareness. I get the feeling that I'm walking yet suspended. As if I'm passing between stars. Or perhaps I am floating through the rippling darkness, caught between two points; what is real and tangible, and what is shadowed and elusive. The darkness seems to stretch on forever though, and something akin to terror spills from my heart and into my lungs and fingertips as I work to wade through it. I *must* get through it. I find myself rushing forward, grappling for purchase, with as much haste as decorum allows within the many folds of my skirt.

And before I can realize that I'm neither here nor there, time itself seems to stutter, and I find myself suddenly standing on a marble floor, gazing wistfully at a band of musicians. As if I have always been here, in this moment. They play a sad, mournful tune that makes me feel melancholy for something unnamed. I yearn for something, and I don't know what exactly. But an alarm going off in my head warns me.

"Whatever you do, Etenya, you must keep your mask on, and speak your name to no one. Even if they are kind. Even if they are your friend. Accept nothing from anyone."

The warning marches within my mind dutifully, though now I cannot remember whose words they belong to... My mother perhaps? But here and now, I can hardly seem to recall my mother— the color of her eyes or whether her skin crinkles between her brows, or even her name. *Perhaps I do not have a mother,* I think. But there seems to be no room for alarm or worry in this faraway place, so I discard my troubled thoughts like a used and crumpled napkin.

"Mask on, no name, mask on, no name," bounces silently between my ears as I look over meaningfully to a table laden with food and drink. My mouth waters. How long have I been here? The solemn processional up the steps of the ballroom feels as if it was an eternity ago, but surely it was only minutes. *Moments.*

The table taunts me, and I feel my stomach concave in on itself as my eyes rove over the decadent spread of lush victuals and sparkling wine. I am reminded of Eve in the Beginning when the serpent tempted her with forbidden fruit.

And yet...

Has the table been here all along? Was it there when I'd been watching the musicians?

The musicians. Dully, I realize that the space they'd filled only moments before is now void, the music softer, like a faded memory. As if they'd moved. Or perhaps *I* had. I am unsure.

"I wouldn't touch the hor d'oeuvres were I you," comes a voice to my right. I swing about, startled at the stranger's casual tone, and, like a vapor on the horizon of my mind, all my thoughts disappear.

"And why is that?" I question cautiously. I squint beneath my mask of linen and black paint, feathers, and beadwork.

Perhaps it is a friend, I think with a rush of hopeful anticipation. But my hopefulness gutters out as I realize that the eyes behind the stranger's bird beak mask are dark, sparkling, and entirely unfamiliar. She moves closer to me, and I think I might have blinked because she is already near me, but it's as if my thoughts don't wish to dwell on her fragmented movements or the way she seems to ripple at the edges of my vision.

Her gown is lavish and extravagant, the beading about the collar exquisite and delicate, the tiniest army of ants sequestered in pairs and groups at the seams, and I can't keep my eyes from following them as they trail down her body. With a rush of warmth in my cheeks, I jerk my head back up. Her smile is sharp, like the icicles that drip and freeze along the awning outside of my window every winter, and I can't help but shiver as she flashes me a grin that is so beautiful, it is painful to witness.

"They are laced with enchantments," the strange woman answers, and her voice is a melody I want to hear sung for the remainder of my days. Her grin turns mischievous, and her tone drops to a conspiratorial whisper. "Or *poison*."

She moves to stand beside me, and I catch the scent of her perfume — an altogether unholy fragrance of summer apples and wormwood, earth berries and musk. To breathe it in is a cathartic experience, I think, and I find myself drawn to her for it, hungry for more.

I cock my head and look back to the table.

"And the punch?" My voice sounds thick and heady in my own ears. As if it belongs to another. As if it does not come from my own mouth.

Again, that hauntingly beautiful smile. "Safe," she tells me with a wink, and I feel a flame of some unfamiliar emotion kindle in my chest. It's so easy to trust her, so easy to believe the words that drip from her full lips like pomegranate juice, and even if they are false, I indistinctly think that it would not matter. Being near her feels like a feast itself, and one I am ravenous to partake of.

She steps past me to the table, pours two flutes of punch, and offers me one as she sips from the other. I accept, and my eyes are loath to tear their gaze from her, but I force myself to look away. To not stare.

"How long have you been here?" I ask, though a voice in my head whispers another warning. I push it away as easily as I blink because I want to hear her speak again. I *need* to hear her speak again.

"Oh, I've been here since the beginning," she answers, her eyes on the room as she tips back the sparkling pink liquid in a swift, graceful movement. Her lips are full and deep—the color of crushed garnet. Distantly, I notice that they do not stain the rim of her glass.

The dance floor that is there now, though a moment ago was not there at all, is sparse. Most of the partygoers stand along walls, chatting soberly with one another, their voices low, their shoulders stiffened nearly up to their ears with tension. Every so often, I notice a clandestine look stolen over a bare shoulder or an uneasy glance from beneath darkened lashes. They are looking at me, but I cannot understand why. I wonder if I might know them, but as I make to approach them, the space they fill is suddenly empty and I wonder if they were ever there at all. Like the musicians.

Absently, I check the tiny silver clock dangling from a bracelet at my wrist.

11pm. A reminder that time is real and passing quickly. I feel as if I ought to be glad of it, but instead, I am unnerved.

I let my eyes skip around the room, observing everything and nothing, before they come to rest, yet again, on *her.* As if she is the only one in the room. The woman sips her punch curiously as she watches me and, for an unsteady moment, I am reminded of the way a cat watches a mouse before he devours it. But the thought passes from me so quickly, I don't think I'd ever even thought it, and my cheeks burn as I notice her attention.

"You are lovely," she tells me suddenly, and I nearly choke on the midnight blue liquid within my crystal glass.

But that can't be right. *Midnight blue? Had it been midnight blue when she'd poured the wine into our glasses from the decanter? Was it* wine *that she'd poured?*

Remotely, as if from over the lip of a fishbowl, I hear another warning. But it's so far away, and she's so close now, closer than she'd been just a moment ago, and she's looking at me with her depthless dark eyes, waiting. Waiting for me.

"I—thank you," I mutter. I am both mortified, and yet secretly pleased, an odd assortment of feelings running through my body. "As are you, of course," I murmur against the rim of my punch glass. My words come out rough and coarse, as if my throat is dry. And perhaps it is. Because my mouth is dry, too. I lick my lips and sip my wine. It is somehow sweeter than I remember it.

The woman flashes me another smile and my chest aches.

"I'm glad you think so," she says, and her voice melts like honey upon my ears, thick, and sweet. I find myself leaning in to hear more.

She licks her own crushed velvet lips, and suddenly, I feel flushed in odd places, my knees and palms, my head and upper lip. The tempo of the music picks up and my heart beats in rhythm with it.

She holds out a pale, delicate hand to me. My eyes flicker to it and I notice it is unadorned with rings or jewels, unlike the other attendees. Unlike myself, even. I wonder why. Who can she be? To have no jewels or gems, no wealth or grandeur. *It is because she is the jewel,* I think. But she is speaking to me, and my thoughts melt like hot wax.

"I am pleased to meet you, miss—?"

"Etenya," I say quickly, easily, stepping forward even, as though I might offer her a silk-wrapped gift. I want my name on her lips, against her tongue, in her mind. Unbidden, the thought comes to me that I want other things there, too. I blush crimson at my own depravity, but another part of me is awakened.

"Etenya," she repeats, and I nearly sigh with a quiet pleasure at how lovely my name sounds in her mouth. I reach politely but eagerly for her hand, grasping it deftly like I might pluck a rose from its thorny stem. To my surprise, she pulls me to her in a swift, graceful motion. There is a hungry desperation in the way she holds me, and my body tenses as if waiting expectantly. Feverishly, I realize I want *more*.

The warning rings through my mind again, louder, but still muffled. Still effortlessly ignored. It has lost its definition anyway—what did it even mean? I can't recall anymore and so much time has passed since *before*. Before I'd come to this ball, before I'd come to know *her*. Weeks have passed, years even. Or has it always been this way? Her and I and this ballroom and the question between her brows and the answer upon my lips?

Her eyes are glittering, and her breath smells sickly-sweet, a scent I know, from somewhere in the far reaches of my mind, but one I've long forgotten. I find I don't mind it though, as her warm breath caresses my neck. Our crystal glasses are gone, and I lucidly wonder when or how it happened. But this moment is too real, and the glasses strangely aren't real, and the thought floats away from me like a lilac cloud on a dusty horizon. Perhaps there had been no glasses. Perhaps there had been no sparkling pink or midnight blue liquid.

Her mouth is close to mine now, and I realize I want it even closer to me—I want it on my mouth, on *me*, and I can't breathe properly, my heart is stuttering with longing and lust, my mouth wet for her. The other guests have melted into nothingness, and the room seems to have fallen away from around us, the ceiling disappearing into a winking darkness not unlike the one I'd traversed so long ago. Except this darkness looks different, feels different. Instead of fear, I sense only a hushed calm. Or is it a foreboding silence? I cannot find it in me to care either way.

Perhaps this is what it is to fall in love, I think vaguely, a flutter of excitement lighting within my ribs. I have never been in love though, so I am not too sure. Or perhaps I have, and I simply can't recall it. I only know that I have wanted it for so long, and here it is, in front of me at last, impossibly delicious.

She pulls me even closer, the nose of her mask brushing against mine, and I find myself reaching up, pulling my own free. She lets me, and I reach for hers next, my hands greedy, my lips parted. I gasp as it falls away. She is stunning, she is glorious, and my heart swells with awe, with love, with *lust* for her.

She is mine, I think. *I am hers.*

As my gaze drops to her mouth, I see that her lips are parted too, and just as her mask slips from my fingers, she reaches a hand around my waist, her grip firm and sure. As certain as the moon is to the night. As certain as my frantic need is for her.

"I want you," she murmurs against my neck, and I can't think or breathe. The warning is but a whisper now, a near-silent myth that has aged with the passing of time and my mind is weary of searching for it.

She pulls me against her, and I let her, and it's like war and peace, crashing waves and a morning breeze through a field of grass. She kisses me, her full mouth upon mine with a delicate ferocity that has my heart slipping and stuttering. She is greedy but gentle, and I sigh deeply with satisfaction. She tastes of salt and earth, pain and longing, joy and terror, and I pull away briefly to catch my breath.

Except, I can't.

Detached, I think that perhaps I should despair. Something isn't quite right. There's a heavy, sodden feeling to the air suddenly, like freshly turned earth on a humid spring night. But I feel only an obscure stillness. Perhaps this moment isn't real, like the musicians and the food-laden table, and the wine wasn't real. I shiver and realize, for the first time since I've passed over the threshold into this tantalizing night, that I'm suddenly dreadfully cold. And it's this realization that causes the fear to rise up undiluted, curling around my spine. It seeps into my skin and coalesces between my fingers and teeth, thick and palpable.

But she smiles down at me then, her own teeth sharp and white—had they always been so sharp, I wonder? The sweetness of her breath has turned, like fruit left to spoil in a tepid sun—pungent and rotten. The music is playing again—a waltz, except it's too loud and the violinist must be playing a wrong note because it drones on excruciatingly, and there are people gathered around us now. I see horror on their faces as they look at me from beneath delicate masks, and I want to ask them, *what is wrong? What is it?* I even push away from her—to think, to *breathe* for a moment, to get my wits about me.

But I cannot.

I cannot move, I cannot form the words. I cannot drag the breath into my lungs and, as I look back to the beautiful stranger, the warning reverberates through me like the toll of a bell, clear and strong and *late*. Much too late.

"*Whatever you do, Etenya, you must keep your mask on, and speak your name to no one. Even if they are kind. Even if they are your friend. Accept nothing from anyone. To survive until sunrise, you must be wise. Death is cunning, and she will dress the darkest transgressions as the sweetest wine to have you.*"

As I lean breathless into Death's embrace, I look to Her.

She is terrible. She is triumphant.

She is smiling.

18

LONG GONE

BY REBECCA CARLYLE

They will find no blood because there was none spilt when she died. It had been an allergic reaction and that is what the police will think. By the time they even utter the word "murder," I'll be long gone—by the time anyone finds her body, I'll be long gone. Not that it mattered. There was no way to prove it was murder. It sincerely looked like an accident.

The Ferris wheel came to a halt and I looked down from the uppermost seat where I had a 360 view. A kaleidoscope of colors assaulted my sensitive eyes from the carnival below. Even from this high up, I couldn't escape the bright lights and loud music. From here I was able to people-watch: excited children tugged at their mother's sleeves pointing at rides and containers of popcorn, impatiently wanting to see everything. Teenagers huddled together and laughed, making fun of performers to each other and imitating their skits. This was a safe place.

-I'll be long gone-

The Ferris wheel jerked back into motion and the young girls on either side of me giggled and shrieked at the way our bench rocked dangerously back and forth. The innocence of youth was literally at my feet. Their trembling terror took me back to when she had collapsed on the dirt footprinted, linoleum floor, shaking from the pain because the inside of her mouth had been so swollen she couldn't make any noise. Her hands had clutched at the countertop as she had started to fall.

-I'll be long gone-

We were let out of our seat and I watched the girls frolic away towards the small, dragon-themed roller coaster, their ponytails swinging and brushing their petite necks and sun-tanned shoulders.

I strolled along in the opposite direction, whistling a tune I couldn't quite place where I knew it was from. There was a slight spring in my step, bouncing on the balls of my feet. With her gone, I felt like a helium balloon, weightless and waiting to be released to drift off into the sky. My eyes flitted from one exploited couple to another. They were easily goaded into playing games: loud popping balloons, dinging bells alerting players the game is about to begin, and milk bottles refusing to be knocked down. The carnies endlessly swindled customers into spending excessive amounts of money on games they could not win.

I was blinded by colorful flashing lights, a sensory overload that I could barely handle. I was left blinking rapidly trying to clear my vision and staggered into an amethyst hued tent. The fabric was soft and heavy, velvety to the touch. It took a moment for my vision to adjust to the light change as a single lantern lit the space. Dust motes floated through the air, stirred by my entrance. Plush cushions were scattered across the ground with a small crate in the center. On the other side of the tent sat the backlit figure of a curvy young woman, gaze buried into colorful cards, oblivious to my presence. Centered atop the crate was a crystal ball that picked up a rosey hue from the satin cloth it rested on—a similar shade to the color *she* wanted to paint their bedroom, the color they had smeared across the walls with brand new paint rollers. I moved a step closer to the orb and its aura began to glow as if it could sense my presence. Slightly alarmed, I backed to the edge of the tent's fabric.

The woman who was kneeling at the crate across from me was startled by the orb's sudden activity, her head snapping up from her lap. She looked into the dark tent, her eyebrows knit together. Bangles adorned both wrists and jingled up and down her forearms as she swept her fingers around and around the orb. She wore a deep plum veil that cascaded down her back, twirling amongst her dark curls. Gold hoops swung by her cheekbones, peeping out and glinting in the lantern light. Thick black eyeliner encircled her large sapphire eyes. Long lashes weighed her eyelids down, her gaze cast at the glowing orb.

"I know you're there." Her raspy voice was deep, filling the space in the tent with its vibrations. She seemed to find me for a moment in the dark shadows, but then her kohl lined eyes flicked away to stare intently at the entrance where a slight line of light from outside trickled in.

-I'll be long gone-

My feet backed further away from the fortune teller and toward the loose tent flap that billowed in the slight breeze.

"Your spirit—I sense something terrible in you. Tell me what you desire. Unburden your guilt to me." Her words rattled around in my mind, bouncing and echoing like a broken record scratching and repeating. I shook my head, trying to shake loose the feeling that I was missing something.

Her head was cocked, waiting for me to answer her, but her gaze was fixated behind me and onto an ornately carved coat rack, void of any jackets or scarves. I cleared my throat, attempting to gain her attention. Her bangles clinked together as she gathered her hands, lacing her fingers on the tabletop.

"Tell me my future." I knew it would be grand now that I was free of *her*, but I was here with a fortune teller, so why not?

Her hands raised to either side of the crystal ball as it grew even brighter than before, brighter even than the lantern behind her. Inside the orb was a milky fog, swirling clockwise in a lethargic manner. She stared into it intently, reading and grasping, pulling whatever information it was providing. Suddenly she recoiled, her hands jerking back as if she had been burned.

"You have no future here; your flame has already been tamped out. But your past will haunt you. The betrayal of a loved one...forces your hand to a place your heart cannot go. Buried beneath your arrogance is deep regret… It fills your aura, forever staining you." Her maroon-painted lips fell still, quivering from the syllables that had spilled out of her.

I wanted to know more, why did I have no future here? But I couldn't voice my question, the words catching in my throat, clawing their way back inside.

-I'll be long gone-

Just as I had stumbled inside by accident, I found my feet pulling themselves and moving of their own accord to get out of the tent filled with unsettled energy. They took me back out into the stifling heat of the midday sun, kicking up clouds of dirt and dust that caught in the slight breeze and swirled about ankles in motion. I walked by a face painter enraptured with her work drawing a sparkling butterfly on a little girl's cheek, a man selling goods made of pungent leather, and another animatedly proclaiming his jewelry and adornments to be only the best quality available.

I walked down the middle of it all, observing girls trying on bedazzled masks, boys trying to best each other in the rifle shooting booth, and parents nervously waiting for their children at the end of rides they insisted on riding alone. There were blue lights, then red, then yellow, screams and whooshing from roller coasters, laughter and bangs from rifles, flashing lights and applause- it was all too much.

-I'll be long gone-

A laughing couple tripped by me, drinks sloshing from their containers, hardly noticing how close they came to colliding with me. Their white-toothed smiles and fingers looped together made my stomach somersault like I had been punched and my breath had flown from my lips and left me behind.

I used to be one of them, but then she went and slept with that guy at work. And she kept seeing him. It was just so easy, she saw him every day. I knew she wasn't dressing up for the office or perfecting her black smudges of eyeliner for me. At least, not anymore. I could remember a time when she used to put on her heels for evenings out on the town with me. We would paint the town red and be home before midnight. I made her feel like a proper

Cinderella. Isn't that just typical? I put everything I had into us and she just had to wreck it all.

That's when I started planning her accident. She said I wasn't fun anymore, that we never did what she wanted to do. Going to the carnival was her idea. My desire to please her, to give her one last gift before departing won me over. A trip to the carnival was in order. We took the day and I fooled her. But when the moment came, she knew. Her eyes glittered with tears as she realized what I'd done. Her pain caused an insatiable desire to laugh in her face.

-I'll be long gone-

Oh...my...dearest love. I would miss her and the way her skin always smelled like candied fruit- no, it was always pomegranates- she smelled like candied pomegranates. It made my mouth water just thinking about it. I headed toward the food court with a vivid array of greasy food and sugary sweets mixing, mingling, and tickling my nose. It pulled me along, the thought of her and the scent of longing.

Mmmm... Hotdogs... Cotton Candy...

I slowly meandered my way closer to the liquor tent and eventually the stench of stale beer overpowered all other smells. There were a few men stumbling over their words, their breath wafting through the air. I chose to sit near the one that was trying and failing to be mobile. Every time he tried to stand his legs wouldn't obey and he would catch himself on the bartop. He chattered to anyone who would listen about how awful his cubicle job was and how his wife had taken the kids and left. I was perched on the edge of a barstool nearest, but the drunk man never noticed me and kept trying to catch the attention of the others-

-I'll be long gone-

A mother walked by with her young son pulling at her arm. He was pleading for her to share her bag of peanuts with him. "Adam..." she hissed. "Stop making a scene." She gave him a small handful. In one swoop he popped them all into his child-sized mouth, and after chewing, he licked the salt off his lips and each of his fingers.

She was deathly allergic to peanuts. It had only taken me an afternoon of research and a trip to the mall to find a chapstick that had the same fatty acids as peanut oil: a mixture that would be toxic for her. She hadn't known about the unassuming weapon I carried or the hunting knife I'd slipped into my coat's hidden pocket as a failsafe. She always took forever to get ready, leaving me plenty of time to prepare. She climbed into the passenger seat of our taupe sedan and kissed me on the cheek. She had smiled, but there was no light in her eyes. She didn't love me anymore. Why couldn't she just say it? Say it and I'll forget the whole thing. But she didn't.

"...And she had her suitcase, man...and didn't look back..." the drunk man was now following around a young couple, warning the boy that one day he would befall the same fate.

"At least your wife didn't cheat on you first and lie about it," I said to the drunk man.

He ignored me and kept following the couple, invading their personal space bubbles. I imagined I could hear their bubble popping, but that could have been the balloon booth. Curious to see how this would end, I followed the three of them at a short distance not wanting to aggravate the drunk more than he already was. The boy was determined to prove to his girl that he thought nothing of the maudlin's ramblings. He pulled her along, looking for someplace private they could slip away to, someplace away from prying eyes— my eyes.

Just like I had done a few hours beforehand. She hadn't noticed the cruel look on my face when I pulled her into the handicapped bathroom with me. She didn't notice how dispassionately I kissed her with the peanut residue on my mouth. Her eyes finally widened in surprise as she clutched for the counter. She tried to ask me one last question but collapsed to the floor before any sound could come out.

-I'll be long gone-

The door of the bathroom was locked and the boy knocked ceaselessly with no answer from inside. With alcohol-induced spittle following him closely, he took out his bi-fold wallet and used his student ID card to unlock the door. Without looking inside, he pulled his girl in with him, shutting the maudlin out. Screams erupted from the small building moments later, the door flew open and the two young people came dashing out. The girl was crying and visibly shaking, even from afar, and the boy had a protective arm around her shoulders and a black flip phone to his ear. His voice was inaudible, drowned out by his girl's sobs and screams. Through the doorway, a set of dusty, worn burgundy Keds was visible. I itched to take another look at her.

-I'll be long gone-

Sirens blared in the distance and I thought to myself of hiding, it took a moment to realize that a crowd had gathered and I could blend in easily. I stood back and watched as police cars pulled up in a frenzy to the nearest fence with their beeping horns and flashing lights. So many flashing lights. Like clowns, they stumbled over each other to get out of their crowded cars. The entire procedure took much less time than I expected: they somehow managed to rope off the bathroom and question the young couple in record time. The girl was still in hysterics and they couldn't get anything out of her, like a harlequin trying to get a smile out of a scared toddler, it just wasn't going to happen. They held up their pens like daisies and their speech bubbles swelled with words as a balloon would with air. A lab monkey holding a camera circled and photographed the body. The camera flashed as he meticulously maneuvered around the body, ensuring he got every angle of the scene.

They'll never figure it out.

"There's so much blood," the cameraman said over his shoulder to a nearby colleague.

What?

A detective pulled up then and stepped out of their own unmarked vehicle. He stopped to speak with one of the uniformed cops.

What was going on? Why were there detectives called to the scene? An accidental allergic reaction shouldn't need this much attention.

Impatience and curiosity got the better of me and I jostled forward through the thick crowd and jogged over to the building, brushing past police who were too busy to notice my presence. At first entry, I couldn't help but stop and stare at all the blood. It was everywhere: dripping from the walls and pooling into a giant puddle on the floor. I had to force myself to pull my stare away from it to look at her body.

She was sprawled on the tile floor in an unnatural position. Her hazel eyes were swollen shut and her cheeks bulged from the swelling of her lips and tongue. There was a hint of blue around her mouth, implying a lack of oxygen before she died. It took me a moment to realize that she was speckled in blood—the blood had sprayed after she had fallen. It was then that I noticed a man's body nearby. He was propped up on the back wall, slouched over a knife that protruded from his bloody mess of a stomach, and a limp hand was loosely draped next to it. The fool had on a silver wedding band. *My wedding ring.* A small breath spilled from between my lips, I realized- *my bloody mess of a stomach, my sharp knife with the ebony handle, my slouched and still body.*

I hesitated, torn between wanting to see what I had become but also wishing it would all go away, that I had stayed in the crowd and continued to be ignorant and blissful. The gypsy's words came back to me then- *'your flame has already been tamped out.'* Is this what she had meant? That I was already dead? I couldn't tear my eyes away from my own body, the way my skin had a sickly pallor, jaw slack and lifeless.

The detective dressed in brown tweed stepped inside the single-person restroom with his jacket tossed over one shoulder. His off-white button-up shirt had horrible yellowed pit stains- it was too hot of a day for his suit. His face was set with hard lines into a grim, pensive look as he surveyed the scene- my scene, my ending act. It felt...wrong to be studied like this. I walked to where he stood and tried to see the room and our bodies through his fresh eyes. I hovered just behind him, peering over his right shoulder. The late afternoon light cascaded through the doorway and fell on her just so, lighting her face, her plump lips. It would have been beautiful if it weren't for the signs of asphyxiation- her pale skin, blue-tinted mouth, and swelling around her neck that pulled a gold chain taut.

I followed the detective as he stepped around to get a better look at my body. My chestnut hair was disheveled as if I had run my fingers through it violently, pulling at clumps here and there in a panic. His stare followed my footprints from where she lay to the countertop and back to her, then the bloody handprint that dragged from shoulder height to about a foot off the floor, right by where my shoulders were slumped. Then my blood-covered hand stretched out, reaching for her cheek- her soft, candied pomegranate cheek.

When I raised my gaze from her face to see what the detective was doing now, I caught sight of the mirror. I wasn't there. I stepped closer so I could see more of the room in the looking glass, but there was nothing. All I found was her still body splayed on the ground, my lifeless, pathetic sack of muscle, and the detective moving between the two of us, piecing together what happened. I couldn't watch him anymore, assessing our relationship and judging everything that I did. As if he would've done anything differently.

With my hands in my pockets, I stepped out of the room and into the hot, stifling air outside. Incessant noise, clanging bells, and grinding wheels followed but I moved through the crowds, focused on nothing but the ground beneath my untethered feet. The gypsy had said '*deep regret*,' but she was dead wrong.

I was long gone.

19

A BITTER JEWEL

BY STEPHANIE ASCOUGH

A tree of death stands in a secret wood
but no choice fruit it bears.
Branches empty, yet they bow
to the hidden
perishing
beneath.

A toadstool circle forms a collar,
tender pearls of broken teeth
that no longer bite.
A burrowed toad watches with night-dark eyes
the loam,
the depths,
the haunted fruit.

There, knotted roots clutch
a broken ember, cold
yet still glowing
a bitter jewel,
a dripping bite of decay

between unyielding fingers.

A bruised berry of avarice,
it feeds on desire
drawing the unwary and unwitting
who wander by.

Like this poor soul,
lured by sweetest hell
and darkest riches,
his fevered eyes aglow.
This is his one desire,
his treasure,
his right.
So close,
he knows it.
So close,
he can feel it.
so close,
he can taste it–

They stay to circle, these who wander
haunted by unseen and cruel promises
that never surface.

The toad, that cluster of warts among pebbles and sour soil,
watches a new, pale head rise
a fractured image of the moon above,
both suspended in darkness.
It joins its fellows in a still dance,
a solemn recognition
of inescapable fate.

20

APPLE SHOOTERS

BY ROSALINE WOODROW

arbage. I look at the litter scattered about the side of the road. How many times have people sat in this turning lane and discarded the items they no longer wanted out the window? Not even items. Just remnants of things already depleted and no longer useful. Cigarette butts, empty vodka shooters.

I wonder how many of those are hers? How many times has she sat at this light and used her vices, believing them to be her antidote? Then, once she was done with them, tossing the vial out and driving off. The antidote bringing her back to life. She never considers that what she left behind affects other people. It never occurs to her that people live lives separate from just being a part of *her* world. How many times have I sat at this light and wondered how many of those things were hers? I really wish this light wouldn't take so long.

Finally, my turn to turn and move on from those thoughts. My palms are getting clammy on the steering wheel. My breaths are coming in short but leave quickly. My heart is racing. This is what happens when I come within proximity of her. When I see her crossing the parking lot at the grocery store, afraid she will see me stop, and we will talk, and our relationship will reconnect again. That's how she is, there's no easing back into it. It's in or out. This road is not as long as I need it to be as I am already turning onto the gravel road. My throat knots at the back of my tongue and I let out a slow breath. It is okay to be anxious; it is not okay to panic. I can't react emotionally right now.

My hands shake on the steering wheel as I pull into the steep driveway at an angle so I don't bottom out. I put the car in park. With my left hand, I lift up my skirt, placing my thumb and index finger against the groove of the .380 tucked into the holster on my thigh. Do I think I will have to shoot him? No, but I want to be prepared. She sounded so scared on the phone. I hadn't heard from her in over a month when she called. I was on my way to meet family for dinner, but I turned around as soon as she asked me to come to get her. My stomach is curling into my chest. I look at my daughter in the rearview mirror. She's content, looking around, blowing raspberries like a typical one-year-old.

When I look back out the windshield to the house, Debbie has walked out the front door, and she is alone. I relax and put my left hand back on the steering wheel, my right hand grabbing the shift handle as I get ready to reverse the car. She opens the door and gets in, placing the large Victoria's Secret tote she hastily packed on the floorboard. It's a lucky tote, the others are stolen from her boyfriend's daughters and sold for five bucks. I pull out of the driveway and speed down the gravel road.

"I'm sorry," she sobs as we turn the corner. "I had to get out of there."

"I'm glad you called me." I force a smile. *Yes, I am thrilled that you once again called me*

over a fight with your shitty boyfriend.

"I just. I had to get out of there." Her eyes are squinted slightly and her words are slurring. She's drunk. Status quo.

I don't know what else to say and my stomach is still in knots because this is the first time I have spoken with her since we had a fight over her, somehow, long-term boyfriend. She thought he should be part of my child's and my life. I disagreed. I wonder why?

"Pppphbbbttt." My daughter tries to create comedic relief in the back. Debbie looks back at her and laughs. Out of the corner of my eye, I see her turn and give me the up-down, taking in that I am in a skirt and my hair is done. A contrast to my typical messy bun and leggings when I am the epitome of stay-at-home-mom.

"Oh, no! You were on your way somewhere. I can go back. Just take me back!" Her voice is erratic.

"No." My hands tighten on the steering wheel. "You called me for a reason, I am not taking you back there, Debbie." I use her first name as a way to protect myself. It may seem petty but ever since she drunkenly told me *let's drop the whole "mom" thing* I never went back. Of course, she was drunk when she said it. I don't know if she even remembers saying it. She never remembers any of the shitty things she says while drunk. If she doesn't remember, then she must be forgiven when sober. Doesn't matter how you feel, she has absolved herself and you must too. To be honest, I don't even think she noticed I stopped calling her the affectionate, familiar term. Using her name helps remind me that there is a boundary between us.

"I'm sorry. I'm just sorry. You were on your way somewhere." She fiddles with her seatbelt. "I just had to get out of there." She attempts to buckle it but she does not have the dexterity in this state to align the metal clip with the slot.

"I am glad you called me," That's a lie. But she won't notice. "What happened?"

"Oh, you know, I saw a text on his phone. He's fooling around with *that* girl again."

Ah yes, *that* girl. The girl who was his girlfriend the moment you two broke up last time. I had to leave Thanksgiving at my in-laws to pick Debbie up. He was taking his new girlfriend to his family's dinner for the holiday instead of Debbie, couldn't leave her drunk and belligerent in his house that she was still living in. He couldn't even wait for Debbie to move out. No, he had another girl lined up. Heaven forbid he has to fold his own laundry or do his own dishes. Shitty human being.

"That doesn't surprise me." *I'm sorry* would be a lie, and I find keeping my words pragmatic and short in these situations protects me from getting emotionally involved.

"Oh, look at you," she motions to my skirt, " I'm sorry. I'm sorry. You can take me back."

"I am *not* taking you back." I look her in the eye when I stop at the stop sign at the end of the gravel road. "You called and I am here now." I nod at her and she nods back.

"He's fooling around with that girl again. He wouldn't let me leave." She tries to pull the seat belt because the alarm is yelling at her that it isn't buckled. *"Here have some wine,"* she imitates his voice. "He dragged me out of the house by my hair last week and ripped the earrings he bought me off my ears when he caught me drinking... but suddenly he is cheating on me and it's *let's get you some wine to calm you down."*

I don't know what to say. He is a shitty person, this is why she and I haven't talked in so long. I refuse to have him be part of my life and she seems to love him and is mad at me for not letting him be around my child. I just peek at Debbie's swollen sad face for a moment and then glance at my daughter in the mirror, her eyelids are getting heavy like her grandmothers are. I am glad to be driving. I don't want to have to keep looking at Debbie's eyes drooping from intoxication. I swear you could just whisper the word alcohol and her eyes would start to do that.

"I'm sorry you were going somewhere, just take me back." Parroting. Another sign she hit the bottle before I picked her up.

"No. You asked me to come. Here I am." I am always a card up her sleeve.

"I did. I told him I was calling you, and he was all, *You called Amy?* And I was like, YES, I called Amy." She gives an emphatic nod.

I am her knight, she calls me and I come sword raised, charging to her rescue. She hides behind me; I am her shield. This, more than anything, is the reason I do not let him in my life. She needs somewhere that she can go that he is not allowed. Somewhere she knows she will always be safe. Even if she hurls insults at me when she demands he be part of my life because she *loves him, he isn't going anywhere.*

"I am glad you called me." This time I meant it. I reach over and squeeze her hand, keeping my eyes on the stoplight. I don't have to look over to know she is slumping, her posture in my peripheral vision reveals what is coming. She buries her face in her hands and starts sobbing.

Well, this is awkward. I glance out the window.

"What am I going to do, Amy?" Her sobs are phlegmy from a life-time of chain-smoking. If the sudden burst of emotion wasn't enough to make me uncomfortable, being stuck listening to that is. I wonder if it would be rude to turn up the radio?

"You take it a moment at a time." I feel wise saying this, nodding as I turn into my neighborhood. She lives too close for me to ever truly relax. I always fear she'll decide to stop by and visit unannounced. I feel like I am always operating at a slight level of caution in my life, my flight or fight system always on standby. "We get you inside. And we take it a day at a time."

"You can just take me back. I want to go back. Just take me back." She nods as I pull into my garage. "You were going somewhere I shouldn't have called."

"Yes, I was. But you called. Here I am. I am not taking you back to him, you called me because you knew I wouldn't let you go back. Now, let's go inside. You can unpack your bag and we will figure out where we go from here." She looks at me like a scared, lost child and nods her head, her half-closed eyes watery from tears and intox-ication.

She is stumbling. I have to make sure she doesn't fall up the stairs as I lead her to the guest room while carrying the toddler. I get a few hangers from my room and bring them to her so she can hang things up from her tote. I am doing my best to make her feel like she is welcome in my home, even though I am not entirely sure she is. I just don't know what other options I have if she is actually going to try and leave him.

"Make yourself comfortable." I smile, nodding, not sure how comfortable she can feel in a makeshift storage room that houses a bed with a box spring that creaks every turn you make. People say beggars can't be choosers, but narcissists with grandiose ideas that they deserve luxury are never satisfied. That's why she stays with him, and my stomach churns looking at her freshly filled nails. Every time I see her and she complains about needing her nails done or her hair blown out, my hope that she will get out of this toxic relationship dies.

"Can I?" she makes the hand motions to smoke, afraid the eighteen-month-old may figure out that Mawmaw smokes, and no longer think she is cool.

"Yeah." I manage. "Out back. Grab a water bottle out of the recycling for your ash and your butts. Please just throw them away." I can make one request of her, right? That is allowed.

"Thanks." She grabs her phone and her pack of cigarettes and chain-smokes on the back porch texting her boyfriend for the next hour.

I don't mind that Debbies's out there. I can pretend to have a normal evening with my daughter. I make her dinner and get her in the bath. That is when I hear the back door slide open, then fumbling in the freezer.

"What do you need?" I know exactly what she needs.

"Look. I just. Can I just like? I need a drink you know?" Clearly, you don't. "I am just feeling a little pukey."

Pukey. I hate the term. It triggers the memory of the weekend a few months ago that I spent cleaning up her vomit. She wanted to get sober but refused to go to a proper facility. My husband and I gave her a shot every hour, then slowly moved her to beer, then finally it was time to tough it out. A shot an hour may seem ridiculous if you have never met a functioning alcoholic. The kind that keeps apple-flavored vodka shooters in their purse to drink room-temperature-straight every hour at work. She managed a full twenty-four hours of sobriety before her boyfriend picked her up, took her to a bar, and she had a Jack and Coke.

"Sure," I say, and I can feel the tight smile on my face. Better than having her falling off the porch from withdrawals again. I don't have time to babysit her. I listen to her get ice and unscrew the lid.

She continues to sit on the porch smoking and drinking vodka on the rocks. I get my child dressed and read to and rocked to sleep. I am glad she is too young to understand any of this. I rub her back and head downstairs. Still on the porch texting him. I don't even bother asking her to come in and eat, it would be a waste to put food on the plate. I head to the basement with the baby monitor. I hear her come in the back door eventually and go to her room. I don't check on her, I don't have it in me to put a polite face on. I go back to my show.

I hear rustling and whimpering on the baby monitor, then I hear Debbie mumble. I race up both flights of stairs. My daughter's door is open and I walk in to find Debbie in the rocking chair with a very sleepy confused child, trying to read her a book.

"What are you doing?" I can't hide my annoyance.

"I was trying to put her to bed." She slurs. "I would have her asleep, but *someone* keeps...interrupting." She snaps at me from the rocking chair. I grab my daughter from her arms.

"She was asleep, if she wakes up we give her a few minutes to put herself back down." As I bring my daughter to my chest I am hit with the overwhelming smell of cigarettes and a liter of perfume to try and cover the cigarette smell. I sit my daughter on the changing table and start taking the clothes off her that the odor has permeated. Debbie has half-opened bloodshot eyes watching me as she rocks on her heels, clearly feeling useless and awkward. Which she is like this.

"I am sorry.." She slurs and pauses her words to blink slowly. "Sorry... I am here." She nods; I don't think her eyes have even reopened since the blink. "I am disrupting everything. Your schedule." I wait but she doesn't complete the sentence. "It's too much. I can go. Just take me back." At this point, I'd love to so I don't have to hear that again.

"*Stop.*" I raise my voice, holding up a hand and cutting off her words. She gives me wide childlike eyes, I didn't realize she could still do that in this state. I hate when she looks at me that way like she isn't supposed to be the adult in our relationship. "It is okay, Debbie. Yes. This"–I motion between her and I–"This is hard. And it will be difficult. But that is no reason to regret the decision you made. We *will* figure it out. It *is* an adjustment. That is all, okay? It isn't easy, but you made the right decision." I let out a slow deep breath. My heart sinks because I see it in her eyes. I struck just the right nerve by raising my voice with her. I nod, trying to soothe the situation between us.

Debbie walks out of the room and I take my toddler, and stroke her hair whispering to her how much I love her as I lay her down in bed. She rolls over giving up her protest, surrendering to her exhaustion. As I rub her back I hear footsteps across the wood floor downstairs, and then the front door shuts. I close my eyes letting out a sigh. Maybe she is stepping out to smoke. That must be what she's doing.

I descend the staircase and look around. She isn't sitting in the living room. I step outside and do a loop around the house. She isn't here. But her cigarette butts litter the porch. *Bitch.* I take out my phone and call her. I hear her phone ringing inside, I step back in and find it next to the glass of melting ice and a nearly empty bottle of vodka on the counter.

This is the problem with living so close to her. Not only do I live in constant fear that she may drive her car into mine on any given day, but she can walk home. I gave her what she needed. She wanted to find a reason to run back to him. Does she want me to chase her? Why do I feel guilty? It isn't my fault she chose to leave, but my heart sinks. I sent her back to him because I snapped. Leave it to her to leave the guilt on me. Leave it to me, to let her.

I shake my head and grab a fresh glass from the cabinet. After a few ice cubes and some orange juice, I pour the rest of the vodka into the glass and drink it quickly before I can make a decision to get in the car. We both use the same antidote for the same poison. Her.

21

THE SWEETNESS WE CAN'T LIVE WITHOUT

BY M. STEVENSON

*S*mooth silver bark cold as a statue against her skin, Guardian presses her ear to the God-Tree, listening. Late winter, the time of beginnings. The time for the sap to run, and for Guardian's work to commence.

The God-Tree is quiet. Guardian leans against its trunk, closing her eyes. This tree is one of many, a slowly growing grove she has tended for centuries; but it is the tree that always runs first, and the one she loves best. She knows the God-Trees don't think, don't feel, but she imagines this one impatient for the new year and the renewal it brings. Like Guardian.

Guardian runs her hand over the bark and thinks of old lovers, their flesh turned cold as stone, the wounds of their loss worn smooth by time. Perhaps the trees are not ready yet. A few more days, a few more weeks–what does it matter? After all, a year is almost nothing to a tree, a sliver of growth thin as a fingernail.

She is about to draw away when she hears it. The soft rush of sap deep within, the tree's lifeblood. The Nectar of the gods, ready to be tapped and decanted.

Guardian smiles and presses her brow to the trunk, a lover's touch. Then she turns away to gather her tapping supplies, and to check her dragons and the hedge of thorns. Her defenses must be ready: with the running sap come the humans, drawn like flies to amber honey. Unable to stay away from their own sweet doom.

Spring comes rushing next, and Guardian's days are full. She unwraps the spiles, each made from a god's little finger, and drives the bones into the God-Trees with gentle taps of her hammer. Soon the constant plink of sap into buckets fills the forest, a chorus of different tones that alternate through harmony and dissonance as the buckets fill. Light from the luminous Nectar diffracts through the forest, painting the trees in the golden aura of sunset.

As each bucket brims with honey-gold sap, Guardian replaces it with an empty pail and carries the trees' precious heartblood to her workshop. She walks slowly, the Nectar's glow lighting her face from beneath. She hasn't been human for centuries; the sap will not burn her. But each drop is priceless, and Guardian must be careful. A spoonful can start a war. A vial can bring down an empire. She has witnessed such disasters before, when she was young and still made mistakes.

As she pours the sap from buckets into amphorae, melts wax to seal it for delivery to the gods, she has company: errant dragons the size of dogs, their jaws a perfect fit for human throats. They flitter through the trees to twine around her legs, purring like kittens. She ought to shout at them for leaving their forest, creating gaps in her defenses through which a determined thief could slip. Instead, relenting, she drips nectar from her fingertip for them to catch on the flickering tips of their tongues.

The dragons writhe in contentment. Guardian smiles and lets them lick the last traces of nectar from her fingers. She has always been too softhearted. But she cannot help the way even their scaly touch makes her heart beat faster, the blood in her ancient veins quickening like springtime sap at this illusion of love.

Abruptly, one of the dragons draws away from her, standing on its back legs. Its slitted nostrils flare and a low growl vibrates in its throat.

At once, the other dragons stop licking the Nectar from Guardian's hands. In unison, their heads swivel towards the trees. Their eyes go bright as flame, and their scales flare around their necks into a threatening ruff.

Guardian follows their gaze and the nectar's heat leaves her at once, leaving her cold and hard as stone.

Stumbling from the trees, honey-colored hair blackened with blood, is a human. Face pale as quartz, legs quivering like aspens, he lurches three steps forward. He meets Guardian's eyes. She stands like a tree herself, transformed into a part of her own grove by a god's wrath or mercy.

The dragons surge forward. Recalled to the present, Guardian makes a terrible sound deep in her throat. The dragons stop in confusion, looking between her and the human.

Guardian gestures at them to stay, slashing her hand through the air. She strides past the dragons, stands over the human. Her hand lifts, wavers, a spear ready to strike.

The human meets her eyes, his gaze so soft and fragile. His lips crack open, a wound.

Then the human collapses.

Guardian lowers her hand. She looks down at the mortal creature crumpled at her feet, pale and motionless. No longer a threat, or so she can fool herself.

She cannot bring herself to kill him, to destroy something so helpless and delicate. She can slay a hydra, but she cannot stomp its unhatched eggs to shards. This has always been her weakness.

"Fuck," Guardian mutters, and gathers the dying human into her arms.

At her hut, she assesses his injuries. A gash to the head that has bled copiously—most likely the work of the sentient stones, Guardian's first line of defense. Bruises along the ribs and back, also the stones' doing. These wounds are not fatal. The scratches are worse. His arms and legs are a pattern of lacerations as complex as the dapple of sunlight on the forest floor. Not deep, but each is stained the bitter black of poison. The human went through the hedge of thorns, and the thorns bit him with their venom teeth.

Guardian brews a cure, crushing herbs with her fingers instead of a pestle. She ignores the voice scratching at the back of her skull, the voice that asks why she is wasting her time on a mortal who will, by nature, only die. Now, later–what difference does it make? She should turn him over to the dragons now. Save her herbs for herself.

A vulture appears at the window and hunches, expectant, awaiting the human's heart. Sometimes Guardian will feed them a part of her meals, stroke their feathers while they gulp rabbit flesh. Today she waves the vulture away, and when it will not leave, shouts so that the bird startles and flaps away, offended.

Guardian turns back to the human in her bed. She smooths poultice along his wounds until the scratches turn from black to red. She sponges the blood from his hair, returning it to the honey bright color of Nectar. When he cries out, unconscious, in pain, she whispers in words that flow like running sap until he stills. And she does not dare to ask herself why she does this, or what comes next.

The human awakes a day later, while Guardian is out tending the God-Trees. When she returns home, her shoulders filling the doorway, he sits up in her bed and looks at her with wild eyes.

"What *are* you?" he asks, his voice wavering on the knife's edge between worship and horror.

Guardian knows what he sees: a woman like a tree, with skin cold and earthen as pottery shards, hair a fall of leaves, eyes the amber of Nectar.

"You came here," she says. "You should know."

The sound of her own voice startles her, a rasp like a footstep scraping over gravel. She doesn't talk much these days. She whispers to the dragons and the trees, and sometimes she sings, but her voice is unaccustomed to conversation. The human's mellifluous tones, even raw as they are with exhaustion and hurt, make her keenly aware of how harsh she sounds.

She expects the human to flinch. He doesn't. His eyes roam over her, more thoughtfully, and then they widen.

"I think I do know," he says. "You're—"

"Guardian." She cuts him off before he can say it, the name of a woman who died centuries ago. She is only Guardian now. "You can call me Guardian."

He knows what she guards, of course. It is why he's here. She does not name it.

"Guardian," says the human. He holds her name on his tongue like a precious drop of Nectar. "Thank you for saving me."

Guardian is not so certain that saving him is what she's done. Guilt, confusion, bite into her heart like poison thorns. She has rid him of fever and the hedge's taint, but the fate he faces is, perhaps, now worse; he can never go back to the mortal world, and when he realizes that, he will call her his jailor. And then he will hate her. Or, if fate is kinder, instead he will go mad.

She turns away abruptly, unwilling to face the inevitable.

"I'm going to get more firewood," she says over her shoulder. "Don't leave the bed. You're not well enough."

She forces herself to not look back to see what he does.

The sap runs on. Another week or so remains before the spring flow slows and Guardian must withdraw the spiles and send her collected Nectar to the gods, to sustain their eternal life. But now she works distracted, collecting and decanting the God-Trees' heartblood as swiftly as she dares. And in between her work, she hurries home to check on the human she can't help but think of as hers.

The human recovers swiftly, now that he is awake. He is still weak, the poison's remnants lingering in his veins, but his mind is fleet. When Guardian is home he watches her with bright eyes, following her every movement until she believes he knows the shape of her body, the cadence of her movements, better than she does herself.

And he talks. Questions, a quest disguised in the form of conversation. Never about the Nectar directly—he is clever, this one. Instead, he asks about Guardian.

Subtle questions, at first. Safe ones. What does she eat? Does she enjoy poetry? What are her favorite birds? Guardian knows his questions are a trick, a drip of slow and subtle poison; the human is interested in the Nectar. Not in her. Never in her. But his interest feels genuine, and when he looks at her with warmth in his eyes, she responds to it, as the God-Trees do to the spring. Sitting on the floor beside the bed, she tells him, drop by drop, of her existence. Her subsistence. Her loneliness, spanning centuries.

The mortal listens, his eyes on hers, as if she is as endlessly fascinating as a fire. As if she were life, personified. And Guardian, for the first time in eons, is aware of her own face. The shape of her lips. The direction and depth of her eyes, and how the firelight, burning gold from the God-trees' wood, limns her in light.

She doesn't ask him questions in return. She doesn't dare. Like a drop of rain in a river, he will be subsumed by time. But his presence is like water in the desert, and Guardian is a flower. She cannot help but drink.

As the human recovers his strength, Guardian helps him rediscover how to walk. He leans on her arm, taking a child's steps around her hut. When he stumbles, she keeps him from falling. And when he takes his first steps without her, hands spread wide for balance, she watches him with the pride of a god admiring its creation.

The human takes another step, catches himself on the wall. Then he turns back to her with a grin free of guile, brimming with the simple joy of an innocent victory. He takes two more steps, this time towards Guardian. He wavers, stumbles.

Guardian catches him in her arms.

The human grips her shoulders, regaining his balance. He looks up into her face, and his smile changes to a look more vulnerable. He lifts a hand and touches fingers, soft and gentle, to her parted lips. His mouth follows.

And Guardian is lost.

~

With physical intimacy, love and trust grow quickly. Now Guardian spends as much of her days as she can with the human, hurrying through her work at the God-Trees. Nights she spends in his bed— her bed—theirs. Guardian has never slept much; now she sleeps even less. The human is still weak, still recovering, and she is no mortal woman; she must be careful with him. But it is enough for her to lie on her side as the moon falls through the window, propped on her elbow, and watch the fragile rise and fall of his chest as he sleeps. It is enough for him to wake to see her watching in the morning, and smile, and kiss her carefully, as if she is the one who could break at a thoughtless touch.

Time passes. The flow of Nectar in the God-Trees slows, the chorus of gathering sweetness ebbing towards silence. It's time to remove the spiles, collect and decant the last of this year's flow, and seal the holes to rest until winter. It is a task that will take Guardian a full day.

She rises as dawn runs a glowing finger along the edge of the horizon. Her lover is asleep in her bed, one arm thrown over the blankets. Guardian lingers for a moment to drink in the sight of him, to marvel at the softness of his mortal body and the way his fingers curl into a beckoning gesture. She devours his touch like Nectar. She cannot stop.

When she's alone, she welcomes how her work takes the hours and days from her shoulders and lightens the burden of eternity. When she is in love, it always seems like there is never time enough in the world.

Soon, though, there will be more time. Never enough, but a gift nonetheless. Guardian's work with the God-Trees will be done for the spring once she finishes this final harvest and delivers the Nectar of Immortality to the gods. Then she will spend every moment with her lover, listening to the cadence of his breath like the pulse of her own heartbeat.

She doesn't wake him as she leaves. He must not follow her. It is better that he sleeps.

Her work takes focus, and soon Guardian is subsumed in coaxing the last trembling drop of Nectar from spile to bucket, ensuring no drops fall unwitnessed from each God-Tree. She eases each hollow bone from its tree and sets it down for the dragons. Disregarding their duty again, the creatures have come swarming to lick the spiles clean and shining until every trace of Nectar is gone. Guardian lets them without reproach. A single stray drop can create a monster. It took only three to make Guardian what she is.

At each God-Tree, Guardian presses her finger to the hole where the spile bit through the bark until it seals beneath her fingers, the trunks once again as smooth and unbroken as the flow of time.

She is drawing forth the last bone spile when the screaming begins.

Guardian's heart stutters, reminding her that it exists.

She has never heard her lover scream, not even when she tended his worst injuries. But that sound, the sound of life being wrested from mortal veins, can only belong to him.

Guardian lets the last spile fall and runs, abandoning the God-Trees and the dragons.

Her lover writhes on the ground beside the rows of decanted nectar in her workshop. A single amphora, wax seal broken, lies on its side, spilling precious Nectar into the earth. Guardian's lover has already drunk. He twists and flails like a snake as the Nectar traces its way through his veins, consuming him from the inside out.

Guardian tries to pull him into her arms, but he is writhing too much to hold, devoured by the agony of Nectar's fire. His thrashing arms threaten to upset the remaining amphorae. She seizes him by the waist and drags him away, into the open forest. The human does not even notice. His eyes, wide and unseeing, their pupils like chasms, are the Nectar-gold of the poison coursing through his veins.

Guardian drops to her knees beside him, her hands hovering uselessly over his thrashing form. Now she regrets that she never asked his name, for she would scream it now, beg him to hear her, to take her hand, even though it would make no difference. She can't save him. Each mortal man believes he alone is different, that he alone can drink the Nectar of the gods and live forever. Each mortal dies.

Her lover's screams intensify. The poison nears his heart, and Guardian's is about to shatter, speared by his piercing cries.

She can't save him. There is only one power that can.

Guardian throws her head back and screams to the skies, to the gods that watch from above. Her voice is an avalanche, shaking the forest.

Even the human falls quiet.

And in the silence, the gods answer.

"Oh, Guardian." She can hear their sigh, the disappointment of a parent whose child has failed. *"You knew that this would happen."*

Guardian raises her face to the heavens. Tears, the honey-gold of Nectar, streak her cheeks. "Please," she begs. "Save him."

"Why? So he can return to the mortal world to boast that he has stolen from the gods and lived? You know that cannot be."

Tears blur Guardian's vision. Her lover has fallen still, no longer writhing. The warmth of human life bleeds from him like spilled Nectar. Within moments his soul will stand at the banks of the river of death.

"Then make him—" The words catch in her throat, but she forces them out. "Make him like me."

"And reward your weakness with a companion?" The gods' voices darken, a shade between sorrow and anger. *"You have failed us, Guardian. A thousand years, and still you have not learned. Your actions merit punishment, not reward."*

Perhaps, then, they mean to take her immortality. Guardian's heart strikes at her chest, but not with fear. She could lose this body of stone, this body that betrays her with its torturous, impossible longings. She could follow her lover across the river of death.

"*No, Guardian.*" This time, the gods' voices brim with unforgiving laughter. "*Death is its own reward. Did you think your price was paid?*"

A desperate thought takes root in Guardian's mind. A way to keep her lover with her forever.

"Punish me, then," she says. "Punish me with a reminder. Place him here so that I can never forget."

The gods consider. She feels the rumble of their thoughts like distant thunder. What Guardian asks for is not a mercy. There is no kindness in it—not for her lover, nor for Guardian.

It does not take them long to decide. The gods, after all, are not merciful.

"*Agreed,*" say the gods, and a force like lightning strikes.

A new tree stands in Guardian's grove, its silver bark smooth as mortal flesh. In the springtime Guardian presses her ear to its trunk, listening for the rush of sap, a cycle as endless as time.

To another's eye, this tree would look the same as all the others, statue-grey and straight as a spear. Guardian knows the difference. This tree, despite its appearance, brims with youth. When she taps it, this tree will gush forth Nectar as sweet and deadly as unrequited love.

Guardian runs a lover's hand over the newest God-Tree's bark. She closes her eyes as if awaiting a lover's kiss.

And, like a heartbeat, she hears it: the rush of Nectar, the flow of a new cycle beginning.

For the briefest moment, Guardian touches her lips to the tree's cold bark. And then she rises, to begin her work anew.

SWEET VENOM

BY CASSANDRA HAMM

*S*he is a song—
      husky and sultry with
notes that steal your senses
and lull your inhibitions.

She is a taste—
    sweet and smooth with a kick,
    her delicious fire tickling its way
    down your eager throat.

She is a star—
    white-hot and blinding,
    luring you to flame
    like a death-hungry moth.

She is beautiful, brazen, slightly mad—
    an intoxicating sort of venom

you'd beg to drink,
a bullet you'd willingly take.
Her touch is blissful destruction.

But if you peer past her bronzed exterior
into the depths of her envy-green eyes,
you'll find emptiness.
You'll see the cracks on her porcelain skin,
her shatter-thin smile,
the deadness behind her laugh.

Beauty is her armor,
yet even that can't stop
the sadness from spreading—
an incurable poison
that will eat her hollow
from the inside out.

23

A LADY'S BONE SONG

BY KAYLA WHITTLE

*T*he door squealed when one of Samiria's graverobbers entered her office. She brought with her the scent of fear and something older, like moldering bread.

"You're late again, Idin," Samiria said, lips pressed into a thin frown. They were painted red as the wax dripping from the candles perched in iron holders on her desk. More hung in sconces on the stone walls, flickering light shadowing the old, half-forgotten room. Dust clung to cobwebs in the corners. Behind Samiria, her shelves were filled with old books, and crumbling maps, and a few murky jars. It was not a welcoming place and had never meant to be one. The king preferred for few to know the details of Samiria's work. It would be unseemly for royalty to associate so closely with graverobbers, particularly when the king needed his kingdom to believe he alone kept them safe. While he was busy waging war far from Aldwater, he wanted Samiria unnoticed. Forgotten, even as she served him.

Idin lowered her head. The bag she held rattled, though she'd done an admirable job of pretending her hands weren't shaking.

"You've been behind all month," Samiria continued. "I doubt you've managed to hit your quota. There's been no word from you. I was beginning to think you'd run off on me."

She pulled her fingers through her long, dark hair—the hair people liked to remark on when they saw her, liked to say how much it made Samiria look exactly like her mother. Reaching past the bottle of wine and pair of glasses set out in front of her, Samiria grasped a golden bauble worth far more than anything else she owned. The hair clip had been her mother's, and belonged to her mother's mother before her. Their gift from the king.

"I think you'll be pleased, Lady," Idin said, stepping forward with disappointingly meek footsteps while Samiria pinned up her hair. "A lead kept me away—a good lead. You'll see. You'll feel it once you touch them."

Another shiver wracked Idin's dirt-stained fingers, rattling the bones tucked inside the bag she held before she set it down on Samiria's desk. One of the glasses rattled when the bag slumped over, away from Samiria. Leaning forward, she sank her fingers into the soft crush of deep red velvet, feeling the sharp, irregular shapes hidden beneath the plush exterior.

She breathed deep. Magic oozed from the bag, leaking between the drawstrings, strong enough to linger like ashes and smoke on Samiria's tongue. Raw power, the kind that could only be found in the bones of those who'd once wielded magic themselves. In death, their abilities sunk down into the marrow, left there for Samiria or anyone who got ahold of their skeletons. With the bones, anyone could control the lives around them, manipulating people, and plants, and animals. With the bones, anyone could have power.

That was why Samiria needed to keep them hidden. It was why the king didn't want them out in Aldwater where the wrong sort of person could get their hands on them. He'd granted her this office, this position, so she could oversee the cleanup of the darkest pieces of Aldwater.

In spite of herself, Samiria was impressed. Before their meeting, she'd anticipated Idin arriving empty-handed after spending so many months away. Those who disappointed her knew they were also indirectly disappointing their king; it was bad business to keep robbers in her employ who couldn't find any graves. Those who failed knew they would be better off leaving the kingdom than returning to report to her their failure. They slipped into the cracks of societies far enough from the crown's reach that Samiria didn't need to go chasing after them.

There were few robbers who met Samiria's standards these days; the bones brought to her desk were few and far between. Samiria, and her mother, and her mother's mother, had ensured that was so. It was good that the work was slowing. It kept the kingdom safer and meant less danger for the king.

Long before Samiria's time, the king's grandfather had narrowly evaded an assassin fueled by magic. His power had focused on the mind, twisting the thoughts of those around him. The assassin had gotten to the queen, magic slinking deep inside her skull until she tipped herself over a high balustrade. He'd nearly gotten to the heir as well, but a sword had been put through him before he could finish. The scars of his power had left the old king's heir broken. The assassin had been stopped, but he'd known the halls to take through the castle. He'd known the royal family's schedules, where they would be throughout the day. He hadn't worked alone, and the stain of betrayal needed to be unrooted.

Magic had been outlawed in Aldwater; any being with the slightest hint of power had been executed, or hunted, or chased far from the kingdom's borders. Left behind were only dusty memories, and the dead, and those who'd been weak or poor enough to hide themselves rather than attempt to escape.

"I found these buried in the woods beyond the old village near Wellington," Idin said as Samiria sorted through the haul. In the bag were a few teeth and metatarsals, alongside the broken pieces of a fibula. "I followed a rumor of a family who'd gone off into the trees a few decades back. Powers manifested late in the family line, I guess. The living moved on eventually, but I found what they left behind. *Who* was left behind. It looked like they tried to destroy whoever they'd lost but I still caught a little of the power calling from underneath the dirt. Dug these up for you."

The edges of some of the bones were sharp, fractured, and warped like someone had tried to return them to dust before burying them. Those few families left with a little magic running through them, those unlucky ones who hadn't escaped, they'd noticed the sunken, disturbed, unsettled graves. Those few families were intelligent; they'd had to be, to survive this long in Aldwater. They knew something was happening to their dead, so they'd done their best to hide the bones of those they lost. When the flesh and muscle and tissue was all stripped away, that power left behind sang something brilliant. Something about those bright, leering skeletons let their magic shine in a way it couldn't in life.

"This is all that remains of the body?" Samiria asked.

Her graverobbers needed to be thorough. Anything forgotten in those woods near Wellington had the potential to disrupt Samiria's standing at the castle. Such power was dangerous if left unchecked.

Few beyond the coin master fueling her operation were allowed to know that Samiria's office even existed down in these dark depths. A forgotten corner of an old portion of the king's castle had been allotted to her grandmother. He wanted them to complete their work, and do it well, but quietly. In the shadows.

"There were no pieces left behind?" Samiria asked, probing when Idin didn't answer.

"No," Idin said, firmly, hastily. "I checked, and I listened for them— felt for the magic. Nothing else called out to me from the soil."

Poking a finger inside the bag, careful of sharp edges and dirt, Samiria's skin met bone. A sharp shock passed across her skin, fighting through her, searching for a way out; the sharp, electric tang of power, crawling and craving and building. Searching for *more*, a longing for wholeness that had been lost at the moment of death. The sensation dissipated like smoke caught in the wind as soon as she pulled her hand away. Unlike Idin, Samiria was better skilled at hiding how her hands wanted to shake. The magic thrilled her to life in a way that felt rare in her damp office.

"This will do," Samiria nodded, pulling the drawstrings tight. Folding her hands over the velvet, her pulse thrummed, enticed by the magic lingering beneath her grip. The soles of her feet burned, as if the power leaked down to the flagstones. It pooled into the air, enough of a taste leftover for Idin to lean close. "For now."

"I am eager to serve you, Lady Samiria," Idin declared. Something in her posture had finally relaxed, hands hanging limp and loose by her sides. "As always."

Samiria's employment inspired loyalty because her graverobbers were well-paid. Their intelligence was recognized; their societal status irrelevant. She compensated those who would never have had such lucrative opportunities otherwise; the king was never particular about the backgrounds of the people she employed, so long as her work was done. Those who found her the bones were enticed to return to her again and again with the promise of more gold, and a hefty, comfortable retirement for those who best impressed her.

Idin had exceeded expectations because Samiria had been prepared to write her off as useless. This find had done her well and solidified her position on Samiria's crew. As the king was still away, Samiria could safely send out her robber again. She hoped she would not be disappointed; she doubted Aldwater would ever fully be freed from these magical bones, and that they would all be safely tucked away with her, but she could do her best to try.

"You'll be given the usual payment at the door and two day's extra pay to enjoy your time in town before you travel for me again," Samiria said, gesturing toward the exit. "Thank you for your service to Aldwater."

"Thank you, Lady Samiria." A smile transformed Idin's expression into something younger, eager, and Samiria found her lips softening in response, hoping Idin would enjoy her pay while it lasted.

Lowering her head again, Idin left. The door squealed horribly to announce her departure. Metal jangled outside as one of the coin master's assistants paid the robber in the hall. The transaction needed to be completed right there, in this quiet, damp place. Samiria's robbers couldn't be found wandering through the castle; questions would be raised.

For most of the kingdom, magic was distant—forgotten, lost in time and legend. The king wanted to keep it so, to honor his grandfather's legacy. Those old laws banning magic had worked well, until commoners began finding the bones. They found them while tilling their fields, or hunting in the woods, or reusing an old gravesite in an overcrowded cemetery. Left-behind pieces sparking with some of the same skill that had made magic so powerful—so hunted—in life. The ability to twist and manipulate people, and objects, and kingdoms.

The king had appointed Samiria's grandmother to lead his graver-obbers and steal away any hint of leftover magic in Aldwater. To force rumors to die out in those streets when the bones were taken away—first forcibly, and more recently when they were pried from the earth. Samiria's mother had overseen the graverobbers next, keeping the bones hidden, keeping the kingdom safe. When she'd died a few winters back, a shade of herself choking on her own sick, Samiria had been named as her replacement. Her family had served the king well.

Standing, Samiria took the bottle of wine and pair of glasses, replacing them onto one of the slumping shelves behind her. She'd been prepared to offer Idin a drink, one her robber would surely feel compelled to accept for fear of offending her superior. Idin's success had changed that conversation.

From among her collection of old books, Samiria pulled down her ledger. Earlier, she'd preemptively scratched out Idin's name from her dwindling list of employees. Grave robbing was dangerous work, and she'd had to retire more of her crew more quickly than she'd have liked. She added Idin's name again, this time to the bottom of the list, like an afterthought.

Slipping the ledger back into place, Samiria reached up to unclasp her hairpin, dark hair swinging forward. When she'd been younger, the first few times she'd stepped into this office, her mother would sweep her hair up and tie it tight, fixing the pin on top like a crown. Back then, there'd been no cobwebs, no dust in the corners. Still, there'd been no visitors. The staff had forgotten this corner of the castle, having been told to avoid it back in her grandmother's time. The real lords and ladies would never descend to such a level. There had only been a different coin master's assistant, now promoted to coin master himself. There had only been Samiria, and her mother, until at last it was Samiria, alone.

Her hand clenched, squeezing tight around the hairclip. Undone, the underside formed the shape of a key.

Lifting her skirt, Samiria tucked the hem into the belt tightened around her waist. Behind her desk, she crouched and dug her fingers into the cracks between flagstones, the spaces where grout had been chipped away long ago. Slowly, begrudgingly, she uncovered a cell door, metal gleaming. Samiria fit her hairpin key into the thick lock.

This door made no sound when it swung open. Behind it, beneath it, stairs descended into darkness. With the bag of bones and one of her candles, Samiria descended. The steps were small, urging her to slip, but she knew the way well. It was a route she'd taken before the job had been hers, back when her mother had been eager to show off the results of her work. Down Samiria went, until the far-off glow of candlelight in her office faded behind her. In the gloom, she paused at the bottom of the stairs. Skulls stared back at her, wide eye sockets half-caught in shadows.

The bones were crowded there, down in the crypt. Shelves lined the short hall that extended from the bottom of the staircase. On them, skeletons lay whole, or in pieces; teeth gleamed white from where they were caught in cracks on the floor. To her left, a pile of discarded bags slumped over. Some were old and weathered, worn down by use by a peasant; some were pretty, fashionable, like the red velvet Idin had left her with.

Samiria shivered, breathing deep. Here, she didn't need to touch the bones to feel their magic. It leaked into the air, reached for her hands, waited for her to reach back. The remains of so many, their leftover power clashing and roiling and crawling over itself. Magic that had once been used to transform faces, bring down buildings, and turn enemies to stone.

Samiria shook Idin's velvet bag, tipping the bones onto a nearby pile. They fell together with a sharp crack. New bones in the crypt always felt like the rumble of thunder, the oppressive weight of heated air before a storm. The piecemeal bits of magic resonated with the rest housed in this overgrown tomb, humming, pulsing. Power that demanded to be used, strength the king wanted hidden because he wasn't clever enough to find a way to wield it as a weapon himself.

She tossed the bag aside to rest with the others discarded there, then dusted off her hands. Beneath her skin, her phalanges felt tight, thrumming, reaching out toward the crypt.

The bones were ready.

She felt them often in her office, the pull of power pulsing against her feet. Removed from the living, the bones didn't comprehend the concept of timing, waiting for the right moment. For the king to return to his castle.

As she turned, Samiria's sleeve caught on the edge of a jawbone, fabric tearing. Sighing through her nose, she reached carefully to untangle herself from the leering skull. Some bones in her crypt held no magic at all.

"Don't look at me like that, Mother," Samiria huffed, nudging the skull farther into the shadows. "We both know you were never willing to do what was necessary."

It'd started with her mother. Never gifted with ambition, happy to remain in the darkness with only shadows and death for company, just as her mother had done before her. She'd had Samiria young, with a robber who'd died not long after, and held no plans for Samiria to take over her position. The only true option for Samiria was to grab onto the life she wanted for herself. That meant forcing her mother into an early retirement. Her mother, who drank tea each morning to stave off winter's chill. She'd been foolish not to suspect anything when Samiria started joining her for her daily tradition. Her death came almost too easily; so many sickened when cold weather came that no one questioned the loss of one Lady. Much less one whose employment, and existence, was already so smothered. It felt like the king had hardly noticed the transition of power taking place beneath him.

Then there'd been the crew to wrangle beneath her, robbers who thought they needn't listen to someone so young. Some who thought they could steal from her. Some who failed her. Some who'd outlived their use, so she offered them the option of retirement, too. A chance at peace for the rest of their days.

No one declined a rich glass of wine if Samiria offered it to them in celebration.

That was an inelegant way of handling things. As the power in the crypt had grown, Samiria had needed a way to practice wrangling the magic. The grave robbers who'd outlived their use were easily misled; their minds simple to pry open. She'd started by giving each of her employees the instruction to exile themselves over ever returning to her empty-handed. Those few like Idin who seemed able to eventually shake off Samiria's influence were dealt with in her old-fashioned way.

She'd planned to add Idin to her crypt, her safekeeping, if she hadn't proven herself useful. If Idin returned with more bones before the king returned from his selfish campaign at the borders, all the better. The power was strong now, and Samiria's hold over it had grown stronger still. She was ready for the minds that bore the weight of Aldwater. Samiria was ready for the king.

Pulling back her shoulders, Samiria ascended. The bones called after her; chill air tugged at her hem, circled the back of her neck. The pull wouldn't be ignored for long, but she had no way to assure the bones that their time aboveground was coming. That one day soon, she would have the power that came from a crown to match the power the bones would help her wield. One day, Samiria and her bones would no longer live in the shadows.

24

OF THE NIGHT

BY CIARA DUGGAN

I was of the night.
And she of the light.
Despite the burn of my skin beneath the
poisonous sun—
The scorching glow that urged my need to run—
Her soothing touch and golden gaze
Resumed my devotion beneath the blaze.

You must endure the pain, *she would whisper in my ear.*
For I promise, upon my heart, the time is coming near.
The time to strip me free of bitter night,
And rid me of my menacing bite.

My peeling skin and ember eyes
Were nothing but a compromise.
Once free of night's impenetrable chains,
I'd no longer thirst for the blood in her veins.

In secret we would lie beneath the softening dark,
And in passion we held hope that her magic would

soon spark.
Should her coven uncover the deception in her heart,
Then her magic seized, and her family torn apart.

For not only my life was at risk beneath such toxic rays,
But her enchantment could be stripped in more
torturous ways.
As perilous as it was for our bodies to entwine,
There was no life without her soft lips upon mine.

When came the inevitable morning, the sun too sharp to bear,
I'd retreat to the darkness where shadows would take care.
I cursed the hours that passed without my beloved's touch,
And seethed at night's unyielding clutch.

But just before the sun would rise, my hope would soon
      refresh.
Perhaps this day would be the last to singe my scarring flesh.
She stood beneath the fading moon, her hair flowing bright.
A warming glow assured to shield my everlasting plight.

And though the sun had deigned to rise,
I knew this daren't be my demise.
For when her gentle hands caressed my face,
I found safety and reverence within her embrace.

This venomous light could cause me pain,
Yet in her arms I would remain.
But luster dimmed behind her loving gaze.
A sorrow that burned beneath the morning haze.

What troubles you on this early morn, *I begged*
my sorceress.
A single tear upon her cheek, My dear, I must confess.
Though my feelings for your gentle soul are ones so

deep in bloom,
The magic that I've fed to you will only lead to doom.

For you are the darkness,
And I am the light.
In nature there can't be such forbidden delight.

My devotion must always remain with the sun.
No binding to the night will ever be undone.
And though you may be my heart's true one,
The magic of my coven you'll never outrun.

Despite the agony her words roused within,
I couldn't help but brush her porcelain skin.
For all I wanted to the end of days,
Was to console her tender grieving gaze.

Only now did I realize the weakness in my soul.
Each rendezvous by her touch would take a heavy toll.
I thought it only the weight of love crossed by stars—
A fear that love could never be ours.

My bones broke beneath the weight of relentless dread,
As her spell sang upon the tears that she shed.
Let the sun take you now, leave ash upon the ground.
Turn your blood to dust, to never more make a sound.

And as blue flames crawled along my cracking skin,
My fangs did grind beneath my tortured grin.
The sun was never what was poison to me,
Rather the love for my witch, I could only now see.

But when you've lived as long as I,
Only one logic there may apply.
I'd rather feel love with my dying breath,

Than nothing at all as I'm slain to death.

As I vanished into the ground—
Nothing but ash to ever be found—
I wished her peace within the light,
As I was forever of the night.

2 5

THE MAD HATTER'S MAD WIFE

BY A.R. FREDERIKSEN

*I*t was fascinating how much damage one single egg could do, let alone several.

Cora studied the jar resting in the palm of her hand, held aloft in mid-air, the yellow-green vinegar of the pickled eggs catching in the fading light from the sash windows.

A slow smile spread across her face as she twisted the jar in the angry slash of light. Slivers of beets and peppers winked at her in between the glossy, bulbous eggs.

"Fascinating," she said. The word slipped out unbidden, from lungs like locked caskets, and startled her enough that she slammed the jar down on the kitchen table. It nearly slipped out of her hand and skidded to the floor. That would've been a waste. All that work for nothing.

"What are you doing here?" Her husband slipped through the door into the kitchen, carrying a monstrosity of a hat sizer. "I thought you'd gone to town for the day."

She moved away from the jar of eggs as easily as a willow in the wind, keeping her eyes fixed on her husband's face. Then it moved to his arms. Hands. He wore gloves today.

"Are you done in the shop already?" she asked.

He jiggled his hatter's device in his arms. "It's broken."

"So you brought it home? What's the logic there?"

Putting the device down on the table, he took off his gloves, wincing and turning his face away as if she hadn't already seen the reaction. The sensitivity must have been bad today if he had taken to wearing gloves in the shop. His condition had started years ago, with restless nights that turned to sleepless nights that turned to weeks of insomnia alongside headaches and tremors leaving him unable to follow through on orders in the shop. The duty always fell on Cora to deliver the news to the unfortunate customers. Mostly, they took it well, though not always.

But the sensitivity was new.

It had started in the last year or so.

Henry brushed it off whenever she brought it up, but Cora felt it at night, when his hands mapped her body in the drenching dark. Felt how he was quick to reactions that had less to do with mapping and more to do with landscape demolition. Only, she hadn't been able to bring it up much lately. If she dared, he became a caricature of himself.

"You can't just leave it there, Henry." She gestured to the hat sizer when he went to exit the kitchen as quickly as he'd entered. "I have an appointment with the doctor in an hour."

He paused in the doorway, holding onto the frame with one hand, favoring his strong leg, the one that hadn't succumbed to the tremors yet. "And you'll be in the kitchen?"

She crossed her arms. "I guess not."

"What's the appointment for?"

"Removing my stitches." She flexed her hand automatically, the one where the stitches pulled at her palm. "It's gone a little over time. He's been busy."

"He'll do it here?" Henry leaned fully into the doorframe, taking all the weight off his bad leg. Either that, or he was settling in for an argument. "Not at the clinic?"

"You know the doctor," she deferred.

"I know he has a liking to you, that's what I know."

The back of her neck tickled and the jar of pickled eggs screamed for her attention as much as she tried to deny it. She couldn't mess this up before it had even begun. "A liking? Only insofar that his wife left him and his bed is growing cold. And it's hardly me, but every woman within town that he's been hounding, you know that. Now, dearest, about that hat sizer?"

"If you don't like it on the table, you can move it."

"Fine. Will you stay while the doctor's here?"

"Is that the bargain? Sure. The sizer stays on the table, and I stay in the house."

When he left this time, idly rubbing the knee of his bad leg that should've lasted him much longer than what it had, Cora didn't stop him. It was good enough that he'd stay. He needed to stay for this. Otherwise, it wouldn't work.

Pressing down on the stitches in her palm, she pulled her lip between her teeth with a hiss. The cut had been hard to make. She'd considered her options first but had gone with the letter opener in the end. She'd cut her dominant right hand, using her left, and had turned the blade the other way around so that the handle pointed away from her. The direction of the wound was important. As was the choice of hand. She hadn't gone into this unprepared.

When the doctor had sewn the stitches for the injury two weeks ago, she'd sowed the seeds of her plan. Those seeds now floated around inside a jar of yellow-green vinegar. She'd gotten the recipe for the pickled eggs from a trusted source. Not trusted by herself, but trusted by others that she trusted, and so it went, on and on, because that was the way for women.

On the way out of the kitchen, Cora put her hand on top of the jar, dragging the pads of her fingers along the glass, the hairs on her arm coming alive, standing on edge.

She'd sowed her seeds well.

Precisely one hour later, the doctor arrived. He entered as all doctors did, expecting ceremony as if they were the King them-selves. Proprietors of order. Upholders of life. In this case, though, Cora didn't mind. Doctor Jameson was her unaware accomplice in today's endeavor, after all, so she'd give him all the ceremony he wanted.

"Doctor, come inside, please. What poor weather today. I apologize for bringing you all the way out here in this. I would have taken the tram to your clinic."

"Rain is healthy for the constitution, Mrs. Hatterson."

She laughed. "I thought fresh air was healthy, not rain."

Waving him inside the parlor, she didn't expect Henry to already be there, seated by the secretary in the corner, the shop ledgers spread out before him. He offered the doctor a curt nod, his glasses perched low on his nose. The doctor offered a nod in return, no less curt than Henry's, and then wrestled his large bag onto the coffee table without knocking over any of the decorative objects on display. Such as the brass candelabra with miniature butterflies and birds carved along the stems. Or the green-painted vase that matched the curtains and which was currently full of foxglove. Cora breathed carefully through her nose. A sigh of relief. The doctor was no large man, and it was no rare occurrence during his consultations that his bag prowled through the house, making victims of the décor in his struggle to contain it.

"Would you like some coffee, Doctor Jameson?"

"I should like to look at that hand of yours first and foremost, Mrs. Hatterson."

The Doctor's eyes shifted to Henry in one surreptitious blink that was gone as soon as it appeared. Henry, understandably, was entirely unaware. Well. Understandably to himself, but not so to the doctor. Hopefully, at least. If not, Cora had failed. But, no, she couldn't have interpreted that look wrong. It had been surreptitious, but not subtle. The doctor believed Henry had cut her hand. Pitied her because of it. Good. Pity worked wonders on men who believed the world was theirs. It hadn't taken much, really. Not when he already suspected Henry of the worst—and with good reason. She'd let a comment slip back when he'd stitched up her hand, and now the doctor blamed Henry for the cut.

"In that case," she said, "let me sit down for you to work."

She chose the couch that put Henry at her back, making it all the easier for the doctor to shoot festering glances at her husband over her shoulder as he worked on her hand.

"No need to be gentle, Doctor. I've had stitches removed before. A long time before moving here, of course, or you'd know. And I'm rambling. Apologies. I will let you work."

It was a lie. She'd never had stitches pulled from her body before, but the insinuation worked its glorious purpose when the doctor's eyes swiveled from her face to a spot behind her. A spot that aligned exactly with where she knew Henry to sit, his nose in his ledgers, weak leg stretched out before him. It was almost too easy.

When the doctor pulled the stitches from her hand, one by one, she curled her toes into the carpet and fixed a faint smile onto her face. Nobody could see that she gritted her teeth behind that smile. Nobody could know she'd lied. For each hot pull of the thread, and for each itchy drag of her protesting flesh, the jar of pickled eggs flashed before her inner eye.

The recipe was foolproof.

She'd replaced the vinegar with a fresh batch, so the liquid wouldn't be bubbly enough for the doctor to notice. If he did, botulism would no doubt spring to his mind. He was a doctor, after all. She'd considered other poisons first, just as she'd considered other ways of cutting her palm open, but had discarded them all. While water hemlock had proven easy enough to get a hold of, she'd struggled to find an excuse for keeping it around. The opposite could be said for the foxglove, currently repurposed for the green-painted vase on the coffee table, but she hadn't been able to make the foxglove potent enough.

But the eggs.

In the end, she'd gone with the eggs. The recipe had fallen into her lap by accident. Or, rather, by word of mouth. You couldn't go around asking for foxglove and water hemlock and not expect the more astute ears to hear you. The ears that were in the know. The soft-scented, powdered ones.

"There," said the doctor. "All done. I should like that coffee now, Mrs. Hatterson. If you are still offering?"

"Of course." She stood up, careful not to disturb her hand. "Henry, darling, will you assist me?"

The doctor's head jerked, but he said nothing. Henry got up from his chair, wincing at his weak leg, and followed Cora into the kitchen. She had thought this through already, but if she acted too fast it would make him suspicious. Her pulse beat hot and steady behind her eyes, urging them towards the jar of eggs on the counter, and when she breathed through her nose, the hairs singed and curled.

She gestured to the drip coffee pot. "Will you pour the water over the grounds?"

"You actually called me here to help? I thought you just wanted to talk in private."

"It's both," she admitted, painful fondness swelling in her chest that he'd read her cues right, but they hadn't been married for nearly a decade without developing habits. "I know I asked you to be here for the consultation, but now that the stitches are gone, I have some other things I'd like to discuss with the doctor. I don't want you privy to those. For your own sake. It's feminine matters. If I could, I wouldn't even have the doctor privy to them."

That should do it. That should chase him away for the next step.

"There." He finished pouring the water. "I suppose I'll go upstairs, then."

She took the pot and put it on a tray together with two cups and milk. "Thank you."

The doctor awaited her inside the parlor, his eyes skirting from her face to the door when nobody entered the parlor after her. "Urgent matters swept my husband away, I'm afraid," she lied. "A commission turned up late. Slipped us by. It happens once in a while. I hope that won't change your decision to have coffee, Doctor?"

"On the contrary, Mrs. Hatterson," said the doctor, chest puffing up. "I'm relieved, to be honest, as I need to talk to you privately about your husband."

She put the tray on the coffee table. Sitting down in the armchair opposite the couch, she put her hands on her lap and feigned surprise at the doctor's statement.

"About my husband?" she asked, pursing her lips. "How so?"

"You have my complete confidence. You no longer need to pretend." A pause. "Your husband cut your hand. You don't need to confirm it. I know it. I must ask, Mrs. Hatterson, has he grown more irritable over the last years? More unpredictable? Volatile, even?"

It was all Cora could do to stop a wide smile from splitting her face in two. She bit her lip, hoping it came off as fear rather than glee. "I'm not sure I fully understand, Doctor."

"You do," he ascertained, seeing a damsel in distress. So easy, this was. "There is a disease. Perhaps you have heard of it? It befalls hatters who've been in the trade for as long as your husband has. It starts with insomnia and tremors in the body. Spasmodic. In some cases, this leads to muscle atrophy. When advanced, this disease also makes the afflicted patient's skin sensitive to foreign touch. I see your husband wears gloves. I see him favoring one leg over the other. I see your dominant hand, with the direction of the cut facing away from you, discounting your claim it was an accident of your own doing. I understand you're afraid of your husband, Mrs. Hatterson, but there are measures we can take. Measures to protect you."

She was taking her own measures already, thank you.

Shifting in her seat, she stared at her lap, modestly avoiding the doctor's eye when all she wanted to do was laugh in his face. "You claim my husband has the hatter's disease?"

She'd known about it for years, having recognized the symptoms in her husband long before the doctor had even entered the picture. Once the doctor began to show an interest in her husband's condition, Cora decided to take preventative action. To nip it in the bud before it bloomed. That was when she'd cut her hand and inserted herself between the doctor and her husband. That was her prerogative. Her marriage. Her life. Hers.

"The measures have been in place for years," the doctor continued as if Cora didn't already know. "The state provides asylum. Mandatory, once the disease is as advanced as it is in your husband. I'm afraid this is no longer your choice, Mrs. Hatterson. I will have to take charge of this. It has already progressed too far, unattended for too long."

Spoken as a man who believed the world was his.

Cora pressed her thumb into her palm where her hands rested in her lap, savoring the pain, letting it ground her so she could continue this farce. "This is my life, doctor."

The doctor shifted forward on the couch, eyes claiming her face like a prize. Or maybe it was claiming her husband as a prize. "And it's at risk, Cora."

She flinched at his use of her name, the first genuine reaction she'd had since reentering the parlor. It was time to end this. He'd never be as pliable as he was now.

Standing up, she said, "Will you allow me more time to think?"

He hesitated. "This has gone on for too long already."

"To say goodbye, then." She widened her eyes. "Please, doctor."

She held her breath. They both did. Then he let go of his, shoulders deflating. "I can grant you a week, I suppose. I understand love myself."

His wife had left him. If he understood love, it wasn't the same kind of love that Cora understood. Not by a long shot. And Cora would take advantage of that, including his pity that sat folded in the curves of his brow.

"I'm so sorry about your wife," Cora said. "If you'll wait here for just a minute, I have something I wish to give you. As an appreciation of your effort and your time."

She went into the kitchen, fingers buzzing when she grabbed the jar of pickled eggs. When she strode back into the parlor, she made sure to walk in a straight line despite the painful thrumming inside her bones, a pain born of an anticipation so strong it felt almost otherworldly. She held up the jar for the doctor to take.

"I've heard this is a favorite of yours," she said, voice breathy. "And I made one too many this week, so this seems only appropriate, don't you think?"

It was hardly appropriate at all, from a patient to a doctor, but he'd called her by her first name, and she'd wrung his pity around her finger in a siren's call. She could see the indecision on his face morph into abashed gratitude. Good. Perfect. Splendid.

"Thank you, Mrs. Hatterson." He cradled the jar of death in his arms. "I will treasure this. And I will reach out to you at the end of the week if I haven't heard from you yet."

"Please do, Doctor."

After he'd left, Cora stood by the closed front door, one hand resting on the wood. She didn't move for a long time, head buzzing, chest hollowing in and out. The wood grew warm under her hand. It was over. She had done it. Now she had to wait. She'd thought that was the easy part, but already she was struggling. Maybe it would be easier tomorrow.

"Did I just watch you pay the doctor with eggs?"

She startled and spun around, slamming her shoulder blades into the door with a wince. Her ribs fluttered inside her chest with her every breath.

"Henry, for pity's sake. Don't scare me like that." She paused, her mind wrenched back to the matter at hand. "Were you snooping?"

He shrugged, hands in his pockets, body leaning as it always did these days. Muscle atrophy. What a fanciful way of putting it. A weak leg was a weak leg. A disease a disease.

"I saw the doctor leave with the jar out the window," he said. "The shop hasn't done well this year, but it hasn't done poorly. Do you need more money? I still don't understand how you cut yourself with that letter opener. All our letters get delivered to the shop, anyway."

She pushed away from the door, pulled her back straight, and walked up to him. Standing on her tiptoes, she kissed his freshly shaven cheek and stroked a thumb along his brow. The fluttering of her ribs subsided.

"The eggs were going bad." If bad meant poisonous, that was. "It was a whim. We never could've eaten them all in time, just the two of us. I'll pay him with money, too, and I have enough, so don't fret. Now, let's go put that leg up. I'll rub it for you, yes?"

Henry let her guide him to the couch where the doctor had sat minutes ago. Maneuvering his leg into her lap, her hands routinely set to work. "My right hand is still a little weak," she apologized with a smile and a tilt of her head, "but I reckon my left can make up for it. You relax now."

"This is more like you," Henry said. "You were so tense earlier."

"It was the appointment. Like I said, feminine matters. I'm sorry."

Her husband might be mad with hats, but Cora was mad with love, and there was no madness strong enough to conquer that.

A TALE OF HAPPINESS

BY RAQUEL GIFFORD

" **W**ould *you like me to read you a story?"*
"Yes, Mommy, please," Elizabeth says with the *brightest smile.*

"Of course love, are you all ready for bed?"

I gently tuck her in as I grab an extra pillow for me to sit next to her.

"Alright, but this has to be a short one, you have school in the morning."

Elizabeth sighs. "Okay Mommy, just a short one."

In a land far far away, where the trees grew wild and the flowers bloomed all year round; there was a giant castle on top of the tallest hill in the kingdom. Now, this was not your ordinary castle. There were no singing birds, there were no pleasantries and there certainly were no honey bees. No my dear, this was a castle filled with the absence of hope. The absence of happiness. But most certainly the absence of love. In this castle lived a beautiful girl with the most tragic past. At the age of five she lost both of her parents in what she was told was a boating accident, but as she grew older she knew it must not be true. There were no articles or anything written about the accident, everything she knew came from her Aunt and Uncle.

"That's sad. Did she live in the castle with her Aunt and Uncle, Mommy?"
"Yes, she did."

Now, her Aunt and Uncle were not the nicest people. She had rules placed upon her that were more harsh than the ones given to her cousins that lived there as well.

Be home right after school.

No friends are allowed over.

You must be in your room studying at all times.

"But Mommy, you always say studying is a good thing."
"You are right, maybe that one isn't so bad."

This Beautiful Girl felt alone in a castle completely filled with people—two adults and six cousins.

"Six cousins?" Elizabeth gasped with utter shock.
"Yes, yes, my dear. Now you must be calm and listen to the story," I say with a smirk on my face.
"Yes, Mommy." She uses her hand to show she is zipping her lips shut and throwing away the key. She brings me so much joy in the littlest of things she does.

This castle was dark and gloomy, with giant statues everywhere of concrete animals. On the outside, it looked like a functioning place, somewhere you could live, but the inside was filled with decay. The stairs creaked every time you stepped on them, the wallpaper was peeling off by the sheets. There were holes in the chairs and dust littered on top of every unused piece of furniture. This was a nightmare for anyone with allergies. This was a place no one could call home. There was only one room that was pristine. The Library Room. This room had wall to wall, ceiling to floor, rows of shelves filled to the top with any book you could dream of. This is where the Beautiful Girl spent all of her days. She had traveled to magical places in this room. Defeated dragons. Married a Prince. Had a fish for a friend. And even fell in love with a Beast. This was the room that brought her happiness.

One day after school, the Beautiful Girl walked inside without saying a word to anyone, went to the kitchen, grabbed a snack, and went straight to the Library Room. She mumbled to her Aunt along the way about having much to study. The Aunt nodded and kept walking. She didn't care what the Beautiful Girl did so long as she was quiet and followed the castle rules.

"Mommy, does she have a name?" Elizabeth whispers.

"She does, but it's a secret. You'll find out once the story is over. But, for now, I like 'Beautiful Girl' don't you?"

"I love it."

She wandered into the Library Room feeling particularly excited. Her attention was focused on the chestnut colored shelves with the books all evenly pressed against each other, trying to find something new to read. Tracing her fingers over the spines of each book, remembering the way they felt in her hand, all familiar– and not new. After ten minutes of going up and down the ladder, she gave up trying to find anything she had yet to read. The Beautiful Girl walked over to the giant stained glass window that had the most stunning shades of blues, purples, reds and gold and sat down on the bench attached to the wall. She leaned back to lie down on the soft pillow. The sun was shining through the window that let a small rainbow appear on a particular book. Squinting her eyes to see the title–she noticed the ribbon bookmark at the end of the book.

"And what does the ribbon at the end mean, Elizabeth?"
"Oh no! The Beautiful Girl has read all of the books." She shrieked.

Letting out a small sigh, shut her eyes, and dozed off. When she woke, the sun had almost fully set and the Beautiful Girl realized that the rainbow on the book had not yet moved, not even an inch. Isn't it odd for the sun to be at its setting point, yet the rainbow remained?

She got up and walked to the shelf, climbing up three steps on the ladder and grabbed the book off of the shelf. Gently, she wiped the dust off the top while she wondered where the book came from. Certainly she has read every single book in this library. She had been to all of the magical places, but this book she had never seen. The book laid there with a layer of dust as if it had been here this whole time. She touched the cover, scanning the front and the back; the book was a marvelous shade of garnet with the most intricate details in marigold. The lines intertwined, making out what looks like a vine of flowers all surrounding a vial of some sort. She descended from the ladder and walked back to the bench.

The book had some wear to it so she made sure to be very careful when opening it. Anxiously scanning the first page she soon realized it isn't in a language she had seen before and certainly she cannot read what the book is about. The Beautiful Girl is then frustrated and tossed the book on the ground.

"SHE.. DID.. NOT!" Elizabeth hissed.
"I am afraid she did."
"You must never treat your books that way, Mommy."
"I know, my dear."

. . .

She closed her eyes and besides the tiny footsteps from her cousins, everything else was quiet and still. Finding peace in the Library Room, she daydreamed of the day she would no longer be stuck in this gloomy castle. Hours later, she woke up feeling a sharp pain in her eyes and suddenly the room was lit with color brighter than the sun. She slowly opened one eye and looked over to the book that was now open on the floor and gleaming with what looked like tiny gold stars all around. There was one page that came loose from the book and was levitating directly over it. Leaping off of the bench she walked towards the page, hesitating as she was afraid that she may get hurt, but proceeded to lift her hand and grab the page. Slowly she brought the paper to eye level, there were pieces of glowing marigolds on the edges of it. This page was different. This page she could read. What was this piece doing in that book, was it put there for her to find? She sat down on the floor and began to read it.

"My dearest beautiful daughter, if you are reading this, I am afraid something terrible has happened to your father and I. We suspected this day may come. I want you to know that you cannot believe what others have told you. We are right here with you, always. All you need to do is unlock the curse that was put on us and this house. I know this may seem like a lot to wrap your head around, but your Aunt Mary and I were both very young when we first discovered our magic. One day we were sitting on the new porch swing that our Grandfather had just built. Moving our feet back and forth, we sat there all day enjoying the cool breeze and the smell of fresh flowers. Soon after, we felt this tiny jolt of electricity and we immediately jumped off. I looked around the house and underneath the swing and I didn't see anything that would cause that jolt. So Instead we walked to our Grandmother's flower garden to pick a colorful arrangement that we could use as decoration for the dinner table. I had my eye on this tulip that was a lovely shade of amber that would go perfectly with the lace tablecloth. As soon as I reached up to grab the flower my hand tingled– as if it had fallen asleep. Holding the tulip I walked back to the house. I looked towards the ground, noticing a bunch of dead flowers in my path. I glanced up and saw Mary reaching to grab flowers herself and seeing the confused look on her face when they all wilted to the ground. Reaching out I felt the tingle again, so I touched one of the dead flowers, and to my surprise, it had come back to life. I remember the cold chill that ran up my spine when I looked over at Mary, she had the most painful look on her face. Mary realized everything she touched would die and everything I touched–lived. She was given dark powers, meant for evil, to bring death upon anything she touched. From that moment on I was dead to her. We never played, picked flowers or went on that swing again. She's never said a word to me since. I wished every night that I would have been the one to get her dark powers–I would have never touched anything again. But Mary was never the same after, she was known as Evil Mary all throughout school and had learned how to make her powers more advanced. One night before going to bed I heard a loud noise come out of Mary's room. Peeking through the tiny hole she had in her door I could see glowing liquids of some kind–like a potion. I have no idea what she was doing, all I remember is her biggest bully in school was never seen again after that day. From that moment on I had a strong reason to believe that her bully was her first test at making someone disappear forever– I would be her last. The curse of being gone can only be undone if we stop her. Once Mary is gone, along with everything she has created–everyone she has ever hurt will be free.

But we are running out of time. I know you are wondering where this book has even come from as it is not one you would have recognized. This book will appear just three days before all hope will be lost–it is your key to getting us back. You must first go to the bench under the stained glass, there you should tap the book with your right hand three times. The marigold foil will release the petals off of the flower stems and the vial filled with poison will float off of the book for you to be able to use. I had created this poison in case this ever happened—as a last resort. We have neglected to tell you that this Library Room is a very magical place. Every book we have read to you and every book you have read in this very room has all prepared you for this very moment, you just didn't know it. You need to take the vial and pour it into their food, make a stew and serve it to them, but you must be careful that it does not touch your lips. I know you can do this my Beautiful Girl."

Until we meet again,

Love, your Ma and Pa.

Silence, as the paper floated from her hand to the ground and a tear fell down the slight curve of her cheek. "They've known this whole time this would happen?" She whispered. "I can... I can bring them back?" Anger flooded her vision. "This cannot be true, HOW can this be true?" She bent down to grab the paper, slowly folded it and placed it into her pocket. A loud crash happened just outside the Library Room. She sprinted towards the bench and tucked the book behind her back.

"There you are, you rotten girl," the Aunt hissed. "You have yet to start our dinner for tonight."

"I am so terribly sorry ma'am, I will get started right away," she said with a hint of sarcasm.

The Aunt let out a tut, turned around and shut the door. The Beautiful Girl grabbed the book from behind her back, placed it on her lap, and tapped with her right hand 3 times. The petals on the book began to release and the vial slowly levitated off of the book.

"Just like Mom said," she whispered with an enourmos smile on her face. She jumped off of the bench and headed toward the kitchen. This will be the best stew she has ever made. The Beautiful Girl pulled out the meat, vegetables, and spices. She washed and peeled the potatoes. Cut the carrots. Measured every spice accordingly. She turned on the stove and carefully started adding each ingredient. The pot began to boil and she took that time to set the table. The Beautiful Girl returned to the kitchen and scooped out a portion for herself into a bowl that she hid in the bottom cabinet. She turned the pot down to a simmer and pulled the vial out from under her apron in the hidden pouch. Careful to not spill even the tiniest drop, she slowly added the full vial of poison into the pot.

"This sounds delicious, Mommy! Can we have stew too? Without the poison?" Elizabeth snuggles deeper into her mother's side.
I let out a soft chuckle. "Of course we can. No poison allowed."

Gently stirring, she took a whiff and noted that the poison is odorless and no one would notice. She made enough for the entire family and hoped that whatever this poison would do, would be quick and pain-less, as her cousins would be eating it as well. She loved her cousins, sure, but the need to bring her parents back was far greater. She grabbed enough bowls for everyone and scooped an equal amount of stew into each bowl. Placing as many bowls as she could carry on a tray–she was ready to set the table. She rang the little gold bell in her pocket to let the family know dinner was now served. There was a loud rumbling as everyone ran down the stairs. She went back into the kitchen to grab the remaining bowls and hers from inside of the cabinet. Placing the rest of the bowls on that table, she made sure to keep an eye on hers. After everyone had a bowl she went to sit at her table in the corner. She wasn't allowed to eat at the same table as everyone, but she was allowed to eat in the same room. Her Uncle takes the very first bite. He made a satisfied sound and said "Very well, very well." The Beautiful Girl tried to hide her excitement and gently smiled at him and said, "Thank you." The Aunt tuts and said "Well yes, it should be good she has been cooking for us for years."

The girl glared, and in that moment wondered how long it would take until the poison kicked in. Mother didn't say in the letter. Will it be mere seconds? Hours? Days? Will it be horrifying to watch? Will they vanish into thin air? Minutes went by that felt like hours. She started to get discouraged and wondered if she found the letter too late or if she missed a step and the poison wasn't working. The rest of the family left the table for her to clean and went back to their rooms.

"Mommy.. Did it not work?" Elizabeth shrieked.
  "You will have to wait and see."

She grabbed all of the bowls and utensils and headed for the kitchen. With tears in her eyes, she washed the dishes. The anger she felt was so strong that she slammed a bowl down and it shattered into tiny pieces–one of which cut her hand. As the hot water ran into the cut she watched the blood slide down into the sink and let out a low sob. The Beautiful Girl came to the horrific realization that she would never see her parents again, and would live forever in this dark, gloomy, miserable castle. She dried her hands and wrapped a paper towel around the cut. Heading into the Library Room, her eyes focused on the bench. The book– but it wasn't there. "Maybe I put it away" She whispered to herself. She raced to the ladder and up the steps to see if the book was back in its place, but the book was nowhere to be found. Was this all a dream? Could the book have vanished? She walked back over to the bench and began to weep. She was hoping maybe, just maybe, there would have been another vial on the cover of the book. Accepting defeat, she pulled out a blanket and pillow from underneath the bench seat and placed them on her. She was much too sad to walk to her room, much too sad to do anything. So, she placed her head on her pillow, wrapped herself tightly in the blanket and closed her eyes.

With tears in her eyes, Elizabeth looks up at me. "Mommy, this makes me so sad."
  It is my dear, but I promise you, I've heard this one before and it will be a happy ending for all."

. . .

The sun rose and the Beautiful Girl tossed over to her side, not wanting to get up—using the blanket to shield her face from the sun. The wind started blowing and the birds started chirping. "Birds.... singing...I must still be dreaming," she said quietly, knowing it had to be all in her head. The chirping became louder and she could feel the sun on her back, filling her with warmth. She turned over to face the window and opened one eye. Her mouth fell open and her eyes instantly filled with tears of joy. She ran out of the Library Room, through the hallway, and right up to the front door. She hesitated for a moment worried none of this may be real. She took both hands and placed them on the cold door knobs and swung both doors open. Just then the sun's warmth hit her face while the cool breeze of the wind blew through her hair. She stepped outside and was absolutely amazed by what she saw. The grass was a vibrant shade of green, the bushes were all alive with gorgeous tones of pink and red roses on them. The giant statues were gone completely and replaced with fountains where ducks swam next to birds flying by. Butterflies were everywhere and even the honeybees were back.

She was filled with so much joy. The poison, it had worked. Something meant to be deadly had restored all of the beauty back into her life. She ran inside and there were no signs of her Aunt or her Uncle, or any of her cousins. The house was completely quiet. There was no more dust, no creaky floors, and no wallpaper falling off of the walls. The entire house inside and out looked like it was brought back to life. With tears of joy she shouted, "MA!, PA!" But there was no one answering her cries. She ran back outside. "MA! PA!" She tried again, but still no one answered. Frantically walking towards the end of the road right where the bushes stopped, she looked left and then right. Stopping to marvel at the purple buds on the bushes that would soon bloom. She tried one last time, "MA! PA!" Tears filled her eyes as the realization set in that no one but herself was there. Completely defeated, she trudged to the front of the castle. She was alone in more ways than most. Would it have been better to have never used the poison? How will she survive living here all alone? The food in the pantry would only last so long; she would have to learn how to grow her own food.

At that moment the wind made a whistling noise. She looked at the trees, but everything was completely still. Maybe she misheard and there was no noise at all. She continued to walk back inside and reached for the door feeling the cold handle on her palm. She hesitated before going in, hoping that her parents would somehow appear.

Just then, she heard the wind whistle again. She spun around on her heels to face the end of the road, and in the distance she could see her parents.

"MA, PA?" she said while her tears threatened to spill down on her cheek. She reluctantly stepped forward one foot at a time trying to control her shaking. The figures of her parents kept moving closer and closer, but she couldn't hear a sound. She tried one last time, "MA, PA?" And then suddenly she heard it, the sweetest sound she has heard in the longest time. "My Beautiful Girl" the figures said. She ran towards them and wrapped her arms around her parents. "You're back! It worked," she shrieked with joy. "Genevieve, my dear, we were always here," her mother says with the same love in her voice she remembered as a child.

"Genevieve?" Elizabeth says to me with her brows furrowed. *"Mommy, but that's your name!"*

"Yes, yes it is."

"Are you the Beautiful Girl in the story?"

"Yes, Elizabeth, that is me. Although the details have been changed, the message still rings true. No matter how gloomy your days can be, you must always look ahead towards the light. You can be in the gloomiest of all castles that used to be beautiful the day before. You can be sad and angry at the way things turn out, but you must always remember that there are beautiful things in this world. "

"Like books and flowers, Mommy?"

Genevieve chuckled. "Yup, books and flowers, and being around the people you love."

I kiss her goodnight and hope that she will be the kind and loving little girl that I know. That she will always look forward to the beautiful days filled with love ahead. And that she will know, no matter what happens, I will always be here.

27

TEA AND TURPENTINE

BY JAY RENEE LAWRENCE

I have been called many things over the centuries. Healer. Herbalist. Charlatan. Witch. I am all of these and none at the same time. I am simply Lilaine de Décès. And, though many have tried to kill me, I will live forever because people never change.

New Orleans is ripe with unsatisfied souls willing to pay any price for beauty, love, vengeance, money, or fame. I have the power to bestow all of these things and more, which is why they end up in my flat, drinking the specially concocted poisons that will grant them their petty desires and grant me more time on this earth.

I'm not sure from whom the young artist received my address, for there are several in the underground circuit who know where to send the most desperate, yet he arrived on my doorstep on a brisk March morning before the sun could steal the dew from the ivy.

I sensed him coming as soon as he'd turned down my street, of course. The mixture of anticipation and fear was hard to miss. It made my skin crawl. I let out a sigh of irritation because I was still in my dressing gown enjoying my coffee while working on a puzzle, but I wasn't about to turn away a customer.

He stood outside for several moments before he plucked up the courage to knock. It was so quiet, I'd barely heard it, but it caused the cats to scatter, seeking refuge in their various hiding places. They, like me, prefer to avoid humans.

"Good day, Ma'am." He said when I opened the door. "I'm looking to find Madame de Décès?"

I hadn't taken a customer to bed in some time, but there was absolutely no temptation to take this one. He was in his late twenties and could have been handsome if he had some meat on his bones. His skin was pallid, his lips were cracked, and there were shadows etched beneath those green, bloodshot eyes. He wore dirty, dark denim that clung to his skinny legs, which was considered fashionable for that decade. Splattered across both his pants and his blue knit sweater were small flecks of dried paint. Worst of all, though, was the stench of desperation, which I have never found attractive, mixed with a faint smell of campfire that clung to his clothing.

"Come in, then." I stepped aside to allow him entrance. He hesitated, eyes darting up and down the sidewalk to make sure there was no one to see him cross my threshold.

"Well? Don't just stand there. You're letting all the heat out."

"Yes, Ma'am." He came in and I closed the door behind him, bolting it as I always do.

He looked out of place in my sitting room, too dark. Too cold. Everything in my home was soft and warm, with pastel colors and fluffy throw pillows.

"Is Madame de Décès here?" he asked.

"Yes. She's here. You're looking at her." I flipped my wavy brown hair over my shoulder, allowing him a moment to admire the smoothness of my skin and the curves of my youthful body. In all the centuries I've lived, I still enjoy the stunned look on his face. He was expecting an old crone, not a beautiful woman who looked to be his own age.

"Oh. Nice to meet you. You have a lovely home," he said quickly to cover up his blushing. He extended his hand towards me and started to say, "I'm—"

"No names, please," I interjected, raising my hand to force his tongue to still. "This way." My bare feet padded across the rugs laid out over my parkett wooden floors. He followed obediently and of his own free will. I'd have liked for him to take his boots off, but I was eager to get things over with and get him out of my house as quickly as possible. As I led him deeper into my apartment, some of the braver felines popped their heads out from behind pastel cushions or around flower pots, but they were quick to withdraw if the stranger got too close.

The dining room is something like a sanctuary to me. It is where I spend most of my time and is usually a bit cluttered, but it was particularly messy that day. Days old coffee mugs stood atop piles of books and the floor was littered with fake mice dragged in by the cats. In the center of the room stood the round, marble-topped table where I ate dinner, brewed potions, and where I'd been working on the puzzle that morning. I quickly and carefully threw a flowery tablecloth over my project and grabbed an armful of clean but unfolded laundry from the extra chair, transferring it to the armchair in the corner of the room.

"I wasn't expecting company today," I said and motioned for him to take a seat. The wicker chair across from mine barely made a sound when he sat his bony ass down.

"Now then. Why have you come to me?" I leaned back, crossed my legs, and pulled the silk robe tighter to cover my exposed chest. I didn't want him getting any ideas.

"Well, I'm here because I've heard you can grant wishes," he whispered. I tried hard not to roll my eyes. *What does he think I am, some Djinn? Grant wishes. Please.*

"All I can do is grant your deepest desire. One, not three. And it comes with a price."

"I don't have any money," he said sheepishly. Obviously, whoever told him where to find me didn't relay the most important bit of information.

"Oh, it isn't money. To bestow that which you want most in the world, I require something much more valuable. Time."

"Time?" His eyebrow furrowed.

"Yes. You must be willing to surrender years of your life. You won't get any older or anything. I'll take them from the end so you'll just die a little sooner than you would have otherwise." A handful of seconds passed while he absorbed what I said. "This isn't some kind of Faustian bargain. I don't take away your soul and there's no fine print. I like to be upfront when I make my deals. So that when you agree—if you agree— you know exactly what you're getting into."

"How many years will you take?"

I shrugged.

"Depends on what it is you want. But, usually, it's a dozen, more or less." I saw that he was struggling through a calculation in his head.

"Does it hurt?" He asked.

"Nope, you won't even notice it's gone. Time's funny that way."

His shoulders slumped and he kept his eyes on the table. "If I don't make this deal, I'll likely be dead soon anyway. I'll pay whatever price I have to." The guilt and self-pity coming from him made me feel nauseous.

"Very well, then. Let's get started." I removed the small key from around my neck and went to the ancient, carved oak armoire that took up nearly an entire wall of my dining room.

The piece is nearly as old as I am and has traveled with me from France to London, then across the Atlantic to New York, and, finally, to Louisiana. Relocating every hundred years or so helps me keep a low profile. Hidden within are shelves filled with various crystals, cursed artifacts, and small blank effigies ready to be dressed to resemble souls and impaled by pins to cause pain and torment. But, most importantly, the cabinet contains neat rows of mason jars. Most of their contents are harmless, some are even beneficial, but a fair few of the herbs are deadly, and not a single jar is labeled.

"Judging by the paint splattered on your clothes, you must be an artist. So I take it you'll be wanting fame and glory?" I started to gather the ingredients that would make the man as famous as Monet himself, though that painter didn't need any magical assistance.

"Yes, I am. An artist, I mean. A painter. But, I don't want fame or glory. I couldn't seem to handle the small amount of it I got on my own."

Without warning, a wave of grief rushed out of the man and stank up the entire room. The air was knocked from my lungs and I could no longer control my gag reflex. I was suffocating. Choking on the intense emotion. The jars I held toppled to the ground as I staggered to the window sill, reaching for a bundle of dried herbs. I set a lighter to it, waved it around to clear the air, and dropped it into the ceramic bowl in the center of the table. At the sight of the flame and smoke, he leaned away as if afraid the tendrils of smoke would reach out and strangle him. His eyes were wide and the waves of emotion intensified causing the cats to yowl and hiss throughout the apartment.

"Are you alright? Hey, calm down!" I ordered, desperately trying to soothe him. But he couldn't seem to hear me, and you wouldn't need to be a witch to know that his eyes were not focused on the present.

In an attempt to regain control of the situation and keep from throwing up my breakfast, I did something rather intrusive. Something I hadn't done to a customer for a very long time—for good reasons.

I closed my eyes and projected myself into his memory.

The world erupted in a swirl of angry colors and smoke. It was hard to tell where we were at first because the scene kept sliding in and out of focus, and the room seemed to be spinning but from what I could make out, it was the artist's small studio and it was on fire. Heady fumes from the turpentine oil fuelling the blaze burned our nostrils and flooded our eyes, but through the tears, I saw flames eating their way through truly beautiful paintings. Stacks of them. Pastoral landscapes and still lifes as real as photographs were turning black and crumbling to ash. Those closest to the epicentre were already lost and I could only wonder as to what beautiful images might have once been stretched across the smouldering skeletal frames.

Who knows how many hours of work, how many thousands of brush strokes, were being obliterated in the mere seconds that passed. I felt an urge to run and save them, but the artist couldn't even seem to stand up straight. We sank to our knees, coughing, helpless to do anything but watch the raging inferno.

As frightening as the backdrop of the memory was, the anguish raging through the young man was even more terrifying. It was a pain I hadn't felt so acutely for at least three hundred years, but I knew it well. For I have also witnessed the burning of the thing I loved most in the world. Though, for me, it wasn't canvas but flesh. The familiarity of it all made it unbearable for me to stay inside his head, so I pulled us back into the present.

We were both panting and he was rocking back and forth with his arms wrapped around his waist. When he began to speak, it was no more than a string of babble. "It's gone. All of it. My life's work. All my fault. Gone."

"What caused the fire?" I asked.

"I did." His eyes finally came back into focus and connected with mine. "I was high. Then, I started drinking. I'm not sure how it started, but I was so out of my mind that I couldn't do anything to stop it. It all just turned to ash while I watched. I would have too, and happily, but a neighbor pulled me out."

"I don't know what you've heard, I can't change what happened."

"I didn't think you could. Nothing can take back what I've done."

"What is it you want, then?"

"Painting is my whole life. It's all I've ever wanted to do and it's all I've ever loved. But, even before the fire, I hadn't so much as picked up a paintbrush in months. I'll never be able to rebuild what I lost if I can't stay sober for more than a few hours. Is it possible for you to take away my addictions?"

"Oui. I can do that," I whispered.

The artist remained silent as I collected the jars from the floor, which were perfectly in-tact thanks to their sturdy design, and returned them to their shelves. I handed him a pen and a pink Post-it Note, because it was the only paper I could find, and told him to write down his desire. Then, I brought the heavy onyx mortar and pestle to the table and placed it in front of him.

"Place the paper inside."

I added five drops of a very special serum on top. The substance is of my own design, which I started putting into the poisons because I was tired of the assassination attempts made by unsatisfied customers. I usually only put in two drops to erase the memory of our bargain, but I added a few extra in hopes of taking away the painful memory of the fire. I didn't know if it would work, but I was feeling kind.

"What's that?" he asked, but I flashed him a look that warned against asking questions.

"Grind until you make a smooth paste," I instructed.

"Do I need to be focusing my energy on it while I work?"

"Bingo," I said. Though, it wasn't true. I just wanted him to be quiet. I could even grind it myself but it's tiresome and hurts my hand.

While he worked, I grabbed the ingredients I needed from the armoire but my mind was in a different place, in a different time.

I rarely thought of Béatrice anymore, because I was never able to relive the good memories without the horrific ones taking over. But what I'd seen in the artist's mind brought them all back to me. The first time I saw her at the market near Montmartre. All the nights we danced naked together worshiping the earth then worshiping each other. And, of course, the night they captured and burned her while I watched, helplessly. What I wouldn't give to forget that final memory, or to erase the guilt of it being all my fault.

"Is this good enough?" The artist showed me the brown paste and I nodded. "I really tried to concentrate on being clean and sober," he added.

"Good for you."

I placed a teacup between us, because not all potions need to be brewed in ugly pewter cauldrons. I had these cups specially made. They each have a little pentagram on the bottom and match my china set. With a teaspoon I added all of the dry ingredients first, then I spooned his mushed-up desire from the mortar and mixed in about a quarter cup of water.

When it was blended, I grabbed my switchblade from the counter next to my keys and wallet. I clicked it open and held the blade, pointing the handle at the artist.

"I'll need a bit of your blood," I said.

"Are you serious?" He looked alarmed.

"Are you surprised?"

He thought for a second and then said, "I guess not."

The potion didn't really require his blood, just some bit of him. It could have been hair or spit or a bit of a fingernail, but I've found that demanding they use their blood makes it all feel a bit more dramatic.

Once he'd added a few drops into the teacup, I cleaned my knife with a paper towel and handed it to him to wrap around his sliced finger.

Then it was time for the final ingredient. The one that would ensure my payment. I reached up and grabbed a section of my hair, carefully counting three thin strands to pluck. Usually, I grab a healthy pinch containing somewhere around ten to twenty, but this bargain was different. I had isolated myself from the world and people for so long, that I'd almost forgotten there were a few souls whose desires are not purely petty. While I couldn't get the love of my life back, his was not lost forever, and without the drugs and alcohol, perhaps he could find it again.

Sprinkling the hairs into the cup, I said an incantation to heat the mixture until it bubbled softly and all the contents were dissolved. Then I carefully slid the steaming cup across the table towards him.

"There you go. Bottoms up."

"With the blood and hair and everything?"

"With the blood and hair and everything," I repeated. "I mean, you don't have to if you don't want to. But this is what will take your addictions away."

He grabbed the cup and lifted it to his cracked lips. The look of disgust on his face was one I'd seen many times before. But, almost no one backs out of the bargain at this point and neither did the artist. He squeezed his eyes shut and drank.

Watching his stubbled throat constrict as he gulped the corrupting liquid, I could feel the delicious energy of life ripple over my skin. But it was just a quick zing since only three of his life years were transferred to me. When the final drop of potion was gone, the effects of the memory-erasing serum started to kick in and his face took on a rather dazed, distant look. I grabbed him by the arm and hoisted him off the chair, leading him back through the kitchen, down the hall, and towards the front door. The cats, sensing the intruder was no longer any sort of threat to them, began to emerge and sniff the air. I deposited the artist on the sidewalk, trusting that he'd make his way wherever he was going, and returned to my puzzle.

It was the lowest price I'd ever accepted. I doubt I'd ever do it again, but I was satisfied with the exchange.

28

LONGING FOR SHADOWS

BY CAITE SAJWAJ

*E*urydice died on her own wedding day. It wasn't early that morning, or late at night after the merriment had ended, no, no, no. It was in the middle of the event, which only served to make the whole ordeal all the more tragic.

The wedding feast lasted well into the evening. Orpheus had never seen so much food, not even in the halls of kings. Quail eggs and figs and crusty bread, pork and roasted hare, semolina custards and cheese pastries and sesame cakes drizzled with honey. And wine, of course. Copious amounts of wine. By the time the festivities moved outside, Orpheus feared he might fall asleep.

The night went on. Orpheus strummed his seven-stringed lyre, watching his wife jump and whirl and stamp her feet in time with the music. After some time, she pulled him into a shadowy corner of the garden, sequestered behind a curtain of ivy.

"Dance with me," Eurydice said. She was resplendent—brown-skinned and dark-haired, wearing a crown of crimson poppies atop her wedding veil. The night was warm. So much dancing had left a thin sheen of sweat on her skin. He kissed her, inhaling the scent of rosewater and marjoram and wine.

"If I dance with you," Orpheus said, "There will be no music."

"Let someone else play a while," she argued, but Orpheus just shook his head. In truth, he was too tired and too full to dance. Later, he would wonder, *Would she still be alive if I'd danced with her? Or, at the very least, would I have died with her?*

Instead, Orpheus returned to playing and Eurydice to dancing. He watched her, as enraptured by her movements as she was by the rhythm. She held a hand over her heart and dipped low, in perfect time with the music, then swept her foot through the grass behind her. The music went on, but Eurydice was no longer dancing. Her mouth opened and closed. Her brows knit together. Orpheus stopped playing and stood, suddenly feeling very awake. Then, Eurydice was falling, falling, falling. There wasn't time to plead with the gods for help, nor even to say goodbye. Within a moment, she was dead, the viper that had bitten her already slithering away, and all Orpheus could think was, *Why did it have to be her?*

It felt as if his lungs had ruptured, every shallow breath forced around a scream held captive in his throat. He sent the wedding guests away and took his wife's body inside, arranging her carefully on what should have been their marriage bed. Now, it was nothing but a tomb.

If Eurydice had family, he might have sent for them, but her father was a river god with fifty daughters or more—so many, surely, that one would not be missed. Her mother was mortal and long-dead. Orpheus prepared her body for burial himself, though there was little point. She was already washed, already anointed with sweet-smelling oils, already wearing her finest gown. Concerning appearances, there was little difference between a wedding and a funeral.

When the work was done, he played her a final song, and sang:
"Sleep among shadows, dear Eurydice.
Why did the gods grant you breath,
if only to take you from me?"

Then, he set his lyre aside, fully intending never to pick it up again. He had never considered that his divine wife might die. Her limbs were hewn from solid oak. Her blood ran the pale gold of sap. She might have lived forever if she had only tread more carefully.

244

"Such a lovely song for such a grim occasion," a voice said.

Orpheus didn't turn. He knew it was Apollo, could feel the heat radiating from him. *Golden Apollo.* He couldn't bear to look at him, brimming with life everlasting while Eurydice lay dead. Some speculated that Apollo was Orpheus' own father. It might be true—the god had given him his first lyre and taught him to play, which was something a father might do. Still, he'd never asked, and now he was afraid to. Divine blood only meant an even longer life without Eurydice.

"I came as soon as I could," Apollo said. His voice was toneless. Clinical. "But it seems your wife is beyond my help,"

"Then begone!" Orpheus cried. "If you cannot help her, I have no use for you!"

There was silence for a moment, then Apollo crept forward to stand beside the bed. His yellow hair was wild beneath a garland of laurel leaves. His bow and quiver were slung across his back. His skin glowed faintly, casting an otherworldly light on Eurydice's body. It was cruel. She almost looked alive.

"I said she is beyond *my* help," Apollo said primly. "Not *yours*."

"Help no one," Apollo had said. It was easier said than done. The Underworld was positively teeming with poor souls in need of *help*. Orpheus passed a child, floundering in the water, screaming, "Help! Help me, please!" He passed an old woman begging for food. He passed a disembodied voice that claimed it had, somehow, *fallen down a well*. Eventually, Orpheus pulled out his lyre and began to strum, slow and soft at first, before slipping into a steady, rising rhythm. He sang a song of grief, of yearning, but also of hope, and the entire Underworld fell silent, listening raptly to the music he made.

He continued on, descending down, down, down into that place of shadows and longing, where Hades ruled beside his dreadful queen, Persephone. With Apollo's guidance, it was easy enough for him to find his way. He paid the ferryman with a silver obol and soothed the three-headed watchdog to sleep with a lullaby. It was the same lullaby his mother had sung to him as a child, and the one he had hoped to sing to his and Eurydice's own children one day. If his quest was successful, perhaps he still could.

It wasn't until he reached the palace that Orpheus began to feel doubt. It was an imposing place, carved of marble the color of old bones, not so different than any other palace, except in the fact that the grounds were empty. No children playing in the fountain, no servants hurrying about the day's chores. There were no soldiers, and no fortifications. Hades and his queen had no need for such things. This was their realm, after all. A place where death was not an intruder, but a cherished guest. Unimpeded, Orpheus strode right into the shadows of the palace and laid himself bare before the god and goddess of the dead.

They lounged together on an oversized throne, carved from the same bone-colored marble as the palace itself and flanked by torches burning with sickly green flames. Hades was a large man, almost impossibly large, barrel-chested and broad-shouldered. He seemed to fill the entire room. His hands were huge, with sanguine rubies on every finger. Beside him, the queen was a wisp, no more substantial than a twig, though her eyes burned more brightly than the torches beside her—an unnatural, poisonous green.

"We know what you would ask of us," Hades said in a voice like dead leaves. "Now tell us why we should give it to you."

Orpheus paused, then raised his lyre and began to play, not from memory, but intuition. Persephone herself had been a goddess of spring once, a long, long time ago. Now, she ruled over nothing but death and dust and darkness. Because of this, Orpheus thought, he *hoped*, the queen might see some of herself in Eurydice, that she might feel some sort of kinship with his dearly departed wife. The song was for her and Eurydice both. It was difficult to sing, at first, with a chest so full of fear. His lungs felt suddenly too small. His voice trembled. Still, Orpheus sang, for all his hopes lay in that moment. He sang of the world above, of dappled sunlight and the whisper of the wind through a meadow. He sang of longing and lone-liness, for surely Hades knew something of that, having been condemned to solitude for so long. What lengths would he go to, if his own wife was taken from him? When the song came to a close, a last, low note echoing through the dark hall, the silence felt all the heavier for its absence.

Husband and wife turned to each other. Finally, Hades sighed.

"Very well," he said. "You may return to the realm of the living with your wife."

"She will not be as she was," Persephone warned, but Orpheus barely heard her. He knelt, half out of gratitude and half because he didn't trust himself to stand. His stomach was roiling with shock, anticipation, and relief. He thought, briefly, that he might vomit, right there at the foot of the throne.

"Trust that she will be behind you and do not look back," Hades said. "Now go. The Underworld is no place for mortals."

Orpheus went, fleeing the palace before the gods could change their minds. He walked, upward and onward, past the three-headed dog Cerberus, all the way to the shores of the river Styx. It wasn't until he was across the river, marching his way toward the distant light of the upper world, that he began to doubt. Was Eurydice truly there, just behind him, or was this some cruel trick? There was no sound of footfall, no harsh breathing from the steep, upward trek. He thought to turn, just to see her face. He almost did, then remembered Hades voice, like the grating of metal against stone. *Do not look back.* So, he didn't, just forged on in spite of his doubts, until, at last, he stood on level ground, with the silver light of the moon above him and the howl of the northern wind at his back. And when he did turn, Eurydice was there, looking back at him.

Somehow, death had made her even more beautiful. Her lips were the pale, bruised color of nightshade. He fell at her feet and kissed her hands, and everything that he'd felt or thought or dreamed since she'd died came pouring from his lips—how frightened he had been, how the grief had nearly killed him, how sorry he was. To this, Eurydice said nothing, only looked at him. Looked and looked and looked, blankly, as if she didn't even know him. Which was, of course, because she didn't. The queen had spoken the truth—Eurydice was not as she once was. She didn't even *remember* him. She had drunk from Lethe, the River of Forgetfulness.

Orpheus took her back to the home they had shared anyway, and made sure she was comfortable. It was no matter that she didn't remember him. Now, they had all the time in the world, and he was certain she would fall in love with him all over again. He could be patient. And patient he was. The first week, Eurydice hardly spoke. Orpheus had explained everything to her, and she wandered the halls like a ghost, staring at a half-melted candle, a rumpled gown, a pot of charcoal eyeliner—anything that might connect her to her old life.

But soon, it became evident that Eurydice's time in the Underworld had altered more than just her memory. Her skin was ashen. She smelled faintly of rot, of crushed rose petals and felled trees and wet soil. She barely ate, even when Orpheus walked to Thrace to bring back her favorite honey candies. She slept most of the day, conserving her energy to wander the halls at night. Orpheus sometimes woke to see her wraithlike shadow slinking by his room.

The only thing that seemed to bring her joy was the garden. They spent their evenings there, roaming amongst violet anemones and sea daffodils, white-trunked fig trees and vines sagging with clusters of dark grapes. They drank wine and listened to the chittering of birds. Sometimes, Orpheus would play his lyre. When he did, he would catch Eurydice drumming her fingers against her leg or humming low in the back of her throat.

It was on an evening such as this Orpheus said, gesturing at the garden, "You grew all of this with your own hands." His limbs were pleasantly heavy from the wine.

Eurydice looked at him. Her eyes, once brown, were the pale, pink color of underripe fruit.

"I wish I could remember." She grimaced as she spoke, as if the words themselves caused her pain.

"So do I," Orpheus said. "But there's soil to spare. Why not plant something new?" He plucked a sprig of myrtle, bursting with white, star-like blooms, and held it out to her. In the amber light of evening, cloistered away in a dark corner of the garden, Orpheus was reminded of their wedding day and of those last, fateful moments before Eurydice had been spirited off to the realm of the dead. "Dance with me," she'd said. He should have. No, he *should* have carried her inside and kissed her until all thoughts of dancing were stripped from her mind.

When Eurydice took the flower from him, a small smile played on her lips. She let her hand linger on his and where their fingers touched, Orpheus felt himself burning, like a flame had been kindled just under his skin. He leaned forward, inhaling that sickly sweet scent. He wanted to drown himself in it.

Eurydice gasped. "Wait, wait!" She cried. She lept away from him and Orpheus felt suddenly cold, all the way down to his bones. Already, he was cursing himself. *Too much. Too soon. Not patient enough. Idiot.*

"Eurydice—" his voice was still so heavy with longing he nearly choked on her name.

She held the myrtle sprig in front of her like a ward, and only then did Orpheus realize it wasn't *him* she was afraid of. The buds were curling, blackened as if held over an open flame. The stem grew shriveled and rotten where her fingers touched it. A single, crumpled leaf, gray with mold, peeled away and floated slowly, slowly to the ground. Orpheus looked down at his hand, where Eurydice had touched him. His knuckles were a brilliant, painful red. A few of his nails had grown purpled and bruised.

"*Eurydice*," he said again.

There were tears in her eyes, thick and murky as bog water.

"You should never have brought me back," she whispered, and then she fled into the house. Orpheus was left alone to wonder, maybe, if she was right.

His hand pained him well into the night, as if a spider had bitten him right in that vulnerable spot between thumb and forefinger. The throbbing kept him awake, so when he saw Eurydice standing in the hallway, a slightly darker shape in the already pervading darkness, he called, "Come here."

She stood at the foot of the bed, beautiful and terrible. Unbidden, a memory crept to the forefront of his mind. Before he had descended into the Underworld, Apollo had asked him: "Is it wise to tamper with the Fates?"

"I love her," had been his answer. And though death and the venom in her veins had left her strange, perhaps even monstrous, he loved her still. He told her so now, breathing the words into the darkness.

Eurydice sat beside him. Even in the dark, he could feel her eyes roving over his hand, trying to assess the damage. "Something is wrong with me," she said, finally.

"Nothing is wrong with you," he argued.

"I hurt you."

"Then, I'll return to Hades," Orpheus insisted. "Surely, he can cure you." Even as he said it, he knew it was a lie. Persephone's words echoed in his mind. *She will not be as she was.*

"I'm sorry, Orpheus." It was the first time Eurydice had said his name since she'd died, and both of them knew what it meant. What cruelty it was, that the Fates had twisted their very souls together while conspiring to keep them apart.

"Please don't go," Orpheus said. He reached for her then, pressing his swollen fingers to her cheek and pulling her to him. She tasted like life and death. Like honey and shadows. It hurt to touch her, but he did it anyway. He was burning again, skin crackling, peeling, breaking apart and birthing something new.

In the morning, Eurydice was gone. He thought he remembered her lips on his feverish forehead, a whispered, "I love you," but memory was such a fragile thing. He might have convinced himself it was a dream, if not for the sharp ache of venom in his veins and the note in the garden that read, *We'll be together on the other side. Please care for the garden in my absence.*

～

Persephone was happy to see Eurydice again, though a little unsure of what to do with her. Having been resurrected, she was neither alive nor dead. In that way, she was much like the queen herself—taken too soon, forced to live a half-life between worlds, belonging to neither one nor the other. Besides that, they were nymphs. They should have lived forever, tending to vines and trees and brambles and other wild things. Yet here they were, two flowers cast underground, without light, without sustenance.

Still, the two of them were able to cultivate life, even in the realm of the dead. The soil was surprisingly fertile, perhaps from all the bonemeal and humus, and together, they tended a garden of wild hemlock, star-leafed castor bean, and nightshade dripping with dark, lustrous berries, of delicate, sweet-scented oleander and wolfsbane with blooms thin as paper—all those toxic things shunned by the above world found a home far below, where they could be admired, loved even, without risk to life or limb.

Eurydice was happy there, where nothing crumbled and died at her touch. She tended her new garden below, while Orpheus tended to the old one above. Someday, she would show him the blooms proudly and say, "I grew this with my own hands." Until then, she was in no hurry.

As for Orpheus, his lips were always a little too cold, his fingers numb where he had touched her. It reminded him, even decades later, that she had been real.

29

THE DEADLIEST POISON

BY JENIFER DALE

*M*any people have fought to discover the deadliest poison, never realizing that it is all around them. Words have the power to infiltrate your mind, sink deep within the recesses of your heart and take time away from your life that should be spent in enjoyment and happiness. That whisper in the dark from years past that makes your heart seize and makes you gasp for air when no one is there. The voice that shouts at you not to eat that cookie or wear that shirt because it will cause you to look imperfect or send a message to people who will hurt you further. Each word stinging as it lets you know that the people around you don't think that you are good enough the way that you are. What occurs then is that you begin to feel bad about yourself, begin to believe it, and it affects your entire life.

No place was safe for me to go. No matter where I went, I heard the poisonous words dripping from their tongues like acid and finding refuge in a mind that was already overwhelmed—fat, freak, demon. So much was placed on how I looked. A skin condition has let people think that they have the freedom to say whatever they will. I've never understood the mindset behind why people believe they have free reign in this manner. Each day I was faced with more words that

THE DEADLIEST POISON

couldn't be taken away, and understanding was never at the forefront. One thing that I had wished for deeply was kindness—one moment of kindness from any source. I never got it, but I believe it would have made a difference for me. It would have made the ugly words more bearable and given me a way to ignore the hatred, even if it was only for a moment. To this day, I believe that one act of kindness can make such a difference to people, and if others like me had had someone care about them, for one moment, we wouldn't have to feel so alone.

It is easy to laugh now when a child tells me that they are glad their face doesn't look like mine because it's so ugly, but while it is easy to laugh, it breaks my heart, and no one should have to pretend it doesn't hurt you when someone says something like this. We should be teaching our next generation to love and accept people who look different instead of showing them that it is alright to hurt people. It saddens me that I have heard people tell me that they shouldn't be exposed to my face and the way I look. I cannot change how I look, but people refuse to change their toxic behavior. I've been told to cover my face, wear gloves and long sleeves. Asked why I can't wear makeup like other people. Upon receiving an explanation, understanding never came. Instead, I would be told to dye my hair to make the condition less noticeable.

Once again, the focus was on changing the way I looked and enforcing the idea that I was not good enough the way I was. While I could freely admit there were things about myself I didn't like, there were many features about my face that I did like. Including the eyes that were covered with this 'sickening issue.' When words about my shape, look, or size wouldn't work, the speech became crueler, taunting my mind, my compassion, and indeed my very character. I had always thought of myself as a kind person who would go above and beyond for other people, and having that called into question threw me for a loop. I wished not for the first time that I could stand up for myself and move past the words, but unable to figure out how to do so.

You wonder why I don't like being home or going to school, why years later, I still wake up in the middle of the night hoping I will be strong enough to scare the words away and feeling victory when I can because that indeed is what it is. Many wonder why people simply don't ignore the words that people spew. If you just ignore it, it won't affect you, right? The problem with that thinking is that it can be challenging to ignore the words thrown at you daily. Unfortunately, we ignore the comments, and it still affects us. The poison still drips, but people can move past it through strength.

It takes a quiet strength to fight a poison that never sleeps, never stops, and reaches deeper than anything else that has hurt you, but that's just it. It wants to hurt you and make you weak. Tear you down little by little until you don't know who you are or what you are doing. The truth, however, is that you will never feel weaker than those who torment you. They live in their own personal Hell, wondering the exact same thing you do. Why do we do what we do? The answer is that they have been poisoned too.

I contemplated this one morning as I walked to class, hearing snickers behind me and shoves when I didn't move fast enough for someone's liking. That I was used to. Saying nothing and simply continuing on my way, ignoring what I heard and pretending it hadn't already gotten inside my mind. My behavior clearly showed how uncomfortable I was. I never looked up in the halls and spent my first year in high school avoiding the cafeteria like the plague, choosing instead to eat in a classroom hallway while it was empty.

There were more important things to consider than ugly words or ugly minds, and I would actively try to ignore the comments as much as I could, but I found that I still struggled with people being so cruel. Reminding myself that things wouldn't be like this one day, I pushed forward each passing day. No one knew my story or my pain. They called me names without getting to know me or what I was about, so it was no wonder they didn't feel remorse. Looking back, I knew that some didn't care, even then. That was what separated me from them. I had always cared about those around me, and when I didn't act the way I should have, I regretted it and wished I could have taken back my ugly words even though I knew I couldn't.

While class time was supposed to be peaceful, I didn't manage to escape there either. A class intended to bring me out of my shy nature and build friendships turned into cruel taunting and more poison being released into a heart that needed to breathe. Our class would play a game where you ask questions to each other. Each time I got paired with someone, they would ask rude questions such as why I was so ugly. Silently, I would stare at the teacher, the one or two people in the class that were kind to me, and plead. Why won't you help me? Isn't this what friends do? As an educator, isn't it your job to protect those in your class from being abused? To my shock and abject horror, the teacher instead decided to laugh and let it continue as I feebly attempted to defend myself as the class behind me watched in silence. They had seen me glance over at the teacher silently asking for help, yet no one said anything. While I didn't blame my friends, I did wonder about the integrity of the educator.

The questions would then get steadily worse. They would ask why I was stupid, poor (as I must have been because of my clothes), why my parents hated me so much, and other questions meant to tear me down. Finally, at my raised voice and hearing me say something mean, I turned to see rolled eyes, and a stern voice called out that enough was enough, but the voice had a teasing edge that let me know that under the seriousness, there was no compassion or empathy at all. The game wasn't stopping because of the cruelty, which hurt more than anything else.

Questions of my own began flooding my mind at once as I attempted to grasp the situation. Was it enough because I had failed to keep the entertainment going? Did it become less fun when you realized one of your students was about to cry? Or maybe it was because I had lost my temper and stooped to their level? Would it not have been enough when the taunting started? Before people saw the true nature of what was happening? A teenager unable to defend herself, being tossed into a viper's nest with people burning her from the inside out? What made the tormentors more worthy of help? Then I wondered something else. Did a teacher care so little for her students and their emotional and mental well-being that they would sit back and do nothing while this occurred and instead take pleasure in it?

Throughout the entire ordeal, it was clear that she hadn't thought anything about what was taking place, and when students had laughed, I had turned to see her smiling. It broke my heart because she should have said something on my behalf and the behalf of the student that I had insulted. The students shouldn't have said anything mean, but I shouldn't have said anything rude either.

An accident that should have been a warning sign that I was drowning. Instead, more cruel words were to be my only reward. Instead of hearing the kind words of someone who loves me, I was asked about the cost of medical treatment, why I was stupid, how I was hurting my family. Screaming and yelling were what I received, and while I honestly felt that I had deserved it, it broke my heart because I began to feel that I was the poison hurting people. I looked away, apologizing for my faults and ruining everything, while inside, I cried silently, screaming. Shouldn't someone want to help me?

Shouldn't someone recognize that the poison is hurting me, changing me? Alas, that wasn't in my future—only looks of disgust and contempt. Only years later, when I took the initiative to apologize for ruining the lives of everyone around me, did I hear praise and see the relationships around me become better. I was suddenly mature, sweet, and kind. I had changed my future outlook, and while it hurt that I didn't get an apology in return, at least I was erasing damage and attempting to make the future better.The pain was still there, and to this day, it remains, but I work hard not to let it overwhelm me.

In many cases, people may not have deserved an apology, but they did in just as many cases. Either way, I wanted to take the initiative to change my life for the better and bring back the person that I liked and wanted to be. Even now, I may not be there, but I'm so much closer now that I've started to fight against a poison that would have each day ending in tears.

My future was essential because I wanted it to be different from my past.That was the turning point for me; I realized that I cared more about losing myself and becoming someone I hated than about paying attention to what people said and letting it affect me. Where I once was kind, I had been cruel. I found myself saying mean things to other people and breaking them down as I had been. Each day passed with me disliking myself more and more. I didn't want to be mean to people. The thing about poison is it eats at you slowly. You feel it first and realize the effects afterward. I had made the mistake of thinking it would only affect me. I was wrong. As I hurt, what was already breaking me began to damage others.

Unkindness has never been something that I had been about. But I had been becoming that way slowly over time. Rightfully so, my attitude cost me friends, damaged the relationships I had tried so hard to form, and ended up losing one of the best friends I had ever had. From that day to this, I wish that I had fought against the pain and poison that had infected me and hoped that I had the opportunity to apologize to the people that I hurt. There was no excuse to be unkind to people. Looking back and remembering the tears that I had caused would make me burst into tears because I had hurt people who didn't deserve it and let myself become the very thing that made me cry and avoid people everywhere I went. The realization made me sick to my stomach.

I grew sadder by the day because I realized that I was letting the people who had hurt me affect how I was treating others. However, I knew that that wasn't entirely fair to say. My behavior was my fault, and I knew that I had to take responsibility for it. While I managed to repair many of my relationships by apologizing, some I couldn't reach anymore and wondered many years after crying if I had ruined their lives with my unkind words. It haunts me to this day, and I wish upon wish that I had never been unkind to anyone.

Words are the pain that finds you when you are alone, simply trying to make it through the day. Laughter, taunting, bullying. Causing tears and hope to fade as you grow older or jaded. Every poison has an antidote, but this one takes years to find. Like the poison itself, the cure is right where many people won't look.

The truth is that it took me a long time to figure out the antidote to the poison was me.

There comes a point where you realize that their words have nothing to do with you and everything to do with them. The words still hurt. They will still slice into you and cause you pain. What changes is how you deal with that poison.

Another turning point for most people is that they have had enough, don't want to take it anymore, and shouldn't have to.

I realized that I was worth something and didn't want to be like the people who were being so mean. That is the hardest part of fighting the poison. The words make you feel like you aren't, and you need to remember that they are nothing but lies because you are worth everything. The reason that these people say unkind things to you is that they have been hurt. Hurt people will hurt others to mask their pain, or for some, as a coping mechanism. While there are many reasons behind this behavior, you need to remember that you don't deserve it and fight against the poison.

The hardest thing in the world is to fight the way people have made you feel your entire life. That is especially true when you have heard these unkind words every day. It starts one day at a time, and slowly you will find that you begin to heal in a healthy manner. Bullies will never stop or take back the nasty words said, but you can become stronger. Tell yourself every day that you are worth something and never forget that there is no one in this world like you. You need to do this so that you can love yourself the way you deserve and use your inner strength. No one deserves to have petty words seep into their soul.

While many people find that the words stay with them years later, knowing who you are and having respect and love for yourself helps you fight those words that are sinking into your heart and mind. It seems contrived to say that loving yourself is all you have to do to fight an issue this strong, but when I realized what I was becoming, I realized that I wanted to like myself instead of hating myself, which changed the tide for me. I didn't want to look at myself for the longest time because of what people had told me, but when I took a long look at myself, I realized some truths about myself that I needed to know.

Despite my family pressuring me to be perfect and using slurs and horrendous language to make me hate myself and my body, I found that, in all honesty, I didn't look so bad. Did I think I was the prettiest girl in the world? Not at all. I was overweight, like they said, but I wasn't a cow. I could lose the weight, but they would be stuck with their personalities. I wasn't perfect either, and after taking a genuine look inside myself, I realized I didn't want to be. My face may be disfigured, and there may be many things about me that other people didn't like, but I didn't want to let the words kill me anymore. Instead, I wanted to like myself and become someone that I could enjoy. If I couldn't do this completely, at least I knew I was trying. After spending so much of my life crying and being unhappy because of others, I wanted to learn how to love myself wholly and truly.

Poison is deadly but remember this: For every poison, there is an antidote. Even if it hasn't been discovered yet, it will be. It may take time to undo the damage, but it can be done over time. The trick to remember is that you should never give up on yourself and because you are an amazing person who deserves to be loved. It may be hard to convince yourself of this, because the bad things that people say are easier to believe. But you should remember that isn't true. The words have no meaning and you need to keep that knowledge with you. The people are only saying horrible things to hurt you and while it does work because the words seep in, remember that the hatred they are spewing isn't true. If someone says that you are ugly, know that you have a true beauty that shines from the inside and out. If you give up and let their words poison you, you let them win and take away your happiness as I did. No one deserves that. Everyone around you has the blessing of being near you. Love yourself, let your spirit shine and always remember that even the deadliest of poisons has a cure. Mine was me, and yours will be you.

30

DEATH CAP

BY DANNIE KINARD

*M*ira's hands bleed, bright red blood beading up through the gashes that paint the backs of her porcelain fingers. Her hands tremble as she holds them out in front of her. Tears are brimming in her eyes, eyes the color of morning fog. An old man looms over her with a slender hazel switch. A cruel, brown whip cut from the hazel tree outside his hut that morning—a hut cloistered from the rest of their village at the edge of a dark, sullen wood. Mira was made to strip off the downy catkins that dangled from the switch herself knowing that it would draw her blood. She doesn't look up to meet the man's gaze. She doesn't want to see the dark, bruise-like circles around his eyes that cause the whites to glow, nor does she want to look upon his scraggly, smoke-stained beard or liver-spotted skin. Besides, there's nothing more to say. Her throat is raw from apologizing and she knows talking more will only stoke his anger.

"Stare at them until you know the difference, stupid girl," he hisses.

He uses one bony hand to clutch a handful of her long fine hair, hair the color of dark loamy earth, and he yanks her head back. The brass rings braided into a slender stripe of her hair jangle as she squeezes her eyes closed, breath hissing through clenched teeth. He forces her head down so she is made to look at the mushrooms strewn across the table. Her face is so close that her nose brushes one of the mushroom caps and she can see every pockmark, scar, and stain decorating the old potion-making table. He releases her and takes his marled wood pipe freshly packed with mugwort and stalks off to a chair heaped with furs in the corner of the room, muttering curses.

Mira looks at fractal mushrooms through rheumy eyes and then drags a linen sleeve over her face clearing her vision. The mushrooms are all so similar—white caps dusted with olive green. White gills, slender stalks. She thought they were the same variety. But she knows now that there is at least one crucial difference according to Oleg— one is an ingredient in his daily health potion and the other would have silently shut down his organs and killed him in a matter of days.

She brushes her fingers over their smooth, silky tops until she notices that some of them, the deadly ones, have a large bulb at the bottom. She remembers her father had once called it a volva when he took her out foraging when she was younger, the explanation doled out in his slow, steady way back when she was his little wild rabbit. The coloring in those is slightly different too, the olive hue a shade or two darker. She bends the stalk of this mushroom and it breaks softly, unevenly. She bends the other and it snaps like chalk. She knows the difference now and she will not soon forget.

"I'll kill him," Arsen says in a low voice almost resembling a growl.

He has one arm slung over Mira's shoulders and he uses his free hand to softly hold one of hers, gently smoothing his fingers over the cuts as though he could erase them. They are standing in line for drinks at the mead hall. The building is large but simple with wooden rafters and rows of long, rough-hewn tables, scarred from years of heavy use. Large hearths roar at opposite ends of the hall and vines with colorful flowers are painted over the ceilings and walls. Their local mead-maker stands against one wall with large casks behind him, dispensing sweet amber *medovukha* into wood-fired mugs. Next to him, carts are lined up selling all manner of food. Spice cakes, kasha drizzled in honey, fresh figs, and roasted quail. The hall is loud and bustling with the evening crowd. Folks shrugging out of their cloaks and sheepskin coats, and woolen hats with thick fur brims. The married women leave their head wraps on, the bands of colorful embroidered cloth wrapped around the forehead adorned with large rings that hang over the temples, similar to the rings braided into Mira's hair. Rings with seven points are common here in the western region of Ravgorod where the Volrichi tribe settled years ago—though the distinction has become less important since being united under the current Grand Prince.

Mira looks up at Arsen, meeting his pale green eyes, the color of grass dusted with early morning frost. His brows are pinched together and his expression is dark. She reaches up to stroke his ash brown hair and she gives a half-smile.

"Maybe I'll kill him," she jokes.

"I'm serious, Mira," he says. "You're going to leave me with no other choice if you keep going back there. He's treating you like a dog, not an apprentice."

Mira feels a pang in her stomach, her already ghostly complexion paling against the deep brown of her hair. She knows it's true, but she blames herself. She knows what kind of animal Oleg is. He's like so many of the men here in Stashka. Brutish, but easy to figure out when it came down to it. The mix up with the mushrooms was a huge misstep, but she can play the game better. She knows she can. She can't say any of that to Arsen though. Not without worrying him more.

"Who else would teach me, Arsen? As long as he's the only other wizard in Stashka, he's my only option. Besides, he has all the books, all the ingredients, and no heirs. You saw my dowry. Inheriting his practice is my only chance to have my own. He said it would be mine. Think of the time and money it would save us when we start our life together. I can endure a typical Stashkan man for a few years for this."

Mira lightly toys with the yarn wrapped around his ring finger. The makeshift ring that serves as a promise.

"I don't like it, Mira."

"It's not forever."

"What's not forever?" says a girl with deep auburn hair and freckles dusting her cheeks as she sidles up to Mira's right side. It's Pasha, her oldest friend.

Arsen barely turns.

"Oleg," he says, his voice as heavy as lead.

"That crotchety bastard?" comes another voice. It's their friend Pavel. He's bounding toward them with bright eyes. The only person in Stashka that doesn't seem affected by the bitter cold sweeping over the village. Pasha gave him the nickname 'the stray' because none of them could remember formally meeting him. He just started following them around one day.

Pavel ropes an arm around Arsen, standing half a head taller than him, and runs his fingers through his dark blond hair which stubbornly strikes out in all directions.

"He's not dead yet?" he adds.

"Well, that's what we were talking about," says Mira, taking a mug brimming with *medovukha* from the mead-maker and handing him one copper *grivna*. "Helping that process along." She winks at Pavel conspiratorially, but Arsen flashes his eyes at her clearly not ready to make light of it.

Pavel doesn't notice. Instead he perks up, glassy blue eyes widening.

"Well, that's got our names written all over it, right Ar?"

"Why, because you're men?" Pasha scoffs, flicking her auburn hair over her shoulder.

"Pasha's right. Why should you have all the fun?" says Mira as they walk to the less populated end of the hall, arms laden with mead.

"I'll tell you why," says Pavel. "Two words. Baba Enok."

Pasha snorts with laughter and covers her mouth.

"You mean like the fairy tales?"

"Exactly like the fairy tales."

Arsen shifts just slightly and Pavel's eyes dart toward him, honing in on his discomfort.

"You haven't heard of her, have you?" he asks with a grin, a delighted glint in his eyes.

"His parents had better sense than to teach him ridiculous fairy stories," Mira says, but that's not entirely true. The truth is his mother was sick throughout most of his childhood before succumbing to her illness and their house was devoid of the fun childish things that most Stashkan children experienced.

"That gives me the pleasure of explaining then," Pavel says lacing his fingers together and pushing his palms outward, cracking his knuckles as they sit down on wooden benches with their mugs. "And to begin, I'll start with the tale of Kiska Barabanov."

"Kiska Barabanov?" says Pasha, scrunching her forehead.

"That name sounds familiar," says Mira.

"She lived a few houses over from me," says Arsen. "She went missing. I remember the search party. Everyone gathering in the square at night, the orange glow of the torches. I was only seven then. I never knew why."

Mira pictured a lonely, young Arsen staring out the window of his hut, the commotion of the search party outside a bleak but exciting break from waiting on his mother and dispensing her usual concoction of mullein—the only meager treatment Oleg would afford their family for the consumption ravaging her body.

"Well, I'll tell you why," says Pavel. "It's said that Kiska Barabanov was the village beauty. She had hair like golden oats."

"Golden oats?" Pasha snorts.

"Shhh, you," says Pavel, "it's my story. Yes, she had hair like golden oats..or..beaten gold..and skin as soft as a new petal. Suitors lined up around the block for the chance to wed her and bed her." Pasha rolls her eyes. "And one day a rich trader from Kesh comes. He is roguishly handsome and money is spilling out of his silk pockets and Kiska and her family knows he is the one. So they marry in a lovely little ceremony on the hill. Kiska's golden hair is done up with an elaborate headdress, a beautiful jeweled *kokoshnik* with strings of pearls hanging down. The wedding is the talk of the village for, as small as it is, no expense is spared. They have a few blissful months together, but then the trader gets mean. Starts hitting poor Kiska. She holds on for a few years, believes him when he says he'll stop. But after one particularly bad beating she breaks. She decides she'll leave, start a new life in a different village where the trader can't find her.

"She packs her bags one night when the trader is out drinking at this very hall. But when she goes to leave, the trader is waiting there in the doorway, swaying and slurring having returned early. The sickly, sweet smell of *modovukha* is issuing from his mouth as he yells obscenities at her. She tries to push past him, but he gets violent. He gets in a few hits and lays Kiska out on the dusty floor of their hut, her lip bleeding, but when he goes in for another hit she spins around on the floor with a fire iron. The trader loses his balance and falls onto it. Blood spills out of him covering Kiska and the floor of their hut. Kiska scrambles up, eyes wide in horror, and grabs her bags. She is even more eager to leave and hastily makes her way to the woods. It is dark, but she dares not take the beaten path when she's soaked in her dead husband's blood.

"She uses the moonlight to guide her when she hears the light tinkling of a bell ring out in the empty wood. The sound comes out of nowhere and fills her with fear. She turns around to find the source, but she cannot find it, so she continues on when she comes across a strange tree. As she nears the tree it uncurls from itself and she sees that it's not actually a tree at all but an old woman with crackled skin like tree bark and long spindly fingers like gnarled old branches. Her eyes are big. Too big. And glowing like lanterns. The tree woman is smiling curiously at her and seems to be waiting for something. Kiska moves to the right to get past her, but the old hag mirrors her, shuffling in the same direction. Kiska steps to the left and she mirrors her again. Kiska's heart is drumming in her chest now and her palms are sweating. She takes one step back and for a moment the hag doesn't move, but then she takes one step toward her, causing Kiska's chest to pound. Her grin is even wider and she is wheezing with excitement. Kiska is terrified. Her chest tightening, pulse hammering visibly beneath her skin. She decides to take another step back. She is relieved when the woman doesn't step toward her. She decides she will turn and run as fast as she can. But all at once the hag barrels toward her with inhuman speed, wheezing and cackling with delight, her jaw unhinging revealing a cavernous mouth. Kiska tries to run, but trips over a root and collapses onto the damp forest floor. That's when the hag descends on her. That's when she eats her up in one swallow."

Mira, Arsen, and Pasha are all staring at Pavel in silence, slowly rediscovering their breath.

"What was the bell about?" Arsen asks.

Pavel shrugs. "Some say the Baba Enok uses it to entice her victims. Others say it's the spirits of other wayward women she's taken trying to warn her new victims."

There is a sense of stillness as they all stare in their mugs, thinking. You can only hear the whisper of their breaths when the tinkling of a bell cuts through the stillness.

They all look up at each other in wide-eyed disbelief and swivel their heads around. That's when they hear it.

"Hot pies!" grumbles a bearded, bear of a man. "Hot pies for purchase!" He is holding up a small brass bell and he rings it again, the light ringing trailing through air as he pushes a rickety wooden cart through the mead hall.

The tension melts from their shoulders as they turn back toward each other and when their eyes meet they erupt in a fit of laughter. Mira is laughing so hard tears form in her eyes, washing away the tears of pain from earlier. She looks at Arsen—at his deep dimples, at the curve of his jaw. His crooked smile that seems impossibly beautiful because of his loss. She thinks that she is lucky she doesn't have to marry a man like the trader, a man like Oleg.

"So how much of that story was true?" Pasha asks, wiping the tears from her own eyes.

"Well, I know that the trader was found dead and Kiska went missing."

"And everything about the Baba Enok?"

"My grandmother swears it was the Baba Enok. Swears she heard the bells that night. I filled in the rest." He winks.

"I honestly worry about you," says Pasha shaking her head, but she secretly smiles into her mug and Mira knows it's because, for all her teasing, she can't help but like Pavel and all his eccentricities. Even if she'd never say it.

"You're not going to leave us for Kazgrad are you? Have your stories published at one of those new printing houses? Produce plays for the Grand Prince?" Arsen asks.

"I don't know why I would," says Pavel. "I have my best audience right here."

They are all hanging on each other laughing in their warm mead cocoons when they leave the hall. The sky is the deepest black, all the scattered stars having been plucked out of the sky and shut away somewhere secret. The only light comes from the flickering lamps lining the streets casting a hazy glow.

"I'll walk the stray home," says Pasha, but she's so drunk she doesn't bother to cloak her words in annoyance. Instead she looks up at Pavel with moony eyes, takes his hand, and pulls him along behind her as he blushes dopily.

Mira and Arsen exchange knowing grins and then Arsen reaches for Mira's hand. She flinches and he looks down at the cuts, remembering, and scowls.

"I'm not okay with this, Mira." He doesn't sound angry. Instead there is a note of desperation in his voice.

"There are two things I want, Arsen. Just two," she says softly. "You and a magic practice that means something. We don't have the money to start from scratch. The books he has each cost a small fortune. Oleg said as long as I do as told, the practice will be mine. Can you think of a better option?"

"Anything would be better than this," says Arsen turning toward her, eyes darkened. They are standing by a lamp post next to delicately latticed wooden buildings and yet his words are the opposite of delicate, they are as heavy and cold as iron. "I will kill him if he does it again."

Mira doesn't press it. Instead she reaches her hand toward the lamp and mutters some words under her breath. She coaxes a ball of light toward her and then cups both her hands around it. When she opens it back up there is a delicate flower made of light. A peony. His mother's favorite.

"That's unfair," he says.

"It's unfair that more wasn't done to save her. It's unfair that her one hope was an uncaring old bastard. We can change things."

Arsen releases a deep sigh.

"I stand by what I said. If he hurts you again…"

"I know."

"But if this is what you want, I'm not going to stop you."

Mira's face brightens. Arsen is leaning against the lamp, orange wool hat pulled low over his his brow. He snuggles into his coat and Mira looks up at him expectantly with her big pale eyes. Arsen opens his coat and wraps her into it with him. She is still holding the flower of light, pressing her cupped hands to Arsen's chest, the glow warm upon their faces. A smile dances onto Mira's face as she stares into the flame and Arsen visibly softens.

Mira stands on the tips of her toes, she plants kisses up his neck and the hard line of his jaw. She looks Arsen in the eyes and he takes his hands and cups her head, fingers laced through her long, dark hair, and he pulls her face to his. Mira lets the flower fall away, the flame hissing out when it hits the cold earth. The night is silent. Tiny white specks are drifting down against the black sky. And somewhere in the still night, the Baba Enok is opening her eyes.

Motes of dust swirl around in the pale golden light flooding in through the small window at the back of Oleg's wooden hut. Leather-bound tomes of every earthy tone are lined up neatly on shelves. The scarred wooden table is cleared off and bottles of potions and raw ingredients are organized in tidy rows in the cabinet, the dried herbs hanging neatly from the rafters in carefully tied bundles. Sprays of mugwort, stinging nettle, crier-weed, wormwood, and more.

Mira's arms ache, but it had not been an entirely bad morning. The cleaning had given her a chance to sift through Oleg's collection, mentally cataloging all his magical items and rare texts. All things that would one day be hers. And, while he was out washing, Mira stole glances at books he'd forbidden her to read and scratched out several spells on a leaf of birchbark to try when she is back home.

Mira stands with one hand on her hip, looking satisfied, and wipes the beads of sweat from her forehead with the back of her other hand while still clutching a dirty rag. Her hair is pulled back in a disheveled bun, wisps of hair springing out at random, some of it spilling down her back. She is trying to think of something else she can do when Oleg hobbles into the doorway. He is drying his face with a rag and tosses it carelessly in the corner grumbling something to himself. For all the washing, his hair is no less yellow. Mira watches as he looks up from beneath his bushy brows. She sees a pause in his gait, the flicker of surprise in his old, milky eyes. He likes what he sees. The hut in order. Mira is pleased too. She knows some old men just need softening. She's playing the game well.

"Get the basket," grumbles Oleg.

A thrill rushes through Mira, which turns to a gentle hum of excitement. This is what she wanted. Why she took extra care cleaning the hut. A trip to the market. She grabs the basket and ropes it onto her arm and then quickly helps Oleg into his thick fur coat and grabs him his staff before he can start grumbling. They step out in the sunlight and start on the dirt path that leads over the hill to the market. It is warmer than usual today, the snow from last night quickly melting into dirty brown puddles. Mira walks beside Oleg, but she yearns to run ahead over the hill. To see what she longs to see.

When they do finally crest the hill, the image that fills her vision is more magnificent than she anticipated. An entourage of men and women in long creamy white woolen *svitas*, toggled at the chest and embroidered in gold, are trotting into the village square on their white horses, tails flicking. Rays of golden sunlight break onto them from between the clouds. Two banner-men follow behind them with white flags, golden suns pasted on them. These are the *druzhina*. The Grand Prince's very own retinue of wizards, made up of his closest advisors. A handful of them tour the country every year performing their miracles in his name, but this is their first time in sleepy old Stashka.

Mira can hear the excited chatter as they descend the hill into the square. Villagers are buzzing about, some of them crowding in around the *druzhina* while they dismount their horses. Oleg, who was busy groaning about his joints a moment ago, finally looks up. He pauses, shifting around, and his expression morphs to one of displeasure, his nose scrunching up like he's smelled something rotten.

"Cattle," he spits. "We'll go tomorrow," he says, beginning to turn.

Mira's heart sinks into her stomach like a heavy stone. She has dreamed her whole life of seeing the *druzhina*, the heroes of the realm. She grew up the only witch in her village with no one of her kind except an ornery old man while she heard tales of their camaraderie in battle, brothers and sisters in magic. She is filled with a sudden pang of longing, followed by a chaotic energy. She has to change his mind. Her mind whirs, fumbling for a way.

"We're out of mugwort," she says finally, trying to keep her tone even. She hopes that Oleg doesn't catch the note of desperation in her voice. She prays that he doesn't get angry because she spoke out of turn. She's gotten the switch for less.

Oleg juts out his chin and scratches his beard, thinking. Mugwort is his favorite herb. In non-magic people it merely induces dreams, but in wizards it gets them high and sends them visions. According to some texts, that is. From what Mira could tell it just gave Oleg a vacant stare and an even fouler demeanor. Mira hopes he won't pass up the opportunity to get more, though she knows she'll likely pay for it later.

"Fine, then what are you standing around like a gaping fish for?" he barks, shooing her on.

The tension that knotted in Mira's shoulders releases, the corners of her rosy lips pulling up, and she continues on into the square. It's lined with latticed wooden buildings, some of them residences and others shops with hanging signs that jut out perpendicularly, their paint faded and peeling. The church looms up at the top of the square.

It's plain and wooden like the rest of the buildings in their small village, but its tower is capped with a tin dome and perched atop it is the heavenly eye with lines radiating out like beams of light. On the side of the church is a large painting of Saint Agniya with a golden halo around her head. The icon Mira was born under. She came so fast into this world, her mother couldn't make it home from her grandmother's. She delivered Mira in the snow under Saint Agniya's watchful eye. Her mother swore it was the saint who made her a witch—her mother likes the new religion, the one god. One people under one eye. But mostly she likes that the missionaries from Lygos taught their people to read and that she no longer has to slaughter her best goat before harvest. Mira's father is of the opposite opinion. He said he doesn't trust a god that doesn't want blood and Mira often caught him whispering to the trees and sacrificing small animals.

Oleg is determined to avoid the crowd when they are in the square. The very place Mira wants to be. Thankfully she is able to catch snatches of the *druzhina* when heads part just right. She follows Oleg as he snakes his way through the market stalls, grumbling, haggling, and tossing things into the basket hooked in the crook of Mira's arm. She tries to look around as much as possible so Oleg doesn't catch her staring. She glances at baskets of plump berries, then back at the *druzhina*. She glances at wheels of cheese, then back at the *druzhina*. She grazes her eyes over barrels of grain, reams of cloth, swathes of leather, then back at the *druzhina*. What she catches in those short snatches is this: An old man is carted out from his shop in a wooden wheelchair, the tanner they call Fabi. A female *druzhinik* with high cheekbones and a white headwrap with gleaming gold temple rings and colorful glass bead bracelets approaches him slowly and raises a hand over his head. Mira's view is blocked for a moment as villagers crowd in to get a better look and the next thing she sees is Fabi walking around on two feet and smiling like a fool.

Mira manages to make it through the market without Oleg noticing her stealing glances. His chums are sitting outside a shabby hut near the end of one of the rows of stalls so he stops to talk to them. Sidor has thick black eyebrows and a stubbly face and Bogdan has a patchy grey beard and potbelly. Both of them smell of heavily fermented *braga*, and she can see the milky white drink dribbling down their chins.

Mira uses Oleg's distraction to watch the *druzhina* longer. They have all broken off and are talking to villagers separately—accepting their praise, performing smaller miracles. Mira aches to talk to them, but she knows it would enrage Oleg. Knows that he can't handle the thought of anyone more successful or powerful than he is. Mira can't take her eyes off the woman. The way she walks as if she owns the world. The way the air around her glitters and crackles with power. She's never seen anyone like her before. She seems like an impossible thing in this little village where daughters are too often traded for goats. For a moment she lets her excitement bubble up in her chest— this woman reminding her why she loved magic to begin with, showing her what she could be.

"What do you say girl?" says Oleg, his voice irritated. Mira startles at his words. She hadn't heard the original question and in her surprise the basket slips from her arm, the contents spilling out onto the ground.

"See, what'd I say? Kasha for brains," Oleg barks. Mira bends over to pick up the fallen herbs. "The girl would be better off as a whore than a witch," he continues.

Sidor leans in, propping his forearm on his thigh, to look her up and down.

"Eh, too thin for my taste," he grumbles. "But she's certainly ripe for the plucking. Her father would be wise to sell her."

"Yeh, I'd have a roll with her," says Bogdan licking his bottom lip.

Mira's body goes rigid, and her eyes form a hard, dark line as she continues picking up the fallen items. Bogdan and Sidor are chuckling breathily. She hears them whispering to themselves, the husky strained whispers of old men, and then she feels the hard underside of a boot on her rear. She barely has time to understand what is happening when she loses her balance, pitches forward, and finds herself chest down in a puddle. Sidor and Bogden are cackling, leaning forward in their chairs using their knees to keep them from

272

crumpling forward completely in their fits. Fits that turn into wheezing and coughing. Worse is Ogden who is baring his crowded yellow teeth and barely making any sound at all, eyes wild and chest convulsing, bony fingers choking his staff.

"And the bitch thinks I'll give her my practice," he rasps. He takes his staff and jabs her hard in the side of the ribs—hot, sharp pain blooming like fire deep within the bone.

In the moment or two Mira is staring into her murky brown reflection, a thousand emotions ripple across her face. White hot rage, disgust, but then something more peculiar, more uncomfortable. Shame, deep shame. But she can't place why.

Mira does not trust herself to speak. Her throat is tightening and she's afraid the sound that'll come out of her will be like that of a strangled animal. Wild and desperate and terrible. She pushes herself up unsteadily, dress pulling down with the weight of the water, a heavy, tight, uncomfortable feeling against her skin. Miry water is dripping off her as she picks up the bottom of her dress, trying to offset the weight.

Mira turns without a word, pale grey eyes set on the communal well situated in the shade of an alley between the blacksmith and the cobbler. Her cheeks burn and tears well up in her eyes, but she takes steady strides over the cobbles. Most of the villagers are too distracted by the *druzhina* in their bright, shiny coats to notice her, like fish drawn to a lure. Only a few sets of eyes follow her, obviously having seen what happened, but it doesn't stop her from feeling as if it were a thousand. In a small village a few eyes are enough. It will make it into the ear of every villager within days.

She is steadying herself on the cool stones of the well when the tears start to flow. She pulls the bucket up, hands clutched tightly around the rope as though it were the thread holding her together. She drags the wooden bucket up out of the well, scraping it against the stone, and rests it on the edge.

She doesn't notice the shadowy figure glide into the alleyway. Not until slender fingers wrap around her shoulder. Her heart drums in her chest as she whips around, clutching the pendant her mother had given her of Saint Agniya. Her eyes are wide as moons and streaming with tears like silver rivers. She is shocked to see the female *druzhinik* gazing upon her seriously. Crow's feet burst from her narrow eyes giving her away to be middle aged. She is undoubtedly beautiful, but not so much that anyone would dismiss her as only that. She has a serious air about her, a firmness. It is clear why. The air around her vibrates with power.

Mira hastily wipes her wet eyes with a clean sleeve, and as she bows down in a low curtsy she sees that it's just about the only clean part of her. Muddy water is soaked through the whole front of her linen dress, her red paneled skirt, her wool stockings, her shoes of hand-woven linden fiber. A tight, crackly feeling tells her it's already drying up her neck as well.

"Do you always let old men kick you around?"

Mira is caught off guard—her expression bewildered, her lips parting slightly in question.

"He's the only one who can teach me," she says finally, sniffling and dragging her hair behind her ear. "He's the only other wizard in Stashka."

The *druzhinik* waves her hand in the air as if swatting her words away like flies.

"I will tell you what I've told few people," she says gliding slowly around the well, brushing her fingertips over its lip. "I grew up in a small village such as this—a village filled with little men pretending they were giants. My own mentor beat me within an inch of my life because I dared question him. It was when I was on the ground, my mouth filling with blood, choking me, that he kneeled down over me, swiped a finger on my cheek, and then licked it. 'It's true what they say,' he laughed, 'a woman's tears are but water.' That's when I buried my knife in his skull." She absently reaches toward the knife on her belt as if remembering and then her eyes flick up at Mira. "There is disapproval in your brow, but hear this—men such as these take lives all the time. Not all at once. They scrape out your pulp little by little, hollow you out like a gourd, till there is nothing left. And they keep doing it, leaving empty, broken shells in their wake. And do you know why?"

Mira shakes her head slowly.

"Because no one stops them."

Mira's lips part to speak, but she doesn't know what to say. She doesn't have to say anything though. The *druzhinik* puts a hand on her shoulder and nods with a knowing glimmer in her eye, as if she knows Mira's pain exactly.

"Bow to no one and take what you want. They do," she says firmly.

With that the *druzhinik* turns, her *svita* whipping out behind her, and walks out of the alley. Two lesser *druzhiniks*, known as *scions*, fall in to step behind her and they all disappear into the sun.

Mira is left in the shadowy alley to think about her words, her tears dried up. All her sadness, her confusion. That feeling she felt earlier. The shame. She knows what it is now. She thought herself clever before. She thought dealing with men like Oleg was a game she could win. She thought that, as bad as men like Oleg were, deep down women like Kiska Barabanov were silly, thoughtless creatures who brought the abuse on themselves. That she was somehow above it. But she was wrong. So wrong. She sees what she has to do now, clear as a shallow pool.

She lifts the bucket from the edge of the well and pours it over the front of her dress letting the cold water run over her. Letting it wash away all the muck, the filth. She does it again one...twice...three times until the water runs clear, until the color of her embroidered linen dress is restored, until the deep red of her paneled wool skirt is vibrant again. She walks out of the alley into the sun, and behind her, something moves in shadows and the single chime of a bell rings out cold and clear.

"I didn't see you today," Arsen says.

Mira is sitting in the window of her hut wearing an unbleached linen nightgown, Arsen's red fur-collared coat slung over her shoulders. Her parents are at her aunts, drinking in celebration as a new calf rips into the world. Arsen is planting kisses up her arm, each spot blooming with heat. Each one making her want to pull his body against her own.

"Pasha and Pavel said they saw Oleg, but not you."

She is grateful for that. They would hear about it in time—what Oleg and his chums did. But not now. It would only make it harder to do what she has to do.

"He ordered me to stay at the hut," she lies.

"Ordered," he says, eyes darkening.

"I know," she says and she runs her fingers through his ash brown hair. He remembers what he was doing and starts kissing up her arm again, up to the delicate lines of her collarbone, up the curve of her neck. She doesn't want it to stop. She hears the words of the *druzhinik* echo in her head. *Bow to no one and take what you want. They do.*

She takes Arsen's fur hat and places it on her head. Then she gently drops down from the ledge, carefully closing the windows behind her. She is barefooted, but the cold doesn't bother her tonight.

"What are you doing?" he whispers.

"Seeing what it's like to be a man," she says looking over her shoulder, and then she takes his hand and leads him into the wood.

"I can't let you do this, Mira."

"Are you ordering me to stop?" Mira says, raising her brows.

"Never," Arsen says emphatically. "But Mira, if anyone saw…"

"They would what? Force us to marry sooner?"

She feels his resistance lessen, sees the protest die on his lips.

Twigs crackle and snap as they step through the forest. The flames from the lamps in the village turning into distant orange specks. They come upon a seat carved from the trunk of a tree, an old fir throne that existed long before they were born. Mira slides into its smooth seat and sits with her legs out wide, arms hooked lazily over the armrests carved with flowers and vines. Totems with unsettling faces stand in a circle around the throne, remnants of the old pagan religion.

Arsen is standing, watching her. She can see tension go in and out of his arms. She can see him clench his jaw. He is trying to work out why this is a bad idea, but Mira won't let him.

"Kneel, Arsen Orlov."

She sees who won the war inside him when he kneels dutifully at her feet. It wasn't reason. Mira extends a lazy hand to him.

"The ring," she says seriously, nodding to the yarn tied around her ring finger.

Arsen looks at her amused now and takes her hand in his. He presses his lips to the yarn.

"Is that all you require of me, Your Highness?"

"Here as well," she says slowly pulling her skirt up and pointing to the inside of her knee.

He presses his lips there, looking up at her. His gaze intense.

"Now here," she says pointing to the inside of her thigh.

Again, he obeys.

His breath is hot on her leg.

Each kiss makes her legs tremble as she slowly leads him up.

In the distance bells are ringing, and the forest holds its breath.

Mira has already beaten the dust from the rugs, emptied the chamber pot, washed and hung the linens. Tasks that are a far cry from the magic she should be doing. But she gets through them easily. And when Oleg takes a backhand to her when she knocks over a bottle of pig's blood, she hardly notices despite her own blood beading up on her lip. She feels an unusual power coursing through her. A gentle thrum. She is buoyed up by memories of last night in the silent wood when only the rhythmic whooshing of her breath could be heard. Arsen would be felling trees in this part of the forest today for a new build. She hears the slow creaking and groaning of splintering wood and then the crash of a tree hitting the forest floor now and she knows he must be close. She wonders if his thoughts are consumed by her. She wonders if he liked being ruled over. But she knows he does. That is the difference between Arsen and other Stashkan men. He can follow just as well as he can lead.

The fog is thick this morning, a hazy white blanket over the forest. Mira is picking her way through the wood, looking for mushrooms for Oleg's health potion. She is a good student. She did not forget her lesson from the other day. She picks the russula mushrooms, the ones without a volva, the ones that snap like chalk, and puts them in her basket. And when she comes across the death caps, she takes those too —tucking them away into the pocket of her apron.

When she enters the hut with her haul she is consumed by a cloud of thick, white smoke. The gentle earthy smell of mugwort filling her nose and lungs until she begins to cough, until she gets dizzy and has to steady herself on the table. She leaves the door open until some of the smoke clears, revealing Oleg sitting in his chair hunched over, clutching his pipe, eyes glazed over, focused on something Mira can't see.

After a moment he starts to blink and then he grumbles.

"Close the door, you brainless witch."

She does, but most of the smoke has already cleared out. Oleg seems to notice this as well and starts muttering curses.

"The selection was good today," says Mira, trying to redirect his energy.

"Well let's see then," he barks standing from his chair and she empties out the basket of russulas on the table in the center of the one-room hut. Oleg brushes his bony hands over them moving them this way and that.

"Hm, fine," he grunts. "Make the potion."

He picks up a book and sits back down with his pipe. A knot forms in the pit of her stomach as she slips a hand into the pocket of her apron and pulls out the three death caps, laying them before her on the table. She is sure her body is shielding the action, but her heart starts to drum when Oleg clears his throat. Her palms are dewy with sweat. Slowly, innocently, she looks over her shoulder at him.

"Yes?"

"Add more hawthorn this time," he grumbles.

Mira nods and directs her eyes back to the table. She squeezes her eyes shut for a moment and pulls in a deep breath, trying to regain her composure.

She mixes the death cap mushrooms in with the russulas and begins chopping them up with a cutting knife, dicing them up so finely they are indistinguishable from one another. The fear she felt just moments ago starts to morph into nervous excitement as it becomes more real. Oleg would be dead soon. Within days. She squeezes her necklace of Saint Agniya and mutters a prayer. Oleg is still puffing away on his pipe, the smoke issuing out in heavy plumes. Mira has to steady herself on the table for a moment. She closes her eyes, presses a few fingers to the center of her forehead. She feels lightheaded, her body slightly tingly. But she takes a breath and returns to her work.

Mira uses a hand to sweep the chopped mushrooms into a wooden bowl and then empties it into a cauldron hanging in the small stone hearth. She adds two handfuls of spindly hawthorn leaves and then some dried yarrow leaves, adder's tongue, blackberry, myrrh, and sheep sorrel. She stirs the mixture in the cauldron with a wooden ladle, the mingled scent of spice and wood, smoke and tart fruit, and the vague smell of musty forest floor wafting through the air.

She stirs for several minutes and then ladles the brew into a mug, letting it run over a square of cheesecloth. She pauses for a long moment, sucks in a deep breath, and then approaches Oleg with the brew. Every step feels like it takes a century, her feet heavy as logs. She is standing in front of Oleg when she begins to have second thoughts. When she thinks maybe it's enough that she knows she could do it.

"I don't think there's enough hawthorn," she hears herself say, intending to take the potion back to the table, to fix it somehow. But her voice sounds far away as if wool is stuffed in her ears. Oleg removes the pipe from his mouth, exhaling a white cloud of smoke in her face.

"Just give it here," he hisses.

The tingly feeling from earlier returns, zipping through her body to the tips of her fingers. She struggles to focus her vision, but hands him the mug as if she's a puppet on strings, as if something else is moving her body now. She hears Oleg grumble and sees him lift the mixture to his wrinkled mouth through blurry eyes.

Her head feels cloudy. She feels like she's slipping, and that's when she sees a flash, quick as lightning. A vision of Oleg coming at her with the cutting knife. Then another. Her hands clutching her bleeding stomach. When the vision fades, her sight quickly returns. She sees that Oleg is no longer holding the mug to his lips. He is blinking the haze out of his own eyes. Mira's heart drops to her stomach when she sees his eyes grow wild, his face twisting into one of rage.

"You little bitch," he rasps.

There is a deep, sharp pain in her chest and Mira feels as though she might vomit. Their eyes are locked for a moment, but in a blink both of them look toward the knife on the table and lunge for it. Mira almost grasps it, but Oleg's bony old fingers fumble for it too and it's pushed off the table, landing in a clatter near the door. Mira tries to right herself, but Oleg smacks Mira across the face with the back of his hand sending a blinding starburst of pain across her vision, causing her to cry out. It takes her a moment before she can stand straight. Once she does, she sees that Oleg's fingers are already wrapping around the wooden scales of the knife.

Her heartbeat picks up like a stampede of horses on the southern steppe. Her mind races for a way out. She whirls her head around and then sees it. Oleg's staff is leaned against a nearby wall. When he turns around wielding the knife, it is already too late. Mira raises the staff over her head and slams it down hard on his skull.

Oleg sways for a moment, eyes glazing over, losing focus. Blood trickles from his hairline and then down his face like a slow, creeping snake. Then Oleg collapses onto his knees and falls flat onto the wood floor with a hard, lifeless thud.

Mira is shaking as she holds the staff out. Mouth open, eyes wide. She peers through a thin break in her hair which has fallen in her face from the force of the blow. It's at this moment that the door of the hut flings open and she sees Arsen standing in the wooden doorframe panting, face flush. His eyes meet Mira's and then flick to Oleg's lifeless body, blood pooling around his head like a crimson halo. When his pale green eyes meet hers for the second time it is like the spell holding her there is broken and she drops the staff, running into his arms. The steadiness of his body presses against her own, a rock in a raging sea.

"How?" Mira chokes out.

"I heard your cry. I knew he would try something, hurt you again," he says closing his eyes and breathing into Mira's hair, clutching it tightly, his voice muffled.

"He didn't," she says in a near whisper. "I tried to poison him," she says through teary eyes. "The mugwort, it grants visions. It showed him. Then I had to..." She glances at the staff lying on the floor, its tip coated in red.

"It's over, Mira," he says squeezing her tighter. "We'll figure this out."

They are like that for several minutes and then Arsen lets go of her. At first she doesn't understand why, but then he kneels next to Oleg's body and puts his fingers to his neck, feeling for his pulse. Everything is moving too fast for her still. Her mind slowed to a crawl. But something registers when Mira sees Oleg's foot twitch. She can barely cry out Arsen's name when the wizard's eyes flick open, glowing and terrible, and he buries the knife deep in Arsen's stomach, removes it, then stabs it in twice more. The sound sharp and wet and final.

At some point during this Mira twists around, locates the staff, and snatches it up. Oleg is groaning and attempting to push himself up to his feet and once again she strikes the wizard in the head. Only this time she doesn't stop. She lands blow after blow, bringing Oleg back to his knees, and she doesn't stop until his face is unrecognizable, until he is lying flat again, and her face and linen dress are speckled in red.

Arsen's face is painted with shock as he looks down to touch the handle of the knife. Mira throws herself to the ground next to him and rips off her apron, balling it up and pressing it to the wound.

"Can you hold this?"

She stumbles over to the cabinet and sifts through bottles, knocking some over, until she finds what she's looking for. She reaches up into the rafters, pulling down herbs, and tosses it all into a wooden bowl. Crushing and mixing the ingredients until it forms a thick, dark, pungent paste. She drops back down onto the floor beside Arsen with a scoop of it in her hand. His eyes are flickering closed and Mira's stomach sinks when she sees how much blood has seeped into the apron, how much has pooled around him. She soaks up as much as she can and presses the paste into the wound and then finds a bandage in the cabinet and wraps it around his torso, struggling to lift him so she can get it under him. But the bandage does little to staunch the bleeding. She puts her balled up apron over it once again, presses it onto the wound, gently but firmly, and mutters spells under her breath. Spells meant to fix, to knit things back together, spells for good health—every spell she can think of.

At one point, Arsen weakly grabs for Mira's hand and she squeezes it and leans in to hear him.

"Mira, I love you," he says weakly, just as the fire in the hearth is on its last tongue, but it sounds like a goodbye and she shakes her head feverishly, tears streaming down her face.

"None of that," she says, stroking his face and giving a weak smile.

"Mira, can you show me the flower?"

It seems like a pathetic piece of magic now in the face of death. A sad little parlor trick. She knows that he wants her to give up on the spells, to let him go, but she won't. She continues to cast spells over him, no indication that anything is sinking in. The only thought in her head that she must keep trying.

Eventually the fire begins to sputter out. Crackling, hissing, popping. Eventually his breath starts to slow.

"No, Arsen, don't. Stay with me," she pleads. But the light flickers from his eyes, and he sighs out his last breath.

She continues to cast until her mind dulls. That's when she realizes she never showed him the flower. She coaxes a ball of light from the meager, low-burning embers in the hearth and closes her hands around it. When she opens her hands, there is the peony, and she holds it to Arsen's chest and sobs.

She doesn't know how long she stays there sobbing onto his chest, her dark hair spilling over him, but eventually she decides she can't stand to be there. She feels suffocated by death and blood—the blood of her lover and her enemy mingling on the floor. The bright, metallic smell choking her senses. She runs out into the foggy wood and doesn't stop running. The dying autumn trees reach toward her through the mist, their spindly fingers cutting her cheeks. One of them catches on her necklace of Saint Agniya, ripping it from her neck. She runs through brambles and past berry bushes, going deep into the wood, deeper than she's ever gone.

There comes a point when her legs give out and she stumbles onto the ground near the edge of a shallow, silver pond. It is then that she notices the wood has stilled. That the wind has ceased blowing, the trees have stopped swaying, and the forest critters have all disappeared. It is then that she feels a dark, unsettling presence looming toward her.

She lifts her head up from the ground, whipping her head around, but there is nothing. Just the eerie stillness. The forest holding its breath. She finally glances down at the pond as she goes to push herself up to her feet. That's when she sees it. Instead of her reflection, the face of an old woman with skin like bark and glowing eyes like lanterns. A grin creeps onto her face and she produces a brass bell. She rings it hard. A heart-stopping jangle. She rings the bell.

Pavel sits in a small, plain room. His dark blonde hair is sticking out in all directions. His eyes look wild and bloodshot as he taps his foot impatiently on the wooden floor. A man sits across from him at a desk. He slowly flicks through parchment, scanning his eyes over the handwritten script.

"Hm," is all he says for a while, but Pavel is paying close attention to the subtle changes in his expression. An eye raise here, a lip purse there. Eventually the man looks up from his spectacles.

"So the Baba Enok eats her, this wayward woman?" asks the man motioning to the thin stack of parchment with one hand while clutching it with the other, his brow furrowed.

"What? She—no," Pavel says, shaking his head and pinching his brows together. "The Baba Enok likes her. We thought the bell was to warn or entice, but the bell is how the Baba Enok says you are arriving at the correct answer. The Baba Enok likes wayward women. She uses them as vehicles to bring down cruel men. Mira was chosen." He sits back in his chair, rubbing his legs, sure he has just ruined his chance.

The man is looking at Pavel like he is mad, and no doubt he sounds mad. Looks mad, too. Though he supposes he was always a little mad before any of this. But the man is rubbing his chin now, looking back down at the parchment and then flicking his narrowed eyes back up at Pavel. He leans back in his chair.

"Our readers won't like that," he says finally, tossing the stack of parchment onto his desk. "Change the ending so the girl is eaten and we'll pay five *grivna*."

Pavel's face is contorted as he wrestles with the idea. How could he explain to this man that this isn't just a story? That the recent rumors of a woman traveling the countryside with two faces—the face of a beautiful young woman and a haggard old witch—is true. That the reason dead men are left in her wake is because she's like a bogey-woman for cruel, abusive men. He certainly couldn't begin to tell him that Arsen woke up, born anew from the blood of old dead Oleg and Mira's lingering spells. Born anew with powers. Nor that he wanders all of Ravgorod searching for his beloved.

He thinks of Pasha back at home with her swelling belly and knows that it is not a war he can wage.

"Okay," he says, gathering up the parchment with a solemn nod and he shakes the man's hand. "I'll have it to you tomorrow."

CPSIA information can be obtained
at www.ICGtesting.com
Printed in the USA
BVHW041712040822
643688BV00020BA/135